Charlotte Mary Yonge

A Reputed Changeling - Or Three Seventh Years Two Centuries Ago

Vol. II

Charlotte Mary Yonge

A Reputed Changeling - Or Three Seventh Years Two Centuries Ago
Vol. II

ISBN/EAN: 9783337111953

Printed in Europe, USA, Canada, Australia, Japan

Cover: Foto ©Andreas Hilbeck / pixelio.de

More available books at **www.hansebooks.com**

A REPUTED CHANGELING

OR

THREE SEVENTH YEARS TWO CENTURIES AGO

BY

CHARLOTTE M. YONGE

IN TWO VOLUMES

VOL. II

London

MACMILLAN AND CO.

AND NEW YORK

1889

CONTENTS

CHAPTER XXVI

CHAPTER XXVII

CHAPTER XXVIII

CHAPTER XXIX

CHAPTER XXX

CHAPTER XXXI

CHAPTER XXXII

CHAPTER XXXIII

CHAPTER XXXIV

CHAPTER XIX

THE DAUGHTER'S SECRET

'Thy sister's naught; O Regan, she hath tied
Sharp-tooth'd unkindness, like a vulture, *here:*
I can scarce speak to thee.' *King Lear.*

'Am I—oh! am I going home?' thought
Anne. 'My uncle will be at Winchester. I
am glad of it. I could not yet bear to see
Portchester again. That Shape would be
there. Yet how shall I deal with what seems
laid on me? But oh! the joy of escaping
from this weary, weary court! Oh, the folly
that took me hither! Now that the Prince
is gone, Lady Strickland will surely speak to
the Queen for my dismissal.'

There had been seventeen days of alarms,
reports, and counter-reports, and now the
King, with the Prince of Denmark, had gone
to join the army on Salisbury Plain, and at

the same time the little Prince of Wales had been sent off to his half-brother, the Duke of Berwick, at Portsmouth, under charge of Lady Powys, there to be embarked for France. Anne had been somewhat disappointed at not going with them, hoping that when at Portsmouth or in passing Winchester she might see her uncle and obtain her release, for she had no desire to be taken abroad; but it was decreed otherwise. Miss Dunord went, rejoicing and thankful to be returning to France, and the other three rockers remained.

There had already been more than one day of alarms and tumults. The Body-guards within were always on duty; the Life-guards without were constantly patrolling; and on the 5th of November, when the Prince of Orange was known to be near at hand, and was in fact actually landing at Torbay, the mob had with difficulty been restrained from burning in effigy, not only Guy Fawkes, but Pope, cardinals, and mitred bishops, in front of the palace, and actually paraded them all, with a figure of poor Sir Edmondbury Godfrey bearing his head in his hand, tied on horseback behind a Jesuit, full before the windows, with yells of

> ' The Pope, the Pope,
>   Up the ladder and down the rope,'

and clattering of warming-pans.

Jane Humphreys was dreadfully frightened. Anne found her crouching close to her bed, with the curtains wrapped round her. ' Have they got in ?' she cried. ' O Miss Woodford, how shall we make them believe we are good Protestants ?'

And when this terror had subsided, and it was well known that the Dutch were at Exeter, there was another panic, for one of the Life-guardsmen had told her to beware, since if the Royal troops at Hounslow were beaten, the Papists would surely take their revenge.

I am to scream from the windows to Mr. Shaw,' she said ; ' but what good will that do if the priests and the Frenchmen have strangled me ? And perhaps he won't be on guard.'

' He was only trying to frighten you,' suggested Anne.

'Dear me, Miss Woodford, aren't you afraid?   You have the stomach of a lion.'

'Why, what would be the good of hurting us?'

However, Anne was not at all surprised, when on the very evening of the Prince's departure, old Mrs. Humphreys, a venerable-looking dame in handsome but Puritanically-fashioned garments, came in a hackney coach to request in her son's name that her grand-daughter might return with her, as her occupation was at an end.

Jane was transported with joy.

'Ay, ay,' said the grandmother, 'look at you now, and think how crazy you were to go to the palace, though 'twas always against my judgment.'

'Ah, I little knew how mortal dull it would be!' said Jane.

'Ye've found it no better than the husks that the swine did eat, eh?   So much the better and safer for your soul, child.'

Nobody wanted to retain Jane, and while she was hastily putting her things together, the grandmother turned to Anne: 'And you, Mistress Woodford, from what I hear, you

have been very good in keeping my silly child
stanch to her religion and true to her duty.
If ever on a pinch you needed a friend in
London, my son and I would be proud to
serve you—Master Joshua Humphreys, at
the Golden Lamb, Gracechurch Street, mind
you. No one knows what may hap in these
strange and troublesome times, and you
might be glad of a house to go to till you
can send to your own friends—that is, if we
are not all murdered by the Papists first.'

Though Anne did not expect such a catas-
trophe as this, she was really grateful for the
offer, and thought it possible that she might
avail herself of it, as she had not been able to
communicate with any of her mother's old
friends, and Bishop Ken was not to her
knowledge still in London.

She watched anxiously for the opportunity
of asking Lady Strickland whether she might
apply for her dismissal, and write to her uncle
to fetch her home.

'Child,' said the lady, 'I think you love
the Queen.'

'Indeed I do, madam.'

'It is well that at this juncture all Protestants should not leave her. You are a gentle-woman in manner, and can speak her native tongue, friends are falling from her, scarcely ladies are left enough to make a fit appearance around her ; if you are faithful to her, remain, I entreat of you.'

There was no resisting such an appeal, and Anne remained in the rooms now left bare and empty, until a message was brought to her to come to the Queen. Mary Beatrice sat in a chair by her fire, looking sad and listless, her eyes red with weeping, but she gave her sweet smile as the girl entered, and held out her hand, saying in her sweet Italian, 'You are faithful, Signorina Anna! you remain! That is well ; but now my son is gone, Anna, you must be mine. I make you my reader instead of his rocker.'

As Anne knelt on one knee to kiss hands with tears in her eyes, the Queen impulsively threw her arms round her neck and kissed her. 'Ah, you loved him, and he loved you, *il mio tesorino !*'

Promotion *had* come — how strangely. She had to enter on her duties at once, and to read some chapters of an Italian version of the *Imitation*. A reader was of a higher grade of importance than a rocker, and for the ensuing days, when not in attendance on the Queen, Anne was the companion of Lady Strickland and Lady Oglethorpe. In the absence of the King and Prince, the Queen received Princess Anne at her own table, and Lady Churchill and Lady Fitzhardinge joined that of her ladies-in-waiting.

Lady Churchill, with her long neck, splendid hair and complexion, short chin, and sparkling blue eyes, was beautiful to look at, but not at all disposed to be agreeable to the Queen's ladies, whom she treated with a sort of blunt scorn, not at all disguised by the forms of courtesy. However, she had, to their relief, a good deal of leave of absence just then to visit her children, as indeed the ladies agreed that she did pretty much as she chose, and that the faithful Mrs. Morley was somewhat afraid of the dear Mrs. Freeman.

One evening in coming up some steps Princess Anne entangled her foot in her pink taffetas petticoat, nearly fell, and tore a large rent, besides breaking the thread of the festoons of seed pearls which bordered it, and scattering them on the floor.

'Lack-a-day! Lack-a-day!' sighed she, as after a little screaming she gathered herself up again. 'That new coat! How shall I ever face Danvers again such a figure? She's an excellent tirewoman, but she will be neither to have nor to hold when she sees that gown —that she set such store by! Nay, I can hardly step for it.'

'I think I could repair it, with Her Majesty's and your Royal Highness's permission,' said Anne, who was creeping about on her knees picking up the pearls.'

'Oh! do! do! There's a good child, and then Danvers and Dawson need know nothing about it,' cried the Princess in great glee. 'You remember Dawson, don't you, little Woodie, as we used to call you, and how she used to rate us when we were children if we soiled our frocks?'

So, in the withdrawing-room, Anne sat on the floor with needle and silk, by the light of the wax candles, deftly repairing the rent, and then threading the scattered pearls, and arranging the festoon so as to hide the darn.

The Princess was delighted, and while the poor wife lay back in her chair, thankful that behind her fan she could give way to her terrible anxieties about her little son, who might be crossing to France, and her husband, suffering from fearful nose-bleeding, and well-nigh alone among traitors and deserters, the step-daughter, on the other side of the great hearth, chattered away complacently to 'little Woodford.'

'Do you recollect old Dawson, and how she used to grumble when I went to sup with the Duchess—my own mother—you know, because she used to give me chocolate, and she said it made me scream at night, and be over fat by day? Ah! that was before you used to come among us. It was after I went to France to my poor aunt of Orleans. I remember she never would let us kiss her for fear of spoiling her complexion, and Mademoiselle and I did so hate living *maigre* on the fast days. I was glad enough to get home at last, and then my sister was jealous because I talked French better than she did.'

So the Princess prattled on without needing much reply, until her namesake had finished her work, with which she was well pleased, and promised to remember her. To Anne it was an absolute marvel how she could thus talk when she knew that her husband had deserted her father in his need, and that things were in a most critical position.

The Queen could not refrain from a sigh of relief when her step-daughter had retired to the Cockpit; and after seeking her sleepless bed, she begged Anne, 'If it did not too much incommode her, to read to her from the Gospel.'

The next day was Sunday, and Anne felt almost as if deserting her cause, when going to the English service in Whitehall Chapel Royal, now almost emptied except of the Princess's suite, and some of these had the bad taste and profanity to cough and chatter all through the special prayer drawn up by the Archbishop for the King's safety.

People were not very reverent, and as all stood up at the end of the Advent Sunday service to let the Princess sweep by in her glittering green satin petticoat, peach-coloured velvet train, and feather-crowned head, she laid a hand on Anne's arm, and whispered, 'Follow me to my closet, little Woodford.'

There was no choice but to obey, as the Queen would not require her reader till after dinner, and Anne followed after the various attendants, who did not seem very willing to forward a private interview with a possible rival, though, as Anne supposed, the object must be to convey some message to the Queen. By the time she arrived and had been admitted to the inner chamber or dressing-room, the Princess had thrown off her more cumbrous finery, and sat at ease in an arm-chair. She nodded her be-curled head, and said, 'You can keep a secret, little Woodie?'

'I can, madam, but I do not love one,' said Anne, thinking of her most burthensome one.

'Well, no need to keep this long. You are a good young maiden, and my own poor mother's godchild, and you are handy and notable. You deserve better preferment than ever you will get in that Popish household, where your religion is in danger. Now, I am not going to be in jeopardy here any longer, nor let myself be kept hostage for His Highness. Come to my rooms at bedtime. Slip in when I wish the Queen good-night, and I'll find an excuse. Then you shall come with me to—no, I'll not say where, and I'll make your fortune, only mum's the word.'

'But—Your Royal Highness is very good, but I am sworn to the Prince and Queen. I could not leave them without permission.'

'Prince! Prince! Pretty sort of a Prince. Prince of brickbats, as Churchill says. Nay, girl, don't turn away in that fashion. Consider. Your religion is in danger.'

'Nay, madam, my religion would not be served by breaking my oath.'

'Pooh! What's your oath to a mere pretender? Besides, consider your fortune. Rocker to a puling babe—even if he was what they say he is. And don't build on the Queen's favour—even if she remains what she is now, she is too much beset with Papists and foreigners to do anything for you.'

'I do not,' Anne began to say, but the Princess gave her no time.

'Besides, pride will have a fall, and if you are a good maid, and hold your tongue, and serve me well in this strait, I'll make you my maid of honour, and marry you so that you shall put Lady before your name. Ay, and get good preferment for your uncle, who has had only a poor stall from the King here.'

Anne repressed an inclination to say this was not the way in which her uncle would wish to get promotion, and only replied, 'Your Royal Highness is very good, but——'

Whereat the Princess, in a huff, exclaimed, 'Oh, very well, if you choose to be torn to pieces by the mob, and slaughtered by the priests, like poor Godfrey, and burnt by the Papists at last, unless you go to Mass, you may stay for aught I care, and joy go with you. I thought I was doing you a kindness for my poor mother's sake, but it seems you know best. If you like to cast in your lot with the Pope, I wash my hands of you.'

Accordingly Anne courtesied herself off, not seriously alarmed as to the various catastrophes foretold by the Princess, though a little shaken in nerves. Here then was another chance of promotion, certainly without treason to her profession of faith, but so offered that honour could not but revolt against it, though in truth poor Princess Anne was neither so foolish nor so heartless a woman as she appeared in the excitement to which an uneasy conscience, the expectation of a great enterprise, and a certain amount of terror had worked her up ; but she had high words again in the evening, as was supposed, with the Queen.   Certainly Anne found her own Royal Mistress weeping and agitated, though she only owned to being very anxious about the health of the King, who had had a second violent attack of bleeding at the nose, and she did not seem consoled by the assurances of her elder attendants that the relief had probably saved him from a far more dangerous attack.   Again Anne read to her till a late hour, but next morning was strangely disturbed.

The Royal household had not been long dressed, and breakfast had just been served to the ladies, when loud screams were heard, most startling in the unsettled and anxious state of affairs.   The Queen, pale and trembling, came out of her chamber with her hair on her shoulders.   'Tell me at once, for pity's sake.   Is it my husband or my son ?' she asked with clasped hands, as two or three of the Princess's servants rushed forward.

'The Princess, the Princess!' was the cry, 'the priests have murdered her.'

'What have you done with her, madam?' rudely demanded Mrs. Buss, one of the lost lady's nurses.

Mary Beatrice drew herself up with grave dignity, saying, 'I suppose your mistress is where she likes to be. I know nothing of her, but I have no doubt that you will soon hear of her.'

There was something in the Queen's manner that hushed the outcry in her presence, but the women, with Lady Clarendon foremost of them, continued to seek up and down the two palaces as if they thought the substantial person of the Princess Anne could be hidden in a cupboard.

Anne, in the first impulse, exclaimed, 'She is gone!'

In a moment Mrs. Royer turned, 'Gone, did you say? Do you know it?'

'You knew it and kept it secret!' cried Lady Strickland.

'A traitor, too!' said Lady Oglethorpe, in

her vehement Irish tone. ' I would not have thought it of Nanny Moore's daughter!' and she turned her eyes in sad reproach on Anne.

'If you know, tell me where she is gone,' cried Mrs. Buss, and the cry was re-echoed by the other women, while Anne's startled ' I cannot tell! I do not know!' was unheeded.

Only the Queen raising her hand gravely said, ' Silence!   What is this?'

' Miss Woodford knew.'

' And never told!' cried the babel of voices.

' Come hither, Mistress Woodford,' said the Queen. ' Tell me, do you know where Her Highness is?'

' No, please your Majesty,' said Anne, trembling from head to foot. ' I do not know where she is.'

' Did you know of her purpose?'

' Your Majesty pardon me.   She called me to her closet yesterday and pledged me to secrecy before I knew what she would say.'

'Only youthful inexperience will permit that pledge to be implied in matters of State,' said the Queen. ' Continue, Mistress Woodford; what did she tell you?'

' She said she feared to be made a hostage

for the Prince of Denmark, and meant to escape, and she bade me come to her chamber at night to go with her.'

'And wherefore did you not? You are of her religion,' said the Queen bitterly.

'Madam, how could I break mine oath to your Majesty and His Royal Highness?'

'And you thought concealing the matter according to that oath? Nay, nay, child, I blame you not. It was a hard strait between your honour to her and your duty to the King and to me, and I cannot but be thankful to any one who does regard her word. But this desertion will be a sore grief to His Majesty.'

Mary Beatrice was fairer-minded than the women, who looked askance at the girl, Princess Anne's people resenting that one of the other household should have been chosen as confidante, and the Queen's being displeased that the secret had been kept. But at that moment frightful yells and shouts arose, and a hasty glance from the windows showed a mass of men, women, and children howling for their Princess. They would tear down Whitehall if she were not delivered up to them.   However, a line of helmeted Life-guards on their heavy horses was drawn up between, with sabres held upright, and there seemed no disposition to rush upon these. Lord Clarendon, uncle to the Princess, had satisfied himself that she had really escaped, and he now came out and assured the mob, in a stentorian voice, that he was perfectly satisfied of his niece's safety, waving the letter she had left on her toilet-table.

The mob shouted, 'Bless the Princess! Hurrah for the Protestant faith! No warm-ing-pans!' but in a good-tempered mood; and the poor little garrison breathed more freely; but Anne did not feel herself forgiven. She was in a manner sent to Coventry, and treated as if she were on the enemy's side. Never had her proud nature suffered so much, and she shed bitter tears as she said to herself, 'It is very unjust! What could I have done? How could I stop Her Highness from speak-ing? Could they expect me to run in and accuse her? Oh, that I were at home again! Mother, mother, you little know! Of what use am I now?'

It was the very question asked by Hester

Bridgeman, whom she found packing her clothes in her room.

'Take care that this is sent after me,' she said, 'when a messenger I shall send calls for it.'

'What, you have your dismissal?'

'No, I should no more get it than you have done. They cannot afford to let any one go, you see, or they will have to dress up the chambermaids to stand behind the Queen's chair. I have settled it with my cousin, Harry Bridgeman, I shall mix with the throng that come to ask for news, and be off with him before the crowd breaks in, as they will some of these days, for the guards are but half-hearted. My Portia, why did not you take a good offer, and go with the Princess?'

'I thought it would be base.'

'And much you gained by it! You are only suspected and accused.'

'I can't be a rat leaving a sinking ship.'

'That is courteous, but I forgive it, Portia, as I know you will repent of your folly. But you never did know which side to look for the butter.'

Perhaps seeing how ugly desertion and defection looked in others made constancy easier to Anne, much as she longed for the Close at Winchester, and she even thought with a hope of the Golden Lamb, Grace-church, as an immediate haven sure to give her a welcome.

Her occupation of reading to the Queen was ended by the King's return, so physically exhausted by violent nose-bleeding, so despondent at the universal desertion, and so broken-hearted at his daughter's defection, that his wife was absorbed in attending upon him.

Anne began to watch for an opportunity to demand a dismissal, which she thought would exempt her from all blame, but she was surprised and a little dismayed by being summoned to the King in the Queen's chamber. He was lying on a couch clad in a loose dressing-gown instead of his laced coat, and a red night-cap replacing his heavy peruke, and his face was as white and sallow as if he were recovering from a long illness.

'Little godchild,' he said, holding out his

hand as Anne made her obeisance, 'the Queen tells me you can read well. I have a fancy to hear.'

Immensely relieved at the kindness of his tone, Anne courtesied, and murmured out her willingness.

'Read this,' he said; 'I would fain hear this; my father loved it. Here.'

Anne felt her task a hard one when the King pointed to the third Act of Shakespeare's *Richard II*. She steeled herself and strengthened her voice as best she could, and struggled on till she came to—

> 'I'll give my jewels for a set of beads,
> My gay apparel for an almsman's gown,
> My figured goblets for a dish of wood,
> My sceptre for a palmer's walking-staff,
> My subjects for a pair of carved saints,
> And my large kingdom for a little grave,
> A little, little grave.'

There she fairly broke down, and sobbed.

'Little one, little one,' said James, 'you are sorry for poor Richard, eh?'

'Oh, sir!' was all she could say.

'And you are in disgrace, they tell me, because my daughter chose to try to entice you away,' said James, 'and you felt bound not to betray her. Never mind; it was an awkward case of conscience, and there's not too much faithfulness to spare in these days. We shall know whom to trust to another time. Can you continue now? I would take a lesson how, "with mine own hands to give away my crown."'

It was well for Anne that fresh tidings were brought in at that moment, and she had to retire, with the sore feeling turned into an enthusiastic pity and loyalty, which needed the relief of sobs and mental vows of fidelity. She felt herself no longer in disgrace with her Royal master and mistress, but she was not in favour with her few companions left— all who could not get over her secrecy, and thought her at least a half traitor as well as a heretic.

Whitehall was almost in a state of siege, the turbulent mob continually coming to shout, ' No Popery!' and the like, though they proceeded no further. The ministers and other gentlemen came and went, but the priests and the ladies durst not venture out for fear of being recognised and insulted, if not injured. Bad news came in from day to day, and no tidings of the Prince of Wales being in safety in France. Once Anne received a letter from her uncle, which cheered her much.

DEAR CHILD—So far as I can gather, your employment is at an end, if it be true as reported that the Prince of Wales is at Portsmouth, with the intent that he should be carried to France; but the gentlemen of the navy seem strongly disposed to prevent such a transportation of the heir of the realm to a foreign country. I fear me that you are in a state of doubt and anxiety, but I need not exhort your good mother's child to be true and loyal to her trust and to the Anointed of the Lord in all things lawful at all costs. If you are left in any distress or perplexity go either to Sir Theophilus Oglethorpe's house, or to that of my good old friend, the Dean of Westminster; and as soon as I hear from you I will endeavour to ride to town and bring you home to my house, which is greatly at a loss without its young mistress.

The letter greatly refreshed Anne's spirits, and gave her something to look forward to, giving her energy to stitch at a set of lawn cuffs and bands for her uncle, and think with the more pleasure of a return that his time of residence at Winchester lay between her and that vault in the castle.

There were no more attempts made at her conversion. Every one was too anxious and occupied, and one or more of the chiefly obnoxious priests were sent privately away from day to day. While summer friends departed, Anne often thought of Bishop Ken's counsel as to loyalty to Heaven and man.

CHAPTER XX

THE FLIGHT

'Storms may rush in, and crimes and woes
    Deform that peaceful bower;
They may not mar the deep repose
    Of that immortal flower.
Though only broken hearts be found
    To watch his cradle by,
No blight is on his slumbers sound,
    No touch of harmful eye.'

KEBLE.

THE news was even worse and worse in that palace of despondency and terror. Notice had arrived that Lord Dartmouth was withheld from despatching the young Prince to France by his own scruples and those of the navy; and orders were sent for the child's return. Then came a terrible alarm. The escort sent to meet him were reported to have been attacked by the rabble on entering

London and dispersed, so that each man had to shift for himself.

There was a quarter of an hour which seemed many hours of fearful suspense, while King and Queen both knelt at their altar, praying in agony for the child whom they pictured to themselves in the hands of the infuriated mob, too much persuaded of his being an imposture to pity his unconscious innocence. No one who saw the blanched cheeks and agonised face of Mary Beatrice, or James's stern, mute misery, could have believed for a moment in the cruel delusion that he was no child of theirs.

The Roman Catholic women were with them. To enter the oratory would in those circumstances have been a surrender of principle, but none the less did Anne pray with fervent passion in her chamber for pity for the child, and comfort for his parents. At last there was a stir, and hurrying out to the great stair, Anne saw a man in plain clothes replying in an Irish accent to the King, who was supporting the Queen with his arm. Happily the escort had missed the Prince of Wales. They had been obliged to turn back to London without meeting him, and from that danger he had been saved.

A burst of tears and a cry of fervent thanksgiving relieved the Queen's heart, and James gave eager thanks instead of the reprimand the colonel had expected for his blundering.

A little later, another messenger brought word that Lord and Lady Powys had halted at Guildford with their charge. A French gentleman, Monsieur de St. Victor, was understood to have undertaken to bring him to London—understood—for everything was whispered rather than told among the panic-stricken women. No one who knew the expectation could go to bed that night except that the King and Queen had—in order to disarm suspicion—to go through the accustomed ceremonies of the *coucher*. The ladies sat or lay on their beds intently listening, as hour after hour chimed from the clocks.

At last, at about three in the morning, the challenge of the sentinels was heard from point to point. Every one started up, and hurried almost pell-mell towards the postern door. The King and Queen were both descending a stair leading from the King's dressing-room, and as the door was cautiously opened, it admitted a figure in a fur cloak, which he unfolded, and displayed the sleeping face of the infant well wrapped from the December cold.

With rapture the Queen gathered him into her arms, and the father kissed him with a vehemence that made him awake and cry. St. Victor had thought it safer that his other attendants should come in by degrees in the morning, and thus Miss Woodford was the only actually effective nursery attendant at hand. His food was waiting by the fire in his own sleeping chamber, and thither he was carried. There the Queen held him on her lap, while Anne fed him, and he smiled at her and held out his arms.

The King came, and making a sign to Anne not to move, stood watching.

Presently he said, 'She has kept one secret, we may trust her with another.'

'Oh, not yet, not yet,' implored the Queen. 'Now I have both my treasures again, let me rest in peace upon them for a little while.'

The King turned away with eyes full of

tears, while Anne was lulling the child to sleep. She wondered, but durst not ask the Queen, where was the tiler's wife; but later she learnt from Miss Dunord, that the woman had been so terrified by the cries of the multitude against the 'pretender,' and still more at the sight of the sea, that she had gone into transports of fright, implored to go home, and perhaps half wilfully, become useless, so that the weaning already commenced had to be expedited, and the fretfulness of the poor child had been one of the troubles for some days. However, he seemed on his return to have forgotten his troubles, and Anne had him in her arms nearly all the next day.

It was not till late in the evening that Anne knew what the King had meant. Then, while she was walking up and down the room, amusing the little Prince with showing by turns the window and his face in a large mirror, the Queen came in, evidently fresh from weeping, and holding out her arms for him, said, after looking to see that there was no other audience—

'Child, the King would repose a trust in

you.   He wills that you should accompany me to-night on a voyage to France to put this little angel in safety.'

'As your Majesty will,' returned Anne; 'I will do my best.'

'So the King said.   He knew his brave sailor's daughter was worthy of his trust, and you can speak French.   It is well, for we go under the escort of Messieurs de Lauzun and St. Victor.   Be ready at midnight.   Lady Strickland or the good Labadie will explain more to you, but do not speak of this to any one else.   You have leave now,' she added, as she herself carried the child towards his father's rooms.

The maiden's heart swelled at the trust reposed in her, and the King's kind words, and she kept back the sense of anxiety and doubt as to so vague a future.   She found Mrs. Labadie lying on her bed awake, but trying to rest between two busy nights, and she was then told that there was to be a flight from the palace of the Queen and Prince at midnight, Mrs. Labadie and Anne alone going with them, though Lord and Lady Powys and Lady Strickland, with the

Queen's Italian ladies, would meet them on board the yacht which was waiting at Gravesend. The nurse advised Anne to put a few necessary equipments into a knapsack bound under a cloak, and to leave other garments with her own in charge of Mr. Labadie, who would despatch them with those of the suite, and would follow in another day with the King. Doubt or refusal there could of course be none in such circumstances, and a high-spirited girl like Anne could not but feel a thrill of heart at selection for such confidential and signal service at her age, scarcely seventeen. Her one wish was to write to her uncle what had become of her. Mrs. Labadie hardly thought it safe, but said her husband would take charge of a note, and if possible, post it when they were safe gone, but nothing of the King's plans must be mentioned.

The hours passed away anxiously, and yet only too fast. So many had quitted the palace that there was nothing remarkable in packing, but as Anne collected her properties, she could not help wondering whether she should ever see them again. Sometimes her spirit rose at the thought of serving her lovely Queen, saving the little Prince, and fulfilling the King's trust ; at others, she was full of vague depression at the thought of being cut off from all she knew and loved, with seas between, and with so little notice to her uncle, who might never learn where she was ; but she knew she had his approval in venturing all, and making any sacrifice for the King whom all deserted ; and she really loved her Queen and little Prince.

The night came, and she and Mrs. Labadie, fully equipped in cloaks and hoods, waited together, Anne moving about restlessly, the elder woman advising her to rest while she could. The little Prince, all unconscious of the dangers of the night, or of his loss of a throne, lay among his wraps in his cradle fast asleep.

By and by the door opened, and treading softly in came the King in his dressing-gown and night-cap, the Queen closely muffled, Lady Strickland also dressed for a journey, and two gentlemen, the one tall and striking-looking, the other slim and dark, in their cloaks, namely Lauzun and St. Victor.

It was one of those supreme moments almost beyond speech or manifestation of feeling.

The King took his child in his arms, kissed him, and solemnly said to Lauzun, ' I confide. my wife and son to you.'

Both Frenchmen threw themselves on their knees kissing his hand with a vow of fidelity. Then giving the infant to Mrs. Labadie, James folded his wife in his arms in a long mute embrace ; Anne carried the basket containing food for the child ; and first with a lantern went St. Victor, then Lauzun, handing the Queen ; Mrs. Labadie with the child, and Anne following, they sped down the stairs, along the great gallery, with steps as noiseless as they could make them. down another stair to a door which St. Victor opened.

A sentry challenged, sending a thrill of dismay through the anxious hearts, but St. Victor had the word, and on they went into the privy gardens, where often Anne had paced behind Mrs. Labadie as the Prince took his airing. Startling lights from the windows fell on them, illuminating the drops of rain that plashed round them on that grim December night, and their steps sounded on the gravel, while still the babe, sheltered under the cloak, slept safely. Another door was reached, more sentries challenged and passed; here was a street whose stones and silent houses shone for a little space as St. Victor raised his lantern and exchanged a word with a man on the box of a carriage.

One by one they were handed in, the Queen, the child, the nurse, Anne, and Lauzun, St. Victor taking his place outside. As if in a dream they rattled on through the dark street, no one speaking except that Lauzun asked the Queen if she were wet.

It was not far before they stopped at the top of the steps called the Horseferry. A few lights twinkled here and there, and were reflected trembling in the river, otherwise a black awful gulf, from which, on St. Victor's cautious hail, a whistle ascended, and a cloaked figure with a lantern came up the steps glistening in the rain.

One by one again, in deep silence, they were assisted down, and into the little boat

that rocked ominously as they entered it.
There the women crouched together over the
child unable to see one another, Anne returning the clasp of a hand on hers, believing
it Mrs. Labadie's, till on Lauzun's exclaiming, '*Est ce que j'incommode sa Majesté?*'
the reply showed her that it was the Queen's
hand that she held, and she began a startled
'Pardon, your Majesty,' but the sweet reply
in Italian was, 'Ah, we are as sisters in this
stress.'

The eager French voice of Lauzun went
on, in undertones certainly, but as if he had
not the faculty of silence, and amid the plash
of the oars, the rush of the river, and the
roar of the rain, it was not easy to tell what
he said, his voice was only another of the
noises, though the Queen made little courteous
murmurs in reply.   It was a hard pull against
wind and tide towards a little speck of green
light which was shown to guide the rowers ;
and when at last they reached it, St. Victor's
hail was answered by Dusions, one of the
servants, and they drew to the steps where
he held a lantern.

'To the coach at once, your Majesty.'

'It is at the inn—ready—but I feared to let it stand.'

Lauzun uttered a French imprecation under his breath, and danced on the step with impatience, only restrained so far as to hand out the Queen and her two attendants. He was hotly ordering off Dusions and St. Victor to bring the coach, when the former suggested that they must find a place for the Queen to wait in where they could find her.

'What is that dark building above?'

'Lambeth Church,' Dusions answered.

'Ah, your Protestant churches are not open; there is no shelter for us there,' sighed the Queen.

'There is shelter in the angle of the buttress; I have been there, your Majesty,' said Dusions.

Thither then they turned.

'What can that be?' exclaimed the Queen, starting and shuddering as a fierce light flashed in the windows and played on the wall.

'It is not within, madame,' Lauzun encouraged; 'it is reflected light from a fire somewhere on the other side of the river.'

'A bonfire for our expulsion. Ah! why should they hate us so?' sighed the poor Queen.

''Tis worse than that, only there's no need to tell Her Majesty so,' whispered Mrs. Labadie, who, in the difficulties of the ascent, had been fain to hand the still-sleeping child to Anne. ' 'Tis the Catholic chapel of St. Roque. The heretic miscreants!'

'Pray Heaven no life be lost,' sighed Anne.

Sinister as the light was, it aided the poor fugitives at that dead hour of night to find an angle between the church wall and a buttress where the eaves afforded a little shelter from the rain, which slackened a little, when they were a little concealed from the road, so that the light need not betray them in case any passenger was abroad at such an hour, as two chimed from the clock over-head.

The women kept together close against the wall to avoid the drip of the eaves. Lauzun walked up and down like a sentinel, his arms folded, and talking all the while, though, as before, his utterances were only an accompaniment to the falling rain and howling wind; Mary Beatrice was murmuring prayers over the sleeping child, which she now held in the innermost corner; Anne, with wide-stretched eyes, was gazing into the light cast beyond the buttress by the fire on the opposite side, when again there passed across it that form she had seen on All Saints' Eve—the unmistakable phantom of Peregrine.

It was gone into the darkness in another second; but a violent start on her part had given a note of alarm, and brought back the Count, whose walk had been in the opposite direction.

'What was it? Any spy?'

'Oh no—no—nothing! It was the face of one who is dead,' gasped Anne.

'The poor child's nerve is failing her,' said the Queen gently, as Lauzun drawing his sword burst out—

'If it be a spy it *shall* be the face of one who is dead;' and he darted into the road, but returned in a few moments, saying no one had passed except one of the rowers returning after running up to the inn to hasten the coach; how could he have been seen from the church wall? The wheels were heard drawing up at that moment, so that the only thought was to enter it as quickly as might be in the same order as before, after which the start was made, along the road that led through the marshes of Lambeth; and then came the inquiry—an anxious one—whom or what mademoiselle, as Lauzun called her, had seen.

'O monsieur!' exclaimed the poor girl in her confusion, her best French failing, 'it was nothing—no living man.'

'Can mademoiselle assure me of that? The dead I fear not, the living I would defy.'

'He lives not,' said she in an undertone, with a shudder.

'But who is he that mademoiselle can be so certain?' asked the Frenchman.

'Oh! I know him well enough,' said Anne, unable to control her voice.

'Mademoiselle must explain herself,' said M. de Lauzun. 'If he be spirit—or phantom —there is no more to say, but if he be in the flesh, and a spy—then——' There was a little rattle of his sword.

'Speak, I command,' interposed the Queen ; 'you must satisfy M. le Comte.'

Thus adjured, Anne said in a low voice of horror : 'It was a gentleman of our neighbourhood ; he was killed in a duel last summer !'

'Ah ! You are certain ?'

'I had the misfortune to see the fight,' sighed Anne.

''That accounts for it,' said the Queen kindly. 'If mademoiselle's nerves were shaken by such a remembrance, it is not wonderful that it should recur to her at so strange a watch as we have been keeping.'

'It might account for her seeing this *revenant* cavalier in any passenger,' said Lauzun, not satisfied yet.

'No one ever was like him,' said Anne. 'I could not mistake him.'

'May I ask mademoiselle to describe him ?' continued the count.

Feeling all the time as if this first mention were a sort of betrayal, Anne faltered the words : 'Small, slight, almost mis-shapen— with a strange one-sided look—odd, unusual features.'

Lauzun's laugh jarred on her. 'Eh! it is not a flattering portrait. Mademoiselle is not haunted by a hero of romance, it appears, so much as by a demon.'

'And none of those monsieur has employed in our escape answer to that description?' asked the Queen.

'Assuredly not, your Majesty. Crooked person and crooked mind go together, and St. Victor would only have trusted to your big honest rowers of the Tamise. I think we may be satisfied that the demoiselle's imagination was excited so as to evoke a phantom impressed on her mind by a previous scene of terror. Such things have happened in my native Gascony.'

Anne was fain to accept the theory in silence, though it seemed to her strange that at a moment when she was for once not thinking of Peregrine, her imagination should conjure him up, and there was a strong feeling within her that it was something external that had flitted across the shadow, not a mere figment of her brain, though the notion was evidently accepted, and she could hear a muttering of Mrs. Labadie that this was the consequence of employing young wenches with their whims and megrims.

The Count de Lauzun did his best to entertain the Queen with stories of *revenants* in Gascony and elsewhere, and with reminiscences of his eleven years' captivity at Pignerol, and his intercourse with Fouquet; but whenever in aftertimes Anne Woodford tried to recall her nocturnal drive with this strange personage, the chosen and very unkind husband of the poor old Grande Mademoiselle, she never could recollect anything but the fierce glare of his eyes in the light of the lamps as he put her to that terrible interrogation.

The talk was chiefly monologue. Mrs. Labadie certainly slept, perhaps the Queen did so too, and Anne became conscious that she must have slumbered likewise, for she found every one gazing at her in the pale morning dawn and asking why she cried, 'O Charles, hold!'

As she hastily entreated pardon, Lauzun was heard to murmur, '*Je parie que le revenant se nomme Charles*,' and she collected her senses just in time to check her contradiction, recollecting that happily such a name as Charles revealed nothing. The little Prince, who had slumbered so opportunely all night, awoke and received infinite praise, and what he better appreciated, the food that had been provided for him. They were near their journey's end, and it was well, for people were awakening and going to their work as they passed one of the villages, and once the remark was heard, ' There goes a coach full of Papists.'

However, no attempt was made to stop the party, and as it would be daylight when they reached Gravesend, the Queen arranged her disguise to resemble, as she hoped, a washerwoman—taking off her gloves, and hiding her hair, while the Prince, happily again asleep, was laid in a basket of linen. Anne could not help thinking that she thus looked more remarkable than if she had simply embarked as a lady ; but she meant to represent the attendant of her Italian friend Countess Almonde, whom she was to meet on board.

Leaving the coach outside a little block of houses, the party reached a projecting point of land, where three Irish officers received them, and conducted them to a boat. Then, wrapped closely in cloaks from the chill morning air, they were rowed to the yacht, on the deck of which stood Lord and Lady Powys, Lady Strickland, Pauline Dunord, and a few more faithful followers, who had come more rapidly. There was no open greeting nor recognition, for the captain and crew were unaware whom they were carrying, and, on the discovery, either for fear of danger or hope of reward, might have captured such a prize.

Therefore all the others, with whispered apologies, were hoisted up before her, and Countess Almonde had to devise a special entreaty that the chair might be lowered again for her poor laundress as well as for the other two women.

The yacht, which had been hired by St. Victor, at once spread her sails; Mrs. Labadie conversed with the captain while the countess took the Queen below into the stifling crowded little cabin. It was altogether a wretched voyage; the wind was high, and the pitching and tossing more or less disabled everybody in the suite. The

Queen was exceedingly ill, so were the countess and Mrs. Labadie. Nobody could be the least effective but Signora Turini, who waited on Her Majesty, and Anne, who was so far seasoned by excursions at Portsmouth that she was capable of taking sole care of the little Prince, as the little vessel dashed along on her way with her cargo of alarm and suffering through the Dutch fleet of fifty vessels, none of which seemed to notice her—perhaps by express desire not to be too curious as to English fugitives.

Between the care of the little one, who needed in the tossing of the ship to be constantly in arms, though he never cried and when awake was always merry, and the giving as much succour as possible to her suffering companions, Anne could not either rest or think, but seemed to live in one heavy dazed dream of weariness and endurance, hardly knowing whether it were day or night, till the welcome sound was heard that Calais was in sight.

Then, as well as they could, the poor travellers crawled from the corners, and put themselves in such array as they could contrive, though the heaving of the waves, as the little yacht lay to, did not conduce to their recovery. The Count de Lauzun went ashore as soon as a boat could be lowered to apprise M. Charot, the Governor of Calais, of the guest he was to receive, and after an interval of considerable discomfort, in full view of the massive fortifications, boats came off to bring the Queen and her attendants on shore, this time as a Queen, though she refused to receive any honours. Lady Strickland, recovering as soon as she was on dry land, resumed her Prince, who was fondled with enthusiastic praises for his excellent conduct on the voyage.

Anne could not help feebly thinking some of the credit might be due to her, since she had held him by land and water nearly ever since leaving Whitehall, but she was too much worn out by her nights of unrest, and too much battered and beaten by the tossings of her voyage, to feel anything except in a languid half-conscious way, under a racking headache; and when the curious old house where they were to rest was reached, and all the rest were eating with ravenous appetites, she could taste nothing, and being conducted by a compassionate Frenchwoman in a snow-white towering cap to a straw mattress spread on the ground, she slept the twenty-four hours round without moving.

CHAPTER XXI

' "Oh, who are ye, young man ?" she said.
"What country come ye frae ?"
" I flew across the sea," he said ;
" 'Twas but this very day." '

Old Ballad.

FIVE months had passed away since the midnight flight from England, when Anne Woodford was sitting on a stone bench flanked with statues in the stately gardens of the Palace of St. Germain, working away at some delicate point lace, destined to cover some of the deficiencies of her dress, for her difficulties were great, and these months had been far from happy ones.

The King was in Ireland, the Queen spent most of the time of his absence in convents, either at Poissy or Chaillot, carrying her son with her to be the darling of the nuns, who had for the most part never even seen a baby, and to whom a bright lively child of a year old was a perfect treasure of delight. Not wishing to encumber the good Sisters with more attendants than were needful, the Queen only took with her one lady governess, one nurse, and one rocker, and this last naturally was Pauline Dunord, both a Frenchwoman and a Roman Catholic.

This was in itself no loss to Anne. Her experience of the nunnery at Boulogne, where had been spent three days in expectation of the King, had not been pleasant. The nuns had shrunk from her as a heretic, and kept their novices and pensionnaires from the taint of communication with her; and all the honour she might have deserved for the Queen's escape seemed to have been forfeited by that moment of fear, which in the telling had become greatly exaggerated.

It was true that the Queen had never alluded to it; but probably through Mrs. Labadie, it had become current that Miss Woodford had been so much alarmed under the churchyard wall that her fancy had conjured up a phantom and she had given a loud scream, which but for the mercy of the Saints would have betrayed them all.

Anne was persuaded that she had done nothing worse than give an involuntary start, but it was not of the least use to say so, and she began to think that perhaps others knew better than she did.   Miss Dunord, who had never been more than distantly polite to her in England, was of course more thrown with her at St. Germain, and examined her closely. Who was it ? What was it ? Had she seen it before ? It was of no use to deny. Pauline knew she had seen something on that All Saints' Eve. Was it true that it was a lover of hers, and that she had seen him killed in a duel on her account ? Who would have imagined it in *cette demoiselle si sage !* Would she not say who it was !

But though truth forced more than one affirmative to be pumped out of Anne, she clung to that last shred of concealment, and kept her own counsel as to the time, place, and persons of the duel, and thus she so far offended Pauline as to prevent that damsel from having any scruples in regarding her as an obnoxious and perilous rival, with a dark secret in her life. Certainly Miss Dunord did earnestly assure her that to adopt her Church, invoke the Saints, and have Masses for the dead was the only way to lay such ghosts; but Anne remained obdurate, and thus was isolated, for there were very few Protestants in the fugitive Court, and those were of too high a degree to consort with her. Perhaps that undefined doubt of her discretion was against her; perhaps too her education and knowledge of languages became less useful to the Queen when surrounded by French, for she was no longer called upon to act as reader; and the little Prince, during his residence in the convent, had time to forget her and lose his preference for her. She was not discharged, but except for taking her turn as a nursery-maid when the Prince was at St. Germain, she was a mere supernumerary, nor was there any salary forthcoming. The small amount of money she had with her had dwindled away, and when she applied to Lady Strickland, who was kinder to her than any one else, she was told that the Queen was far too much distressed for money wherewith to aid the King to be able to pay any one, and that they must all wait till the King had his own again.   Her clothes were wearing out, and scarcely in condition for attendance on the Prince when he was shown in state to the King of France.   Worse than all, she seemed entirely cut off from home. She had written several times to her uncle when opportunity seemed to offer, but had never heard from him, and she did not know whether her letters could reach him, or if he were even aware of what had become of her. People came with passports from England to join the exiled Court, but no one returned thither, or she would even have offered herself as a waiting-maid to have a chance of going back.   Lady Strickland would have forwarded her, but no means or opportunity offered, and there was nothing for it but to look to the time that everybody declared to be approaching when the King was to be reinstated, and they would all go home in triumph.

Meanwhile Anne Woodford felt herself a supernumerary, treated with civility, and no more, as she ate her meals with a very feminine Court, for almost all the gentlemen were in Ireland with the King. She had a room in the entresol to herself, in Pauline's absence, and here she could in turn sit and dream, or mend and furbish up her clothes—a serious matter now—or read the least scrap of printed matter in her way, for books were scarcer than even at Whitehall; and though her 'mail' had safely been forwarded by Mr. Labadie, some jealous censor had abstracted her Bible and Prayer-book. Probably there was no English service anywhere in France at that time, unless among the merchants at Bordeaux—certainly neither English nor Reformed was within her reach—and she had to spend her Sundays in recalling all she could, and going over it, feeling thankful to the mother who had made her store Psalms, Gospels, and Collects in her memory week by week.

She was so far forgotten that active attempts to convert her had been dropped, except by Pauline. Perhaps it was thought that isolation would be effectual, but in fact the sight of popular Romanism not kept in check by Protestant surroundings shocked her, and made her far more averse to change than when she saw it at its best at Whitehall. In fine, the end of her ambition had been neglect and poverty, and the real service that she had rendered was unacknowledged, and marred by that momentary alarm. No wonder she felt sore.

She had never once been to Paris, and seldom beyond the gardens, which happily were free in the absence of the Queen, and always had secluded corners apart from the noble terraces, safe from the intrusion of idle gallants. Anne had found a sort of bower of her own, shaded by honeysuckles and wild roses, where she could sit looking over the slopes and the windings of the Seine and indulge her musings and longings.

The lonely life brought before her all the anxieties that had been stifled for the time by the agitations of the escape. Again and again she lived over the scene in the ruins. Again and again she recalled those two strange appearances, and shivering at the thought of the anniversary that was approaching in another month, still felt sometimes that, alive or dead, Peregrine's would be a home face, and framed to herself imaginary scenes in which she addressed him, and demanded whether he could not rest in his unhallowed grave. What would Bishop Ken say? Sometimes even she recollected the strange theory which had made him crave execution from the late King, seven years, yes, a little more than seven years ago, and marvel whether at that critical epoch he had indeed between life and death been snatched away to his native land of faëry. Imagination might well run riot in the solitary, unoccupied condition to which she was reduced ; and she also brooded much over the fragments of doubtful news which reached her.

Something was said of all loyal clergy being expelled and persecuted, and this of course suggested those sufferings of the clergy during the Commonwealth, of which she had often heard, making her very anxious about her uncle, and earnestly long for wings to fly to him. The Archfields too! Had Charles returned, and did that secret press upon him as it did upon her? Did Lucy think herself utterly forgotten and cast aside, receiving no word or message from her friend? ' Perhaps,' thought Anne, ' they fancy me sail-

ing about at Court in silks and satins, jewels
and curls, and forgetting them all, as I remember Lucy said I should when she first heard
that I was going to Whitehall.   Nay, and
I even took pleasure in the picture of myself
so decked out, though I never, never meant
to forget her.   Foolish, worse than foolish,
that I was!   And to think that I might now
be safe and happy with good Lady Russell,
near my uncle and all of them.   I could
almost laugh to think how my fine notions of
making my fortune have ended in sitting here,
neglected, forgotten, banished, almost in rags!
I suppose it was all self-seeking, and that I
must take it meekly as no more than I deserve.   But oh, how different! how different
is this captivity!   "Oh that I had wings like
a dove, for then I would flee away, and be at
rest."   Swallow, swallow! you are sweeping
through the air.   Would that my spirit could
fly like you! if only for one glimpse to tell
me what they are doing.   Ah! there's some
one coming down this unfrequented walk,
where I thought myself safe.   A young
gentleman!   I must rise and go as quietly as
I can before he sees me.   Nay,' as the action

following the impulse, she was gathering up her work, ''tis an old abbé with him! no fear! Abbé? Nay, 'tis liker to an English clergyman! Can a banished one have strayed hither? The younger man is in mourning. Could it be? No, graver, older, more manly —Oh!'

'Anne! Anne! We have found you!'

'Mr. Archfield! You!'

And as Charles Archfield, in true English fashion, kissed her cheek, Anne fairly choked with tears of joy, and she ever after remembered that moment as the most joyful of her life, though the joy was almost agony.

'This is Mistress Anne Woodford, sir,' said Charles, the next moment. 'Allow me, madam, to present Mr. Fellowes, of Magdalen College.'

Anne held out her hand, and courtesied in response to the bow and wave of the shovel hat.

'How did you know that I was here?' she said.

'Dr. Woodford thought it likely, and begged us to come and see whether we could do anything for you,' said Charles; 'and you may believe that we were only too happy to do so.   A lady to whom we had letters, who is half English, the Vicomtesse de Bellaise, was so good as to go to the convent at Poissy and discover for us from some of the suite where you were.'

'My uncle—my dear uncle—is he well?'

'Quite well, when last we heard,' said Charles.   'That was at Florence, nearly a month ago.'

'And all at Farcham, are they well?'

'All just as usual,' said Charles, 'at the last hearing, which was at the same time. I hoped to have met letters at Paris, but no doubt the war prevents the mails from running.'

'Ah! I have never had a single letter,' said Anne.   'Did my uncle know anything of me?   Has he never had one of mine?'

'Up to the time when he wrote, last March, that is to say, he had received nothing.   He had gone to London to make inquiries——'

'Ah! my dear good uncle!'

'And had ascertained that you had been chosen to accompany the Queen and Prince

in their escape from Whitehall. You have
played the heroine, Miss Anne.'

'Oh! if you knew——'

'And,' said Mr. Fellowes, 'both he and
Sir Philip Archfield requested us, if we
could make our way home through Paris,
to come and offer our services to Mistress
Woodford, in case she should wish to send
intelligence to England, or if she should
wish to make use of our escort to return
home.'

'Oh sir! oh sir! how can I thank you
enough!   You cannot guess the happiness
you have brought me,' cried Anne with
clasped hands, tears welling up again.

'You *will* come with us then,' cried
Charles.   'I am sure you ought.   They
have not used you well, Anne; how pale and
thin you have grown.'

'That is only pining! I am quite well,
only home-sick,' she said with a smile. 'I
am sure the Queen will let me go. I am
nothing but a burthen now. She has plenty
of her own people, and they do not like a
Protestant about the Prince.'

'There is Madame de Bellaise,' said Mr.

Fellowes, 'advancing along the walk with Lady Powys.   Let me present you to her.'

'You have succeeded, I see,' a kind voice said, as Anne found herself making her courtesy to a tall and stately old lady, with a mass of hair of the peculiar silvered tint of flaxen mixed with white.

'I am sincerely glad,' said Lady Powys, 'that Miss Woodford has met her friends.'

'Also,' said Madame de Bellaise, 'Lady Powys is good enough to say that if mademoiselle will honour me with a visit, she gives permission for her to return with me to Paris.'

This was still greater joy, except for that one recollection, formidable in the midst of her joy, of her dress.   Did Madame de Bellaise divine something ? for she said, 'These times remind me of my youth, when we poor cavalier families well knew what sore straits were.   If mademoiselle will bring what is most needful, the rest can be sent afterwards.'

Making her excuses for the moment, Anne with light and gladsome foot sped along the stately alley, up the stairs to her chamber, round which she looked much as if it had been a prison cell, fell on her knees in a gush of intense thankfulness, and made her rapid preparations, her hands trembling with joy, and a fear that she might wake to find all again a dream. She felt as if this deliverance were a token of forgiveness for her past wilfulness, and as if hope were opened to her once more. Lady Powys met her as she came down, and spoke very kindly, thanking her for her services, and hoping that she would enjoy the visit she was about to make.

'Does your ladyship think Her Majesty will require me any longer?' asked Anne timidly.

'If you wish to return to the country held by the Prince of Orange,' said the Countess coldly, 'you must apply for dismissal to Her Majesty herself.'

Anne perceived from the looks of her friends that it was no time for discussing her loyalty, and all taking leave, she was soon seated beside Madame de Bellaise, while the coach and four rolled down the magnificent avenue, and scene after scene disappeared, beautiful and stately indeed, but which she was as glad to leave behind her as if they had been the fetters and bars of a dungeon, and she almost wondered at the words of admiration of her companions.

Madame de Bellaise sat back, and begged the others to speak English, saying that it was her mother tongue, and she loved the sound of it, but really trying to efface herself, while the eager conversation between the two young people went on about their homes.

Charles had not been there more recently than Anne, and his letters were at least two months old, but the intelligence in them was as water to her thirsty soul. All was well, she heard, including the little heir of Archfield, though the young father coloured a little, and shuffled over the answers to the inquiries with a rather sad smile. Charles was, however, greatly improved. He had left behind him the loutish, unformed boy, and had become a handsome, courteous, well-mannered gentleman. The very sight of him handing Madame de Bellaise in and out of her coach was a wonder in itself when Anne recollected how he had been wont to hide himself in the shrubbery to prevent being called upon for such services, and how uncouthly in the last extremity he would perform them.

Madame de Bellaise was inhabiting her son's great Hôtel de Nidemerle. He was absent in garrison, and she was presiding over the family of grandchildren, their mother being in bad health. So much Anne heard before she was conducted to a pleasant little bedroom, far more home-like and comfortable than in any of the palaces she had inhabited. It opened into another, whence merry young voices were heard.

'That is the apartment of my sister's youngest daughter,' said Madame de Bellaise, ' Noémi Darpent. I borrowed her for a little while to teach her French and dancing, but now that we are gone to war, they want to have her back again, and it will be well that she should avail herself of the same escort as yourself. All will then be *selon les convenances*, which had been a difficulty to me,' she added with a laugh.

Then opening the door of communication she said : ' Here, Noémi, we have found your countrywoman, and I put her under your care. Ah ! you two chattering little pies, I knew the voices were yours. This is my grand-daughter, Marguerite de Nidemerle, and my niece—*à la mode de Bretagne*—Cécile d'Aubépine, all bestowing their chatter on their cousin.'

Noémi Darpent was a tall, fair, grave-faced maiden, some years over twenty, and so thoroughly English that it warmed Anne's heart to look at her, and the other two were bright little Frenchwomen—Marguerite a pretty blonde, Cécile pale, dark, and sallow, but full of life. Both were at the age at which girls were usually in convents, but as Anne learnt, Madame de Bellaise was too English at heart to give up the training of her grandchildren, and she had an English governess for them, daughter to a Romanist cavalier ruined by sequestration.

She was evidently the absolute head of the family. Her daughter-in-law was a delicate little creature, who scarcely seemed able to bear the noise of the family at the long supper-table, when all talked with shrill French voices, from the two youths and their abbé tutor down to the little four-year-old Lolotte in her high chair. But to Anne, after the tedious formality of the second table at the palace, stiff without refinement, this free family life was perfectly delightful and refreshing, though as yet she was too much cramped, as it were, by long stiffness, silence, and treatment as an inferior to join, except by the intelligent dancing of her brown eyes, and replies when directly addressed.

After Mrs. Labadie's homeliness, Pauline's exclusive narrowness, Jane's petty frivolity, Hester's vulgar worldliness, and the general want of cultivation in all who treated her on an equality, it was like returning to rational society ; and she could not but observe that Mr. Archfield altogether held his own in conversation with the rest, whether in French or English. Little more than a year ago he would hardly have opened his mouth, and would have worn the true bumpkin look of contemptuous sheepishness. Now he laughed and made others laugh as readily and politely as—Ah! With whom was she comparing him? Did the thought of poor Peregrine dwell on his mind as it did upon hers? But perhaps things were not so terrible to a man as to a woman, and he had not seen those apparitions! Indeed, when not animated, she detected a certain thoughtful melancholy on his brow which certainly had not belonged to former times.

Mr. Fellowes early made known to Anne that her uncle had asked him to be her banker, and the first care of her kind hostess was to assist her in supplying the deficiencies of her wardrobe, so that she was able to go abroad without shrinking at her own shabby appearance.

The next thing was to take her to Poissy to request her dismissal from the Queen, without which it would be hardly decorous to depart, though in point of fact, in the present state of affairs, as Noémi said, there was nothing to prevent it.

'No,' said Mr. Fellowes; 'but for that reason Miss Woodford would feel bound to show double courtesy to the discrowned Queen.'

'And she has often been very kind to me —I love her much,' said Anne.

'Noémi is a little Whig,' said Madame de Bellaise. 'I shall not take her with us, because I know her father would not like it, but to me it is only like the days of my youth to visit an exiled queen. Will these gentlemen think fit to be of the party?'

'Thank you, madam, not I,' said the Magdalen man. 'I am very sorry for the poor lady, but my college has suffered too much at her husband's hands for me to be very anxious to pay her my respects; and if my young friend will take my advice, neither will he. It might be bringing his father into trouble.'

To this Charles agreed, so M. L'Abbé undertook to show them the pictures at the Louvre, and Anne and Madame de Bellaise were the only occupants of the carriage that conveyed them to the great old convent of Poissy, the girl enjoying by the way the comfort of the kindness of a motherly woman, though even to her there could be no confiding of the terrible secret that underlay all her thoughts. Madame de Bellaise, however, said how glad she was to secure this companionship for her niece. Noémi had been more attached than her family realised to Claude Merrycourt, a neighbour who had had the folly, contrary to her prudent father's advice, to rush into Monmouth's rebellion, and it had only been by the poor girl's agony when he suffered under the summary barbarities of Kirke that her mother had known how much her heart was with him. The depression of spirits and loss of health that ensued had been so alarming that when Madame de Bellaise, after some months, paid a long visit to her sister in England, Mrs. Darpent had consented to send the girl to make acquaintance with her French relations, and try the effect of change of scene. She had gone, indifferent, passive, and broken-hearted, but her aunt had watched over her tenderly, and she had gradually revived, not indeed into a joyous girl, but into a calm and fairly cheerful woman.

When she had left home, France and England were only too closely connected, but now they were at daggers drawn, and probably would be so for many years, and the Revolution had come so suddenly that Madame de Bellaise had not been able to make arrangements for her niece's return home, and Noémi was anxiously waiting for an opportunity of rejoining her parents.

The present plan was this. Madame de Bellaise's son, the Marquis de Nidemerle, was Governor of Douai, where his son, the young Baron de Ribaumont, with his cousin, the Chevalier d'Aubépine, were to join him with their tutor, the Abbé Leblanc. The war on the Flemish frontier was not just then in an active state, and there were often friendly relations between the commandants of neighbouring garrisons, so that it might be possible to pass a party on to the Spanish territory with a flag of truce, and then the way would be easy. This passing, however, would be impossible for Noémi alone, since etiquette would not permit of her thus travelling with the two young gentlemen, nor could she have proceeded after reaching Douai, so that the arrival of the two Englishmen and the company of Miss Woodford was a great boon. Madame de Bellaise had already despatched a courier to ask her son whether he could undertake the transit across the frontier, and hoped to apply for passports as soon as his answer was received. She told Anne her niece's history to prevent painful allusions on the journey.

'Ah, madame!' said Anne, 'we too have a sad day connected with that unfortunate insurrection. We grieved over Lady Lisle, and burnt with indignation.'

'M. Barillon tells me that her judge, the Lord Chancellor, was actually forced to commit himself to the Tower to escape being torn to pieces by the populace, and it is since reported that he has there died of grief and shame. I should think his prison cell must have been haunted by hundreds of ghosts.'

'I pray you, madame! do you believe that there are apparitions?'

'I have heard of none that were not explained by some accident, or else were the produce of an excited brain;' and Anne said no more on that head, though it was a comfort to tell of her own foolish preference for the chances of Court preferment above the security of Lady Russell's household, and Madame de Bellaise smiled, and said her experience of Courts had not been too agreeable.

And thus they reached Poissy, where Queen Mary Beatrice had separate rooms set apart for visitors, and thus did not see them from behind the grating, but face to face.

'You wish to leave me, signorina,' she said, using the appellation of their more intimate day, as Anne knelt to kiss her hand. 'I cannot wonder. A poor exile has nothing wherewith to reward the faithful.'

'Ah! your Majesty, that is not the cause; if I were of any use to you or to His Royal Highness.'

'True, signorina; you have been faithful and aided me to the best of your power in my extremity, but while you will not embrace the true faith I cannot keep you about the person of my son as he becomes more intelligent. Therefore it may be well that you should leave us, until such time as we shall be recalled to our kingdom, when I hope to reward you more suitably. You loved my son, and he loved you—perhaps you would like to bid him farewell.'

For this Anne was very grateful, and the Prince was sent for by the mother, who was too proud of him to miss any opportunity of exhibiting him to an experienced mother and grandmother like the vicomtesse. He was a year old, and had become a very beautiful child, with large dark eyes like his mother's, and when Mrs. Labadie carried him in, he held out his arms to Anne with a cry of glad recognition that made her feel that if she could have been allowed the charge of him she could hardly have borne to part with him.   And when the final leavetaking came, the Queen made his little hand present her with a little gold locket, containing his soft hair, with a J in seed pearls outside, in memory, said Mary Beatrice, of that night beneath the church wall.

'Ah, yes, you had your moment of fear, but we were all in terror, and you hushed him well.'

Thus with another kiss to the white hand, returned on her own forehead, ended Anne Jacobina's Court life.   Never would she be Jacobina again — always Anne or sweet Nancy!   It was refreshing to be so called, when Charles Archfield let the name slip out, then blushed and apologised, while she begged him to resume it, which he was now far too correct to do in public.   Noémi quite readily adopted it.

'I am tired of fine French names,' she said: 'an English voice is quite refreshing; and do you call me Naomi, not Noémi. I did not mind it so much at first, because my father sometimes called me so, after his good old mother, who was bred a Huguenot, but it is like the first step towards home to hear Naomi—Little Omy, as my brothers used to shout over the stairs.'

That was a happy fortnight. Madame de Bellaise said it would be a shame to let Anne have spent a half year in France and have seen nothing, so she took the party to the theatre, where they saw the *Cid* with extreme delight. She regretted that the season was so far advanced that the winter representations of *Esther*, at St. Cyr by the young ladies, were over, but she invited M. Racine for an evening, when Mr. Fellowes took extreme pleasure in his conversation, and he was prevailed on to read some of the scenes. She also used her *entrée* at Court to enable them to see the fountains at Versailles, which Winchester was to have surpassed but for King Charles's death.

'Just as well otherwise,' remarked Charles

to Anne. 'These fine feathers and flowers of spray are beautiful enough in themselves, but give me the clear old Itchen not tortured into playing tricks, with all the trout killed; and the open down instead of all these terraces and marble steps where one feels as cramped as if it were a perpetual minuet. And look at the cost! Ah! you will know what I mean when we travel through the country.'

Another sight was from a gallery, whence they beheld the King eat his dinner alone at a silver-loaded table, and a lengthy ceremony it was. Four plates of soup to begin with, a whole capon with ham, followed by a melon, mutton, salad, garlic, *pâté de foie gras*, fruit, and confitures. Charles really grew so indignant, that, in spite of his newly-acquired politeness, Anne, who knew his countenance, was quite glad when she saw him safe out of hearing.

'The old glutton!' he said; 'I should like to put him on a diet of buckwheat and saw-dust like his poor peasants for a week, and then see whether he would go on gormandis-ing, with his wars and his buildings, starving his poor. It is almost enough to make a Whig of a man to see what we might have come to. How can you bear it, madame?'

'Alas! we are powerless,' said the vicomtesse. 'A seigneur can do little for his people, but in Anjou we have some privileges, and our peasants are better off than those you have seen, though indeed I grieved much for them when first I came among them from England.'

She was perhaps the less sorry that Paris was nearly emptied of fashionable society since her guest had the less chance of uttering dangerous sentiments before those who might have repeated them, and much as she liked him, she was relieved when letters came from her son undertaking to expedite them on their way provided they made haste to forestall any outbreak of the war in that quarter.

Meantime Naomi and Anne had been drawn much nearer together by a common interest. The door between their rooms having some imperfection in the latch swung open as they were preparing for bed, and Anne was aware of a sound of sobbing, and saw one of the white-capped, short-petticoated *femmes de chambre* kneeling at Naomi's feet, ejaculating, 'Oh, take me! take me, mademoiselle!   Madame is an angel of goodness, but I cannot go on living a lie.   I shall do something dreadful.'

'Poor Suzanne! poor Suzanne!' Naomi was answering; 'I will do what I can, I will see if it is possible——'

They started at the sound of the step, Suzanne rising to her feet in terror, but Naomi, signing to Anne and saying, 'It is only Mademoiselle Woodford, a good Protestant, Suzanne.   Go now; I will see what can be done; I know my aunt would like to send a maid with us.'

Then as Suzanne went out with her apron to her eyes, and Anne would have apologised, she said, 'Never mind; I must have told you, and asked your help.   Poor Suzanne, she is one of the Rotrous, an old race of Huguenot peasants whom my aunt always protected; she would protect any one, but these people had a special claim because they sheltered our great-grandmother, Lady Walwyn, when she fled after the S. Barthélémi.   When the Edict of Nantes was revoked, the two brothers fled. I believe she helped them, and they got on board ship, and brought a token to my father; but the old mother was feeble and imbecile, and could not move, and the monks and the dragoons frightened and harassed this poor wench into what they called conforming. When the mother died, my aunt took Suzanne and taught her, and thought she was converted; and indeed if all Papists were like my aunt it would not be so hard to become one.'

'Oh yes! I know others like that.'

'But this poor Suzanne, knowing that she only was converted out of terror, has always had an uneasy conscience, and the sight of me has stirred up everything. She says, though I do not know if it be true, that she was fast drifting into bad habits, when finding my Bible, though it was English and she could not read it, seems to have revived everything, and recalled the teaching of her good old father and pastor, and now she is wild to go to England with us.'

'You will take her?' exclaimed Anne.

'Of course I will. Perhaps that is what I was sent here for. I will ask her of my aunt,

and I think she will let me have her. You
will keep her secret, Anne.'

'Indeed I will.'

Madame de Bellaise granted Suzanne to
her niece without difficulty, evidently guessing
the truth, but knowing the peril of the situation too well to make any inquiry. Perhaps
she was disappointed that her endeavours to
win the girl to her Church had been ineffec-
tual, but to have any connection with one
'relapsed' was so exceedingly perilous that
she preferred to ignore the whole subject,
and merely let it be known that Suzanne was
to accompany Mademoiselle Darpent, and
this was only disclosed to the household on
the very last morning, after the passports had
been procured and the mails packed, and she
hushed any remark of the two English girls
in such a decided manner as quite startled
them by the manifest need of caution.

'We should have come to that if King
James were still allowed to have his own
way,' said Naomi.

'Oh no! we are too English,' said Anne.

'Our generation might not see it,' said
Naomi ; 'but who can be safe when a Popish

king can override law?   Oh, I shall breathe
more freely when I am on the other side of
the Channel.   My aunt is much too good for
this place, and they don't approve of her, and
keep her down.'

CHAPTER XXII

REVENANTS

' But soft, behold ! lo, where it comes again !
I'll cross it, though it blast me.'

Hamlet.

FLOODS of tears were shed at the departure
of the two young officers of sixteen and seventeen.　The sobs of the household made the
English party feel very glad when it was
over and the cavalcade was in motion.　A
cavalcade it was, for each gentleman rode
and so did his body-servant, and each horse
had a mounted groom.　The two young
officers had besides each two chargers, re-
quiring a groom and horse boy, and each
conducted half a dozen fresh troopers to join
the army.　A coach was the regulation mode
of travelling for ladies, but both the English
girls had remonstrated so strongly that

Madame de Bellaise had consented to their riding, though she took them and Suzanne the first day's journey well beyond the ken of the Parisians in her own carriage, as far as Senlis, where there was a fresh parting with the two lads, fewer tears, and more counsel and encouragement, with many fond messages to her son, many to her sister in England, and with affectionate words to her niece a whisper to her to remember that she would not be in a Protestant country till she reached Holland or England.

The last sight they had of the tall dignified figure of the old lady was under the arch of the cathedral, where she was going to pray for their safety. Suzanne was to ride on a pillion beside the Swiss valet of Mr. Fellowes, whom Naomi had taken into her confidence, and the two young ladies each mounted a stout pony. Mr. Fellowes had made friends with the Abbé Leblanc, who was of the old Gallican type, by no means virulently set against Anglicanism, and also a highly culti-vated man, so that they had many subjects in common, besides the question of English Catholicity. The two young cousins, Ribaumont and D'Aubépine, were chiefly engaged in looking out for sport, setting their horses to race with one another, and the like, in which Charles Archfield sometimes took a share, but he usually rode with the two young ladies, and talked to them very pleasantly of his travels in Italy, the pictures and antiquities which had made into an interesting reality the studies that he had hated when a boy, also the condition of the country he had seen with a mind which seemed to have opened and enlarged with a sudden start beyond the interests of the next fox-hunt or game at bowls. All were, as he had predicted, greatly shocked at the aspect of the country through which they passed : the meagre crops ripening for harvest, the hay-carts, sometimes drawn by an equally lean cow and woman, the haggard women bearing heavy burthens, and the ragged, barefooted children leading a wretched cow or goat to browse by the wayside, the gaunt men toiling at road-mending with their poor starved horses, or at their seigneur's work, alike unpaid, even when drawn off from their own harvests. And in the villages the only sound buildings were the church and *presbytère* by its side, the dwellings being miserable hovels, almost sunk into the earth, an old crone or two, marvels of skinniness, spinning at the door, or younger women making lace, and nearly naked children rushing out to beg. Sometimes the pepper-box turrets of a château could be seen among distant woods, or the walls of a cloister, with a taper spire in the midst, among greener fields ; and the towns were approached through long handsome avenues, and their narrow streets had a greater look of prosperity, while their inns, being on the way to the place of warfare, were almost luxurious, with a choice of dainty meats and good wines. Everywhere else was misery, and Naomi said it was the vain endeavour to reform the source of these grievances that had forced her father to become an exile from his native country, and that he had much apprehended that the same blight might gradually be brought over his adopted land, on which Charles stood up for the constitution, and for the resolute character of Englishmen, and Anne, as in duty bound, for the good intentions of her godfather.

Thus they argued, and Anne not only felt herself restored to the company of rational beings, but greatly admired Charles's sentiments and the ability with which he put them forward, and now and then the thought struck her, and with a little twinge of pain of which she was ashamed, would Naomi Darpent be the healer of the wound nearly a year old, and find in him consolation for the hero of her girlhood? Somehow there would be a sense of disappointment in them both if so it were.

At length the spires and towers of Douai came in sight, fenced in by stern lines of fortification according to the science of Vauban —smooth slopes of glacis, with the terrible muzzles of cannon peeping out on the summits of the ramparts, and the line of salient angle and ravelin with the moat around, beautiful though formidable. The Marquis de Nidemerle had sent a young officer and sergeant's party to meet the travellers several miles off, and bring them unquestioned through the outposts of the frontier town, so closely watched in this time of war, and at about half a mile from the gates he himself, with a few attendants, rode out all glittering and clanking in their splendid uniforms and accoutrements.   He doffed his hat with the heavy white plume, and bowed his greeting to the ladies and clergymen, but both the young Frenchmen, after a military salute, hastily dismounted and knelt on one knee, while he sprang from his horse, and then, making the sign of the Cross over his son, raised him, and folding him in his arms pressed him to his breast and kissed him on each cheek, not without tears, then repeated the same greeting with young D'Aubépine.   He then kissed the hand of his *belle cousine*, whom, of course, he knew already, and bowed almost to the ground on being presented to Mademoiselle Woodford, a little less low to Monsieur Archfield, who was glad the embracing was not to be repeated, politely received Mr. Fellowes, and honoured the domestic abbé with a kindly word and nod.   The gradation was amusing, and he was a magnificent figure, with his noble horse and grand military dress, while his fine straight features, sunburnt though naturally fair, and his tall powerful frame, well became his surroundings

—'a true white Ribaumont,' as Naomi said, as she looked at the long fair hair drawn back and tied with ribbon. 'He is just like the portrait of our great-grandfather who was almost killed on the S. Barthélémi!' However, Naomi had no more time to talk *of* him, for he rode by her side inquiring for his mother, wife, and children, but carefully doing the honours to the stranger lady and gentlemen.

Moat and drawbridge there were at Portsmouth, and a sentry at the entrance, but here there seemed endless guards, moats, bridges, and gates, and there was a continual presenting of arms and acknowledging of salutes as the commandant rode in with the travellers. It was altogether a very new experience in life. They were lodged in the governor's quarters in the fortress, where the accommodation for ladies was of the slenderest, and M. de Nidemerle made many apologies, though he had evidently given up his own sleeping chamber to the two ladies, who would have to squeeze into his narrow campbed, with Suzanne on the floor, and the last was to remain there entirely, there being

no woman with whom she could have her
meals.   The ladies were invited to sup with
the staff, and would, as M. de Nidemerle
assured them, be welcomed with the greatest
delight.   So Naomi declared that they must
make their toilet do as much justice as possible to their country; and though full dress
was not attainable, they did their best with
ribbons and laces, and the arrangement of
her fair locks and Anne's brown ones, when
Suzanne proved herself an adept; the ladies
meantime finding no small amusement in the
varieties of swords, pistols, spurs, and other
accoutrements, for which the marquis had
apologised, though Naomi told him that they
were the fittest ornaments possible.

'And my cousin Gaspard is a really good
man,' she said, indicating to her friend the
little shrine with holy-water stoup, ivory
crucifix, print of the Madonna, two or three
devotional books, and the miniatures of
mother, wife, and children hung not far off;
also of two young cavaliers, one of whom
Naomi explained to be the young father whom
Gaspard could not recollect, the other, that of
the uncle Eustace, last Baron Walwyn and

Ribaumont, of whom her own mother talked with such passionate affection, and whose example had always been a guiding star to the young marquis.

He came to their door to conduct them down to supper, giving his arm to Miss Woodford as the greatest stranger, while Miss Darpent was conducted by a resplendent ducal colonel. The supper-room was in festal guise, hung round with flags, and the table adorned with flowers; a band was playing, and never had either Anne or Naomi been made so much of. All were eagerly talking, Charles especially so, and Anne thought, with a thrill, ‘Did he recollect that this was the very anniversary of that terrible 1st of July?’

It was a beautiful summer evening, and the supper taking place at five o’clock there was a considerable time to spare afterwards, so that M. de Nidemerle proposed to show the strangers the place, and the view from the ramparts.

‘In my company you can see all well,’ he said, ‘but otherwise there might be doubts and jealousies.’

He took them through the narrow Flemish

streets of tall houses with projecting upper
stories, and showed them that seminary which
was popularly supposed in England to be the
hotbed of truculent plots, but where they only
saw a quiet academic cloister and an exquisite
garden, green turf, roses and white lilies in
full perfection, and students flitting about in
cassocks and square caps, more like an Oxford
scene, as Mr. Fellowes said, than anything he
had yet seen.   He was joined by an English
priest from his own original neighbourhood.
The Abbé Leblanc found another acquaintance, and these two accompanied their friends
to the ramparts.   The marquis had a great
deal to hear from his cousin about his home,
and thus it happened that Charles Archfield
and Anne found themselves more practically
alone together than they had yet been.   As
they looked at the view over the country, he
told her of a conversation that he had had
with an officer now in the French army, but
who had served in the Imperial army against
the Turks, and that he had obtained much
useful information.

'Useful?' asked Anne.

'Yes.   I have been watching for the

moment to tell you, Anne ; I have resolved what to do. I intend to make a few campaigns there against the enemy of Christendom.'

'O Mr. Archfield !' was all she could say.

'See here, I have perceived plainly that to sink down into my lady's eldest son is no wholesome life for a man with all his powers about him. I understand now what a set of oafs we were to despise the poor fellow you wot of, because he was not such a lubber as ourselves. I have no mind to go through the like.'

'You are so different ; it could not be the same.'

'Not quite ; but remember there is nothing for me to do. My father is still an active man, and I am not old enough to take my part in public affairs, even if I loved greatly either the Prince of Orange or King James. I could not honestly draw my sword for either. I have no estate to manage, my child's inherit- ance is all in money, and it would drive me mad, or worse, to go home to be idle. No ; I will fight against the common enemy till I have made me a name, and won reputation and standing ; or if I should not come back, there's the babe at home to carry on the line.'

'Oh, sir! your father and mother—Lucy —all that love you.   What will they say?'

'It would only put them to needless pain to ask them.   I shall not.   I shall write explaining all my motives—all except one, and that you alone know, Anne.'

She shuddered a little, and felt him press her arm tightly.   They had fallen a good deal behind the marquis and his cousin, and were descending as twilight fell into a narrow, dark, lonely street, with all the houses shut up. 'No one has guessed, have they?' she faltered.

'Not that I know of.   But I cannot—no! I can*not* go home, to have that castle near me, and that household at Oakwood.   I see enough in my dreams without that.'

'See!   Ah, yes!'

'Then, Anne, you have suffered then too— guiltless as you are in keeping my terrible secret!   I have often thought and marvelled whether it were so with you.'

She was about to tell him what she had seen, when he began, 'There is one thing in this world that would sweeten and renew my life—and that?'

Her heart was beating violently at what was so suddenly coming on her, when at that instant Charles broke off short with 'Good Heavens!   What's that?'

On the opposite side of the street, where one of the many churches stood some way back, making an opening, there was a figure, essentially the same that Anne had seen at Lambeth, but bare-headed, clad apparently in something long and white, and with a pale bluish light on the ghastly but unmistakable features.

She uttered a faint gasping cry scarcely audible, Charles's impulse was to exclaim, ' Man or spirit, stand!' and drawing his sword to rush across the street; but in that second all had vanished, and he only struck against closed doors, which he shook, but could not open.

' Mr. Archfield! Oh, come back! I have seen it before,' entreated Anne; and he strode back, with a gesture of offering her support, and trembling, she clung to his arm. ' It does not hurt,' she said.   ' It comes and goes——'

'You have seen it before!'

'Twice.'

No more could be said, for through the gloom the white plume and gold-laced uniform of the marquis were seen.   He had missed them, and come back to look for them, beginning to apologise.

'I am confounded at having left mademoiselle behind.—*Comment!*'—as the sound betrayed that Charles was sheathing his sword.   'I trust that monsieur has met with no unpleasant adventure from my people.'

'Oh no, monsieur,' was the answer, as he added—

'One can never be sure as to these fiery spirits towards an Englishman in the present state of feeling, and I blame myself extremely for having permitted myself to lose sight of monsieur and mademoiselle.'

'Indeed, sir, we have met with no cause of complaint,' said Charles, adding as if casually, 'What is that church?'

''Tis the Jesuits' Church,' replied the governor.   'There is the best preaching in the town, they say, and Jansenists as we are, I was struck with the Lenten course.'

Anne went at once to her room on returning to the house. Naomi, who was there already, exclaimed at her paleness, and insisted on administering a glass of wine from what the English called the rere supper, the French an *encas*, the substantial materials for which had been left in the chamber. Then Anne felt how well it had been for her that her fellows at the palace had been so uncongenial, for she could hardly help disclosing to Naomi the sight she had seen, and the half-finished words she had heard. It was chiefly the feeling that she could not bear Naomi to know of the blood on Charles's hand which withheld her in her tumult of feeling, and made her only entreat, 'Do not ask me, I cannot tell you.' And Naomi, who was some years older, and had had her own sad experience, guessed perhaps at one cause for her agitation, and spared her inquiries, though as Anne, tired out by the long day, and forced by their close quarters to keep herself still, dropped asleep, strange mutterings fell from her lips about 'The vault—the blood—come back. There he is. The secret has risen to forbid. O, poor Peregrine!'

Between the July heat, the narrow bed, and the two chamber fellows, Anne had little time to collect her thoughts, except for the general impression that if Charles finished what he had begun to say, the living and the dead alike must force her to refuse, though something within forboded that this would cost her more than she yet durst perceive, and her heart was ready to spring forth and enclose him as it were in an embrace of infinite tenderness, above all when she thought of his purpose of going to those fearful Hungarian wars.

But after the hot night, it was a great relief to prepare for an early start. M. de Nidemerle had decided on sending the travellers to Tournay, the nearest Spanish town, on the Scheldt, since he had some acquaintance with the governor, and when no campaign was actually on foot the courtesies of generous enemies passed between them. He had already sent an intimation of his intention of forwarding an English kinswoman of his own with her companions, and bespoken the good offices of his neighbour, and they were now to set off in very early morning under the escort of a flag of truce, a trumpeter, and a party of troopers, commanded by an experienced old officer with white moustaches and the peaked beard of the last generation, contrasting with a face the colour of walnut wood.

The marquis himself and his son, however, rode with the travellers for their first five miles, through a country where the rich green of the natural growth showed good soil, all enamelled with flowers and corn crops run wild ; but the villages looked deserted, the remains of burnt barns and houses were frequent, and all along that frontier, it seemed as if no peaceful inhabitants ventured to settle, and only brigands often rendered such by misery might prowl about. The English party felt as if they had never understood what war could be.

However, in a melancholy orchard run wild, under the shade of an apple-tree laden with young fruit, backed by a blackened gable half concealed by a luxuriant un-trimmed vine, the *avant couriers* of the commandant had cleared a space in the rank grass, and spread a morning meal, of cold *pâté*, fowl and light wines, in which the French officers drank to the good journey of their friends, and then when the horses had likewise had their refreshment the parting took place with much affection between the cousins. The young Ribaumont augured that they should meet again when he had to protect Noémi in a grand descent on Dorsetshire in behalf of James, and she merrily shook her fist at him and defied him, and his father allowed that they were a long way from that.

M. de Nidemerle hinted to Mr. Archfield that nobody could tell him more about the war with the Turks than M. le Capitaine Delaune, who was, it appeared, a veteran Swiss who had served in almost every army in Europe, and thus could give information by no means to be neglected. So that, to Anne's surprise and somewhat to her mortification, since she had no knowledge of the cause, she saw Charles riding apart with this wooden old veteran, who sat as upright as a ramrod on his wiry-looking black horse, leaving her to the company of Naomi and Mr. Fellowes. Did he really wish not to pursue the topic which had brought Peregrine from his grave? It would of course be all the better, but it cost her some terrible pangs to think so.

There were far more formalities and delays before the travellers could cross the Tournay bridge across the Scheldt. They were brought to a standstill a furlong off, and had to wait while the trumpeter rode forward with the white flag, and the message was referred to the officer on guard, while a sentry seemed to be watching over them. Then the officer came to the gateway of the bridge, and Captain Delaune rode forward to him, but there was still a long weary waiting in the sun before he came back, after having shown their credentials to the governor, and then he was accompanied by a Flemish officer, who, with much courtesy, took them under his charge, and conducted them through all the defences, over the bridge, and to the gate where their baggage had to be closely examined. Naomi had her Bible in her bosom, or it would not have escaped; Anne heartily wished she had used the same precaution on her flight from England, but she

had not, like her friend, been warned before-
hand.

When within the city there was more
freedom, and the Fleming conducted the
party to an inn, where, unlike English inns,
they could not have a parlour to themselves,
but had to take their meals in common with
other guests at a sort of *table d'hôte*, and the
ladies had no refuge but their bedroom, where
the number of beds did not promise privacy.
An orderly soon arrived with an invitation to
Don Carlos Arcafila to sup with the Spanish
governor, and of course the invitation could
not be neglected. The ladies walked about
a little in the town with Mr. Fellowes, looking without appreciation at the splendid five-
towered cathedral, but recollecting with due
English pride that the place had been con-
quered by Henry VIII. Thence they were
to make for Ostend, where they were certain
of finding a vessel bound for England.

It was a much smaller party that set forth
from Tournay than from Paris, and soon
they fell into pairs, Mr. Fellowes and Naomi
riding together, sufficiently out of earshot of
the others for Charles to begin—

'I have not been able to speak to you, Anne, since that strange interruption — if indeed it were not a dream.'

'Oh, sir, it was no dream! How could it be?'

'How could it, indeed, when we both saw it, and both of us awake and afoot, and yet I cannot believe my senses.'

'Oh, I can believe it only too truly! I have seen him twice before. I thought you said you had.'

'Merely in dreams, and that is bad enough.'

'Are you sure? for I was up and awake.'

'Are *you* sure? I might ask again. I was asleep in bed, and glad enough to shake myself awake. Where were you?'

'Once on Hallowmas Eve, looking from the window at Whitehall; once when waiting with the Queen under the wall of Lambeth Church, on the night of our flight.'

'Did others see him then?'

'I was alone the first time. The next time when he flitted across the light, no one else saw him; but they cried out at my start. Why should he appear except to us?'

'That is true,' muttered Charles.

'And oh, sir, those two times he looked as he did in life—not ghastly as now. There can be no doubt now that——'

'What, sweet Anne?'

'Sir, I must tell you! I could bear it no longer, and I *did* consult the Bishop of Bath and Wells.'

'Any more?' he asked in a somewhat displeased voice.

'No one, not a soul, and he is as safe as any of the priests here; he regards a confession in the same way. Mr. Archfield, forgive me. He seemed divinely sent to me on that All Saints' day! Oh, forgive me!' and tears were in her eyes.

'He is Dr. Ken—eh? I remember him. I suppose he is as safe as any man, and a woman must have some relief. You have borne enough indeed,' said Charles, greatly touched by her tears. 'What did he say?'

'He asked, was I certain of the—death,' said she, bringing out the word with difficulty; 'but then I had only seen *it* at Whitehall; and these other appearances, in such places too, take away all hope that it is otherwise!'

'Assuredly,' said Charles ; 'I had not the least doubt at the moment. I know I ran my sword through his body, and felt a jar that I believe was his backbone,' he said with a shudder, 'and he fell prone and breathless ; but since I have seen more of fencing, and heard more of wounds, the dread has crossed me that I acted as an inexperienced lad, and that I ought to have tried whether the life was in him, or if he could be recovered. If so, I slew him twice, by launching him into that pit. God forgive me !'

'Is it so deep ?' asked Anne, shuddering. 'I know there is a sort of step at the top ; but I always shunned the place, and never looked in.'

'There are two or three steps at the top, but all is broken away below. Sedley and I once threw a ball down, and I am sure it dropped to a depth down which no man could fall and *live*. I believe there once were underground passages leading to the harbour on one hand, and out to Portsdown Hill on the other, but that the communication was broken away and the openings destroyed when Lord Goring was governor of Portsmouth, to secure the castle. Be that as it may, he could not have been living after he reached that floor. I heard the thud, and the jingle of his sword, and it will haunt me to my dying day.'

'And yet you never intended it. You did it in defence of me. You did not mean to strike thus hard. It was an accident.'

'Would that I could so feel it!' he sighed. 'Nay, of course I had no evil design when my poor little wife drove me out to give you her rag of ribbon, or whatever it was ; but I hated as well as despised the fellow. He had angered me with his scorn—well deserved, as now I see—of our lubberly ways. She had vexed me with her teasing commendations—out of harmless mischief, poor child. I hated him more every time you looked at him, and when I had occasion to strike him I was glad of it. There was murder in my heart, and I felt as if I were putting a rat or a weasel out of the way when I threw him down that pit. God forgive me! Then, in my madness, I so acted that in a manner I was the death of that poor young thing.'

'No, no, sir.   Your mother had never thought she would live.'

'So they say; but her face comes before me in reproach.   There are times when I feel myself a double murderer.   I have been on the point of telling all to Mr. Fellowes, or going home to accuse myself. Only the thought of my father and mother, and of leaving such a blight on that poor baby, has withheld me; but I cannot go home to face the sight of the castle.'

'No,' said Anne, choked with tears.

'Nor is there any suspicion of the poor fellow's fate,' he added.

'Not that I ever heard.'

'His family think him fled, as was like enough, considering the way in which they treated him,' said Charles.   'Nor do I see what good it would do them to know the truth.'

'It would only be a grief and bitterness to all.'

'I hope I have repented, and that God accepts my forgiveness,' said Charles sadly. 'I am banishing myself from all I love, and there is a weight on me for life; but, unless suspicion falls on others, I do not feel bound to make it worse for all by giving myself up. Yet those appearances—to you, to me, to us both! At such a moment, too, last night!'

'Can it be because of his unhallowed grave?' said Anne, in a low voice of awe.

'If it were!' said Charles, drawing up his horse for a moment in thought. 'Anne, if there be one more appearance, the place shall be searched, whether it incriminate me or not. It would be adding to all my wrongs towards the poor fellow, if that were the case.'

'Even if he were found,' said Anne, 'suspicion would not light on you. And at home it will be known if he haunts the place. I will——'

'Nay, but, Anne, he will not interrupt me now. I have much more to say. I want you to remember that we were sweethearts ere ever I, as a child of twelve, knew that I was contracted to that poor babe, and bidden to think only of her. Poor child! I honestly did my best to love her, so far as I knew how, and mayhap we could have rubbed on through life passably well as things go. But—but—— It skills not talking of things gone by, except to show that it is a whole heart—not the reversion of one—that is yours for ever, mine only love.'

'Oh, but—but—I am no match for you.'

'I've had enough of grand matches.'

'Your father would never endure it.'

'My father would soon rejoice. Besides, if we are wedded here—say at Ostend—and you make me a home at Buda, or Vienna, or some place at our winter quarters, as my brave wench will, my father will be glad enough to see us both at home again.'

'No; it cannot be. It would be plain treachery to your parents; Mr. Fellowes would say so. I am sure he would not marry us.'

'There are English chaplains. Is that all that holds you back?'

'No, sir. If the Archbishop of Canterbury were here himself, it could not make it other than a sin, and an act of mean ingratitude, for me, the Prince's rocker, to take advantage of their goodness in permitting you to come and bring me home—to do what would be pain, grief, and shame to them.'

'Never shame.'

'What is wrong is shame! Cannot you see how unworthy it would be in me, and how it would grieve my uncle that I should have done such a thing?'

'Love would override scruples.'

'Not *true* love.'

'True! Then you own to some love for me, Anne.'

'I do—not—know. I have guarded—I mean—cast away—I mean—never entertained any such thought ever since I was old enough to know how wicked it would be.'

'Anne! Anne!' (in an undertone very like rapture), 'you have confessed all! It is no sin *now*. Even you cannot say so.'

She hung her head and did not answer, but silence was enough for him.

'It is enough!' he said; 'you will wait. I shall know you are waiting till I return in such sort that nothing can be denied me. Let me at least have that promise.'

'You need not fear,' murmured Anne. 'How could I need? The secret would withhold me, were there nothing else.'

'And there is something else? Eh.

sweetheart ?   Is that all I am to be satisfied with ?'

'Oh, sir !— Mr. Archfield, I mean — O Charles !' she stammered.

Mr. Fellowes turned round to consult his pupil as to whether the halt should be made at the village whose peaked roofs were seen over the fruit trees.

But when Anne was lifted down from the steed it was with no grasp of common courtesy, and her hand was not relinquished till it had been fervently kissed.

Charles did not again torment her with entreaties to share his exile.   Mayhap he recognised, though unwillingly, that her judgment had been right, but there was no small devotion in his whole demeanour, as they dined, rode, and rested on that summer's day amid fields of giant haycocks, and hostels wreathed with vines, with long vistas of sleek cows and plump dappled horses in the sheds behind.   The ravages of war had lessened as they rode farther from the frontier, and the rich smiling landscape lay rejoicing in the summer sunshine ; the sturdy peasants looked as if they had never heard of marauders, as

they herded their handsome cattle and responded civilly when a draught of milk was
asked for the ladies.

There was that strange sense of Eden
felicity that sometimes comes with the knowledge that the time is short for mutual enjoy-
ment in full peace. Charles and Anne would
part, their future was undefined; but for the
present they reposed in the knowledge of
each other's hearts, and in being together.
It was as in their childhood, when by tacit
consent he had been Anne's champion from
the time she came as a little Londoner to be
alarmed at rough country ways, and to be
easily scared by Sedley. It had been then
that Charles had first awakened to the
chivalry of the better part of boyhood's
nature, instead of following his cousin's lead,
and treating girls as creatures meant to be
bullied. Many a happy reminiscence was
shared between the two as they rode together,
and it was not till the pale breadth of sea
filled their horizon, broken by the tall spires
and peaked gables and many-windowed steep
roofs of Ostend, that the future was permitted
to come forward and trouble them. Then

Anne's heart began to feel that persistence in her absolute refusal was a much harder thing than at the first, when the idea was new and strange to her. And there were strange yearnings that Charles should renew the proposal, mixed with dread of herself and of her own resolution in case of his doing so. As her affections embraced him more and more she pictured him sick, wounded, dying, out of reach of all, among Germans, Hungarians, Turks,—no one at hand to comfort him or even to know his fate.

There was even disappointment in his acquiescence, though her better mind told her that it was in accordance with her prayers against temptation. Moreover, he was of a reserved nature, not apt to discuss what was once fixed, and perhaps it showed that he respected her judgment not to try to shake her decision. Though for once love had carried him away, he might perhaps be grateful to her for sparing him the perplexities of dragging her about with him and of giving additional offence to his parents. The affection born of lifelong knowledge is not apt to be of the vehement character that disregards all obstacles or possible miseries to the object thereof. Yet enough feeling was betrayed to make Naomi whisper at night, ' Sweet Nan, are you not some one else's sweet ?'

And Anne, now with another secret on her heart, only replied with embraces, and, ' Do not talk of it ! I cannot tell how it is to be. I cannot tell you all.'

Naomi was discreet enough only to caress.

With strict formalities at outworks, moat, drawbridge, and gates, and the customary in- quisitorial search of the luggage, the travellers were allowed to repair to a lofty inn, with the Lion of Flanders for its sign, and a wide courtyard, the successive outside galleries covered with luxuriant vines. Here, as usual, though the party of females obtained one bedroom together, the gentlemen had to share one vast sleeping chamber with a variety of merchants, Dutch, Flemish, Spanish, and a few English. Meals were at a great *table d'hôte* in the public room, opening into the court, and were shared by sundry Spanish, Belgic, and Swiss officers of the garrison, who made this their mess-room. Two young

English gentlemen, like Charles Archfield, making the grand tour, whom he had met in Italy, were delighted to encounter him again, and still more so at the company of English ladies.

'No wonder the forlorn widower has recovered his spirits!' Anne heard one say with a laugh that made her blush and turn away; and there was an outcry that after a monopoly of the fair ones all the way from Paris, the seats next to them must be yielded.

Anne was disappointed, and could not bring herself to be agreeable to the obtrusive cavalier with the rich lace cravat and perfumed hair, both assumed in her honour.

The discussion was respecting the vessels where a passage might be obtained. The cavaliers were to sail in a couple of days for London, but another ship would go out of harbour with the tide on the following day for Southampton, and this was decided on by acclamation by the Hampshire party, though no good accommodation was promised them.

There was little opportunity for a *tête-à-tête*, for the young men insisted on escorting the ladies to the picture galleries, palaces, and gardens, and Charles did not wish to reawaken the observations that, according to the habits of the time, might not be of the choicest description.   Anne watched him under her eyelashes, and wondered with beating heart whether after all he intended to return home, and there plead his cause, for he gave no token of intending to separate from the rest.

The *Hampshire Hog* was to sail at daybreak, so the passengers went on board over night, after supper, when the summer twilight was sinking down and the far-off west still had a soft golden tint.

Anne felt Charles's arm round her in the boat and grasping her hand, then pulling off her glove and putting a ring on her finger—all in silence.   She still felt that arm on the deck in the confusion of men, ropes, and bales of goods, and the shouts and hails on all sides that nearly deafened her.   There was imminent danger of being hurled down, if not overboard, among the far from sober sailors, and Mr. Fellowes urged the ladies to go below at once, conducting Miss Darpent himself as soon as he could ascertain where to go.   Anne felt herself almost lifted down. Then followed a strong embrace, a kiss on brow, lips, and either cheek, and a low hoarse whisper—'So best!   Mine own!   God bless you,'—and as Suzanne came tumbling aft into the narrow cabin, Anne found herself left alone with her two female companions, and knew that these blissful days were over.

CHAPTER XXIII

> ' When ye gang awa, Jamie,
>   Far across the sea, laddie,
> When ye gang to Germanie
>   What will ye send to me, laddie ? '
>
> *Huntingtower.*

Fides was the posy on the ring. That was
all Anne could discover, and indeed only this
much with the morning light of the July sun
that penetrated the remotest corners. For
the cabin was dark and stifling, and there
was no leaving it, for both Miss Darpent and
her attendant were so ill as to engross her
entirely.

She could hardly leave them when there
was a summons to a meal in the captain's cabin,
and there she found herself the only passenger
able to appear, and the rest of the company,

though intending civility, were so rough that she was glad to retreat again, and wretched as the cabin was, she thought it preferable to the deck.

Mr. Fellowes, she heard, was specially prostrated, and jokes were passing round that it was the less harm, since it might be the worse for him if the crew found out that there was a parson on board.

Thus Anne had to forego the first sight of her native land, and only by the shouts above and the decreased motion of the vessel knew when she was within lee of the Isle of Wight, and on entering the Solent could encourage her companions that their miseries were nearly over, and help them to arrange themselves for going upon deck.

When at length they emerged, as the ship lay to in sight of the red roofs and white steeples of Southampton, and of the green mazes of the New Forest, Mr. Fellowes was found looking everywhere for the pupil whom he had been too miserable to miss during the voyage. Neither Charles Archfield nor his servant was visible, but Mr. Fellowes's own man coming forward, delivered to the bewildered tutor a packet which he said that his comrade had put in his charge for the purpose. In the boat, on the way to land, Mr. Fellowes read to himself the letter, which of course filled him with extreme distress. It contained much of what Charles had already explained to Anne of his conviction that in the present state of affairs it was better for so young a man as himself, without sufficient occupation at home, to seek honourable service abroad, and that he thought it would spare much pain and perplexity to depart without revisiting home. He added full and well-expressed thanks for all that Mr. Fellowes had done for him, and for kindness for which he hoped to be the better all his life. He enclosed a long letter to his father, which he said would, he hoped, entirely exonerate his kind and much-respected tutor from any remissness or any participation in the scheme which he had thought it better on all accounts to conceal till the last.

'And indeed,' said poor Mr. Fellowes, 'if I had had any inkling of it, I should have applied to the English Consul to restrain him as a ward under trust. But no one would

have thought it of him.   He had always
been reasonable and docile beyond his years,
and I trusted him entirely.   I should as soon
have thought of our President giving me the
slip in this way.   Surely he came on board
with us.'

'He handed me into the boat,' said Miss
Darpent.   'Who saw him last?   Did you,
Miss Woodford?'

Anne was forced to own that she had seen
him on board, and her cheeks were in spite
of herself such tell-tales that Mr. Fellowes
could not help saying, 'It is not my part to
rebuke you, madam, but if you were aware of
this evasion, you will have a heavy reckoning
to pay to the young man's parents.'

'Sir,' said Anne, 'I knew indeed that he
meant to join the Imperial army, but I knew
not how nor when.'

'Ah, well! I ask no questions.   You need
not justify yourself to me, young lady; but
Sir Philip and Lady Archfield little knew
what they did when they asked us to come
by way of Paris.   Not that I regret it on all
accounts,' he added, with a courteous bow to
Naomi which set her blushing in her turn.

He avoided again addressing Miss Woodford, and she thought with consternation of the prejudice he might excite against her. It had been arranged between the two maidens that Naomi should be a guest at Portchester Rectory till she could communicate with Walwyn, and her father or brother could come and fetch her.

They landed at the little wharf, among the colliers, and made their way up the street to an inn, where, after ordering a meal to satisfy the ravenous sea-appetite, Mr. Fellowes, after a few words with Naomi, left the ladies to their land toilet, while he went to hire horses for the journey.

Then Naomi could not help saying, 'O Anne! I did not think you would have done this. I am grieved!'

'You do not know all,' said Anne sadly, 'or you would not think so hardly.'

'I saw you had an understanding with him. I see you have a new ring on your finger; but how could I suppose you would encourage an only son thus to leave his parents?'

'Hush, hush, Naomi!' cried Anne, as the

uncontrollable tears broke out. 'Don't you believe that it is quite as hard for me as for them that he should have gone off to fight those dreadful bloodthirsty Turks? Indeed I would have hindered him, but that—but that—I know it is best for him. No! I can't tell you why, but I *know* it is; and even to the very last, when he helped me down the companion-ladder, I hoped he might be coming home first.'

'But you are troth-plight to him, and secretly?'

'I am not troth-plight; I know I am not his equal, I told him so, but he thrust this ring on me in the boat, in the dark, and how could I give it back!'

Naomi shook her head, but was more than half-disarmed by her friend's bitter weeping. Whether she gave any hint to Mr. Fellowes Anne did not know, but his manner remained drily courteous, and as Anne had to ride on a pillion behind a servant she was left in a state of isolation as to companionship, which made her feel herself in disgrace, and almost spoilt the joy of dear familiar recognition of hill, field, and tree, after her long year's absence, the longest year in her life, and substituted the sinking of heart lest she should be returning to hear of misfortune and disaster, sickness or death.

Her original plan had been to go on with Naomi to Portchester at once, if by inquiry at Fareham she found that her uncle was at home, but she perceived that Mr. Fellowes decidedly wished that Miss Darpent should go first to the Archfields, and something within her determined first to turn thither in spite of all there was to encounter, so that she might still her misgivings by learning whether her uncle was well. So she bade the man turn his horse's head towards the well-known poplars in front of Archfield House.

The sound of the trampling horses brought more than one well-known old 'blue-coated serving-man' into the court, and among them a woman with a child in her arms. There was the exclamation, 'Mistress Anne! Sure Master Charles be not far behind,' and the old groom ran to help her down.

'Oh! Ralph, thanks. All well? My uncle?'

'He is here, with his Honour,' and in

scarcely a moment more Lucy, swift of foot, had flown out, and had Anne in her embrace, and crying out—

'Ah, Charles! my brother! I don't see him.'

Anne was glad to have no time to answer before she was in her uncle's arms. 'My child, at last! God bless thee! Safe in soul and body!'

Sir Philip was there, too, greeting Mr. Fellowes, and looking for his son, and with the cursory assurance that Mr. Archfield was well, and that they would explain, a hasty introduction of Miss Darpent was made, and all moved in to where Lady Archfield, more feeble and slow of movement, had come into the hall, and the nurse stood by with the little heir to be shown to his father, and Sedley Archfield stood in the background. It was a cruel moment for all, when the words came from Mr. Fellowes, 'Sir, I have to tell you, Mr. Archfield is not here. This letter, he tells me, is to explain.'

There was an outburst of exclamation, during which Sir Philip withdrew into a window with his spectacles to read the letter, while all to which the tutor or Anne ventured to commit themselves was that Mr. Archfield had only quitted them without notice on board the *Hampshire Hog.*

The first tones of the father had a certain sound of relief, ' Gone to the Imperialist army to fight the Turks in Hungary!'

Poor Lady Archfield actually shrieked, and Lucy turned quite pale, while Anne caught a sort of lurid flush of joy on Sedley Archfield's features, and he was the first to exclaim, ' Undutiful young dog!'

' Tut! tut!' returned Sir Philip, ' he might as well have come home first, and yet I do not know but that it is the best thing he could do.   There might have been difficulties in the way of getting out again, you see, my lady, as things stand now.   Ay! ay! you are in the right of it, my boy.   It is just as well to let things settle themselves down here before committing himself to one side or the other.   'Tis easy enough for an old fellow like me who has to let nothing go but his Commission of the Peace, but not the same for a stirring young lad; and he is altogether right as to not coming back to idle here as a

rich man. It would be the ruin of him. I
am glad he has the sense to see it. I was
casting about to obtain an estate for him to
give him occupation.'

'But the wars,' moaned the mother; 'if
he had only come home we could have persuaded him.'

'The wars, my lady! Why, they will be
a feather in his cap; and may be if he had
come home, the Dutchman would have
claimed him for his, and let King James be
as misguided as he may, I cannot stomach
fighting against his father's son for myself or
mine. No, no; it was the best thing there
was for the lad to do. You shall hear his
letter, it does him honour, and you, too, Mr.
Fellowes. He could not have written such
a letter when he left home barely a year ago.'-

Sir Philip proceeded to read the letter
aloud. There was a full explanation of the
motives, political and private, only leaving
out one, and that the most powerful of all of
those which led Charles Archfield to absent
himself for the present. He entreated pardon
for having made the decision without obtain-
ing permission from his father on returning

home ; but he had done so in view of possible obstacles to his leaving England again, and to the belief that a brief sojourn at home would cause more grief and perplexity than his absence. He further explained, as before, his reasons for secrecy towards his travelling companion, and entreated his father not to suppose for a moment that Mr. Fellowes had been in any way culpable for what he could never have suspected ; warmly affectionate messages to mother and sister followed, and an assurance of feeling that 'the little one' needed for no care or affection while with them.

Lady Archfield was greatly disappointed, and cried a great deal, making sure that the poor dear lad's heart was still too sore to brook returning after the loss of his wife, who had now become the sweetest creature in the world ; but Sir Philip's decision that the measure was wise, and the secrecy under the circumstances so expedient as to be pardonable, prevented all public blame. Mr. Fellowes, however, was drawn apart, and asked whether he suspected any other motive than was here declared, and which might make his pupil unwilling to face the parental brow, and he had declared that nothing could have been more exemplary than the whole demeanour of the youth, who had at first gone about as one crushed, and though slowly reviving into cheerfulness, had always been subdued, until quite recently, when the meeting with his old companion had certainly much enlivened his spirits. Poor Mr. Fellowes had been rejoicing in the excellent character he should have to give, when this evasion had so utterly disconcerted him, and it was an infinite relief to him to find that all was thought comprehensible and pardonable.

Anne might be thankful that none of the authorities thought of asking her the question about hidden motives; and Naomi, looking about with her bright eyes, thought she had perhaps judged too hardly when she saw the father's approval, and that the mother and sister only mourned at the disappointment at not seeing the beloved one.

The Archfields would not hear of letting any of the party go on to Portchester that evening. Dr. Woodford, who had ridden over for consultation with Sir Philip, must remain, he would have plenty of time for his niece by and by, and she and Miss Darpent must tell them all about the journey, and about Charles; and Anne must tell them hundreds of things about herself that they scarcely knew, for not one letter from St. Germain had ever reached her uncle.

How natural it all looked! the parlour just as when she saw it last, and the hall, with the long table being laid for supper, and the hot sun streaming in through the heavy casements.   She could have fancied it yesterday that she had left it, save for the plump rosy little yearling with flaxen curls peeping out under his round white cap, who had let her hold him in her arms and fondle him all through that reading of his father's letter. Charles's child! ' He was her prince indeed now.

He was taken from her and delivered over to Lady Archfield to be caressed and pitied because his father would not come home 'to see his grand-dame's own beauty,' while Lucy took the guests upstairs to prepare for supper, Naomi and her maid being bestowed in the best guest-chamber, and Lucy taking her friend to her own, the scene of many a con-fabulation of old.

'Oh, how I love it!' cried Anne, as the door opened on the well-known little wainscotted abode. 'The very same beau-pot. One would think they were the same clove-gilly flowers as when I went away.'

'O Anne dear, and you are just the same after all your kings and queens, and all you have gone through;' and the two friends were locked in another embrace.

'Kings and queens indeed! None of them all are worth my Lucy.'

'And now, tell me all; tell me all, Anne, and first of all about my brother. How does he look, and is he well?'

'He looks! O Lucy, he is grown such a noble cavalier; most like the picture of that uncle of yours who was killed, and that Sir Philip always grieves for.'

'My father always hoped Charley would be like him,' said Lucy. 'You must tell him that. But I fear he may be grave and sad.'

'Graver, but not sad now.'

'And you have seen him and talked to

him, Anne? Did you know he was going
on this terrible enterprise?'

'He spoke of it, but never told me when.'

'Ah! I was sure you knew more about it
than the old tutor man. You always were
his little sweetheart before poor little Madam
came in the way, and he would tell you anything near his heart. Could you not have
stopped him?'

'I think not, Lucy; he gave his reasons
like a man of weight and thought, and you
see his Honour thinks them sound ones.'

'Oh yes; but somehow I cannot fancy
our Charley doing anything for grand, sound,
musty reasons, such as look well marshalled
out in a letter.'

'You don't know how much older he is
grown,' said Anne, again, with the tell-tale
colour in her cheeks. 'Besides, he cannot
bear to come home.'

'Don't tell me that, Nan. My mother
does not see it; but though he was fond of
poor little Madam in a way, and tried to
think himself more so, as in duty bound, she
really was fretting and wearing the very life
—no, perhaps not the life, but the temper—

out of him. What I believe it to be the cause is, that my father must have been writing to him about that young gentlewoman in the island that he is so set upon, because she would bring a landed estate which would give Charles something to do. They say that Peregrine Oakshott ran away to escape wedding his cousin ; Charley will banish himself for the like cause.'

'He said nothing of it,' said Anne.

'O Anne, I wish you had a landed estate ! You would make him happier than any other, and would love his poor little Phil ! Anne ! is it so ? I have guessed !' and Lucy kissed her on each cheek.

'Indeed, indeed I have not promised. I know it can never, never be—and that I am not fit for him. Do not speak of it, Lucy ! He spoke of it once as we rode together——'

'And you could not be so false as to tell him you did not love him ? No, you could not ;' and Lucy kissed her again.

'No,' faltered Anne ; 'but I would not do as he wished. I have given him no troth-plight. I told him it would never be per-mitted. And he said no more, but he put this ring on my finger in the boat without a word. I ought not to wear it; I shall not.'

'Oh yes, you shall. Indeed you shall. No one need understand it but myself, and it makes us sisters. Yes, Anne, Charley was right. My father will not consent now, but he will in due time, if he does not hear of it till he wearies to see Charles again. Trust it to me, my sweet sister that is to be.'

'It is a great comfort that you know,' said Anne, almost moved to tell her the greater and more perilous secret that lay in the background, but withheld by receiving Lucy's own confidence that she herself was at present tormented by her cousin Sedley's courtship. He was still, more's the pity, she said, in garrison at Portsmouth, but there were hopes of his regiment being ere long sent to the Low Countries, since it was believed to be more than half inclined to King James. In the meantime he certainly had designs on Lucy's portion, and as her father never believed half the stories of his debaucheries that were rife, and had a kindness for his only brother's orphan, she did not feel secure against his yielding so as to provide for Sedley without continuance in the Dutch service.

'I could almost follow the example of running away!' said Lucy.

'I suppose,' Anne ventured to say, faltering, 'that nothing has been heard of poor Mr. Oakshott.'

'Nothing at all. His uncle's people, who have come home from Muscovy, know nothing of him, and it is thought he may have gone off to the plantations. The talk is that Mistress Martha is to be handed on to the third brother, but that she is not willing.' It was clear that there could have been no spectres here, and Lucy went on, 'But you have told me nothing yet of yourself and your doings, my Anne. How well you look, and more than ever the Court lady, even in your old travelling habit. Is that the watch the King gave you?'

In private and in public there was quite enough to tell on that evening for intimate friends who had not met for a year, and one of whom had gone through so many vicissitudes. Nor were the other two guests by any means left out of the welcome, and the evening was a very happy one.

Mr. Fellowes intimated his intention of going himself to Walwyn with the news of Miss Darpent's arrival, and Naomi accepted the invitation to remain at Portchester till she could be sent for from home.

It was not till the next morning that Anne Woodford could be alone with her uncle. As she came downstairs in the morning she saw him waiting for her; he held out his hands, and drew her out with him into the walled garden that lay behind the house.

'Child! dear child!' said he, 'you are welcome to my old eyes. May God bless you, as He has aided you to be faithful alike to Him and to your King through much trial.'

'Ah, sir! I have sorely repented the folly and ambition that would not heed your counsel.'

'No doubt, my maid; but the spirit of humility and repentance hath worked well in you. I fear me, however, that you are come back to further trials, since probably Portchester may be no longer our home.'

'Nor Winchester?'

'Nor Winchester.'

'Then is this new King going to persecute as in the old times you talk of?   He who was brought over to save the Church!'

'He accepts the English Church, my maid, so far as it accepts him.   All beneficed clergy are required to take the oath of allegiance to him before the first of August, now approaching, under pain of losing their preferments. Many of my brethren, even our own Bishop and Dean, think this merely submission to the powers that be, and that it may be lawfully done ; but as I hear neither the Archbishop himself, nor my good old friends Doctors Ken and Frampton can reconcile it to their conscience, any more than my brother Stanbury, of Botley, nor I, to take this fresh oath, while the King to whom we have sworn is living.   Some hold that he has virtually renounced our allegiance by his flight.   I cannot see it, while he is fighting for his crown in Ireland.   What say you, Anne, who have seen him ; did he treat his case as that of an abdicated prince ?'

'No, sir, certainly not.   All the talk was of his enjoying his own again.'

'How can I then, consistently with my duty and loyalty, swear to this William and Mary as my lawful sovereigns? I say not 'tis incumbent on me to refuse to live under them a peaceful life, but make oath to them as my King and Queen I cannot, so long as King James shall live. True, he has not been a friend to the Church, and has wofully trampled on the rights of Englishmen, but I cannot hold that this absolves me from my duty to him, any more than David was freed from duty to Saul. So, Anne, back must we go to the poverty in which I was reared with your own good father.'

Anne might grieve, but she felt the gratification of being talked to by her uncle as a woman who could understand, as he had talked to her mother.

'The first of August!' she repeated, as if it were a note of doom.

'Yes; I hear whispers of a further time of grace, but I know not what difference that should make. A Christian man's oath may not be broken sooner or later. Well, poverty is the state blessed by our Lord, and it may be that I have lived too much at mine ease;

but I could wish, dear child, that you were safely bestowed in a house of your own.'

'So do not I,' said Anne, 'for now I can work for you.'

He smiled faintly, and here Mr. Fellowes joined them ; a good man likewise, but intent on demonstrating the other side of the question, and believing that the Popish, persecuting King had forfeited his rights, so that there need be no scruple as to renouncing what he had thrown up by his flight. It was an endless argument, in which each man could only act according to his own conscience, and endeavour that this conscience should be as little biassed as possible by worldly motives or animosity.

Mr. Fellowes started at once with his servant for Walwyn, and Naomi accompanied the two Woodfords to Portchester. In spite of the cavalier sentiments of her family, Naomi had too much of the spirit of her Frondeur father to understand any feeling for duty towards the King, who had so decidedly broken his covenant with his people, and moreover had so abominably treated the Fellows of Magdalen College ; and her pity for Anne as a sufferer for her uncle's whim quite angered her friend into hot defence of him and his cause.

The dear old parsonage garden under the gray walls, the honeysuckle and monthly roses trailing over the porch, the lake-like creek between it and green Portsdown Hill, the huge massive keep and towers, and the masts in the harbour, the Island hills sleeping in blue summer haze—Anne's heart clave to them more than ever for the knowledge that the time was short and that the fair spot must be given up for the right's sake. Certainly there was some trepidation at the thought of the vault, and she had made many vague schemes for ascertaining that which her very flesh trembled at the thought of any one suspecting ; but these were all frustrated, for since the war with France had begun, the bailey had been put under repair and garrisoned by a detachment of soldiers, the vault had been covered in, there was a sentry at the gateway of the castle, and the postern door towards the vicarage was fastened up, so that though the parish still repaired to church through the wide court, solitary wanderings there were no longer possible, nor indeed safe for a young woman, considering what the soldiery of that period were.

The thought came over her with a shudder as she gazed from her window at the creek where she remembered Peregrine sending Charles and Sedley adrift in the boat.

The tide was out, the mud glistened in the moonlight, but nothing was to be seen more than Anne had beheld on many a summer night before, no phantom was evoked before her eyes, no elfin-like form revealed his presence, nor did any spirit take shape to upbraid her with his unhallowed grave, so close at hand.

No, but Naomi Darpent, yearning for sympathy, came to her side, caressed her on that summer night, and told her that Mr. Fellowes had gone to ask her of her father, and though she could never love again as she had once loved, she thought, if her parents wished it, she could be happy with so good a man.

CHAPTER XXIV

IN THE MOONLIGHT

ANNE WOODFORD sat, on a sultry summer
night, by the open window in Archfield
House at Fareham, busily engaged over the
tail of a kite, while asleep in a cradle in the
corner of the room lay a little boy, his apple-
blossom cheeks and long flaxen curls lying
prone upon his pillow as he had tossed when
falling asleep in the heat.

The six years since her return had been
eventful. Dr. Woodford had adhered to his
view that his oath of allegiance could not be
forfeited by James's flight; and he therefore
had submitted to be ousted from his prefer-

ments, resigning his pleasant prebendal house, and his seaside home, and embracing poverty for his personal oath's sake, although he was willing to acquiesce in the government of William and Mary, and perhaps to rejoice that others had effected what he would not have thought it right to do.

Things had been softened to him as regarded his flock by the appointment of Mr. Fellowes to Portchester, which was a Crown living, though there had been great demur at thus slipping into a friend's shoes, so that Dr. Woodford had been obliged to asseverate that nothing so much comforted him as leaving the parish in such hands, and that he blamed no man for seeing the question of Divine right as he did in common with the Non-jurors. The appointment opened the way to the marriage with Naomi Darpent, and the pair were happily settled at Portchester.

Dr. Woodford and his niece found a tiny house at Winchester, near the wharf, with the clear Itchen flowing in front and the green hills rising beyond, while in the rear were the ruins of Wolvesey, and the buildings of the Cathedral and College. They retained no servant except black Hans, poor Peregrine's legacy, who was an excellent cook, and capable of all that Anne could not accomplish in her hours of freedom.

It was a fall indeed from her ancient aspirations, though there was still that bud of hope within her heart. The united means of uncle and niece were so scanty that she was fain to offer her services daily at Mesdames Reynaud's still flourishing school, where the freshness of her continental experiences made her very welcome.

Dr. Woodford occasionally assisted some student preparing for the university, but this was not regular occupation, and it was poorly paid, so that it was well that fifty pounds a year went at least three times as far as it would do in the present day. Though his gown and cassock lost their richness and lustre, he was as much respected as ever. Bishop Mews often asked him to Wolvesey, and allowed him to assist the parochial clergy when it was not necessary to utter the royal name, the vergers marshalled him to his own stall at daily prayers, and he had free access to Bishop Morley's Cathedral library.

The Archfield family still took a house in the Close for the winter months, and there a very sober-minded and conventional court-ship of Lucy took place by Sir Edmund Nutley, a worthy and well-to-do gentleman settled on the borders of Parkhurst Forest, in the Isle of Wight.

Anne, with the thought of her Charles burning within her heart, was a little scandal-ised at the course of affairs. Sir Edmund was a highly worthy man, but not in his first youth, and ponderous—a Whig, moreover, and an intimate friend of the masterful governor of the island, Lord Cutts, called the 'Salamander.' He had seen Miss Arch-field before at the winter and spring Quarter Sessions, and though her father was no longer in the Commission of the Peace, the residence at Winchester gave him oppor-tunities, and the chief obstacle seemed to be the party question. He was more in love than was the lady, but she was submissive, and believed that he would be a kind hus-band. She saw, too, that her parents would

be much disappointed and displeased if she
made any resistance to so prosperous a settle-
ment, and she was positively glad to be out
of reach of Sedley's addresses.   Such an
entirely unenthusiastic acceptance was the
proper thing, and it only remained to provide
for Lady Archfield's comfort in the loss of
her daughter.

For this the elders turned at once to
Anne Woodford.   Sir Philip made it his
urgent entreaty that the Doctor and his
niece would take up their abode with him,
and that Anne would share with the grandmother the care of the young Philip, a
spirited little fellow who would soon be
running wild with the grooms, without the
attention that his aunt had bestowed on him.

Dr. Woodford himself was much inclined
to accept the office of chaplain to his old
friend, who he knew would be far happier
for his company ; and Anne's heart bounded
at the thought of bringing up Charles's child,
but that very start of joy made her blush
and hesitate, and finally surprise the two old
gentlemen by saying, with crimson cheeks—

'Sir, your Honour ought to know what

might make you change your mind. There have been passages between Mr. Archfield and me.'

Sir Philip laughed. 'Ah, the rogue! You were always little sweethearts as children. Why, Anne, you should know better than to heed what a young soldier says.'

'No doubt you have other views for your son,' said Dr. Woodford, 'and I trust that my niece has too much discretion and sense of propriety to think that they can be interfered with on her account.'

'Passages!' repeated Sir Philip thoughtfully. 'Mistress Anne, how much do you mean by that? Surely there is no promise between you?'

'No, sir,' said Anne; 'I would not give any; but when we parted in Flanders he asked me to—to wait for him, and I feel that you ought to know it.'

'Oh, I understand!' said the baronet. 'It was only natural to an old friend in a foreign land, and you have too much sense to dwell on a young man's folly, though it was an honourable scruple that made you tell me, my dear maid. But he is not come or coming yet, more's the pity, so there is no need to think about it at present.'

Anne's cheeks did not look as if she had attained that wisdom; but her conscience was clear, since she had told the fact, and the father did not choose to take it seriously. To say how she herself loved Charles would have been undignified and nothing to the purpose, since her feelings were not what would be regarded, and there was no need to mention her full and entire purpose to wed no one else. Time enough for that if the proposal were made.

So the uncle and niece entered on their new life, with some loss of independence, and to the Doctor a greater loss in the neighbourhood of the Cathedral and its library; for after the first year or two, as Lady Archfield grew rheumatic, and Sir Philip had his old friend to play backgammon and read the *Weekly Gazette*, they became unwilling to make the move to Winchester, and generally stayed at home all the winter.

Before this, however, Princess Anne had been at the King's House at Winchester for a short time; and Lady Archfield paid due respects to her, with Anne in attendance. With the royal faculty of remembering everybody, the Princess recognised her namesake, gave her hand to be kissed, and was extremely gracious. She was at the moment in the height of a quarrel with her sister, and far from delighted with the present *régime*. She sent for Miss Woodford, and, to Anne's surprise, laughed over her own escape from the Cockpit, adding, 'You would not come, child. You were in the right on't. There's no gratitude among them! Had I known how I should be served I would never have stirred a foot! So 'twas you that carried off the child! Tell me what he is like.'

And she extracted by questions all that Anne could tell her of the life at St. Germain, and the appearance of her little half-brother. It was impossible to tell whether she asked from affectionate remorse or gossiping interest, but she ended by inquiring whether her father's god-daughter were content with her position, or desired one — if there were a vacancy—in her own household, where she might get a good husband.

Anne declined courteously and respectfully,

and was forced to hint at an engagement
which she could not divulge. She had heard
Charles's expressions of delight at the arrangement which gave his boy to her tender care,
warming her heart.

Lady Archfield had fits of talking of
finding a good husband for Anne Woodford
among the Cathedral clergy, but the maiden
was so necessary to her, and so entirely a
mother to little Philip, that she soon let the
idea drop. Perhaps it was periodically
revived, when, about three times a year, there
arrived a letter from Charles. He wrote in
good spirits, evidently enjoying his campaigns,
and with no lack of pleasant companions,
English, Scotch, and Irish Jacobites, with
whom he lived in warm friendship and wholesome emulation. He won promotion, and
the county Member actually came out of his
way to tell Sir Philip what he had heard from
the Imperial ambassador of young Archfield's
distinguished services at the battle of Salank-
amen, only regretting that he was not fighting
under King William's colours. Little Philip
pranced about cutting off Turks' heads in
the form of poppies, 'like papa,' for whose

safety Anne taught him to pray night and morning.

Pride in his son's exploits was a compensation to the father, who declared them to be better than vegetating over the sheepfolds, like Robert Oakshott, or than idling at Portsmouth, like Sedley Archfield.

That young man's regiment had been ordered to Ireland during the campaign that followed the battle of Boyne Water. He had suddenly returned from thence, cashiered: by his own story, the victim of the enmity of the Dutch General Ginkel; according to another version, on account of brutal excesses towards the natives and insolence to his commanding officer. Courts-martial had only just been introduced, and Sir Philip could believe in a Whig invention doing injustice to a member of a loyal family, so that his doors were open to his nephew, and Sedley haunted them whenever he had no other resource; but he spent most of his time between Newmarket and other sporting centres, and contrived to get a sort of maintenance by bets at races, cock-fights, and bull-baitings, and by extensive gambling. Evil reports of him came from time to time, but Sir Philip was loth to think ill of the son of his brother, or to forbode that as his grandson grew older, such influence might be dangerous.

In his uncle's presence Sedley was on his good behaviour ; but if he caught Miss Woodford without that protection, he attempted rude compliments, and when repelled by her dignified look and manner, sneered at the airs of my lady's waiting-woman, and demanded how long she meant to mope after Charley, who would never look so low. 'She need not be so ungracious to a poor soldier. She might have to put up with worse.'

Moreover, he deliberately incited Philip to mischief, putting foul words into the little mouth, and likewise giving forbidden food and drink, lauding evil sports, and mocking at obedience to any authority, especially Miss Woodford's. Philip was very fond of his Nana, and in general good and obedient : but what high-spirited boy is proof against the allurements of the only example before him of young manhood, assuring him that it was manly not to mind what the women said, nor to be tied to the apron-strings of his grand-dame's abigail?

The child had this summer thus been actually taken to the outskirts of a bull-fight, whence he had been brought home in great disgrace by Ralph, the old servant who had been charged to look after his out-door amusements, and to ride with him. The grandfather was indeed more shocked at the danger and the vulgarity of the sport than its cruelty, but Philip had received his first flogging, and his cousin had been so sharply rebuked that—to the great relief of Anne and of Lady Archfield—he had not since appeared at Fareham House.

The morrow would be Philip's seventh birthday, a stage which would take him farther out of Anne's power. He was no longer to sleep in her chamber, but in one of his own with Ralph for his protector, and he was to begin Latin with Dr. Woodford. So great was his delight that he had gone to bed all the sooner in order to bring the great day more quickly, and Anne was glad of the opportunity of finishing the kite, which was to be her present, for Ralph to help him fly upon Portsdown Hill.

That great anniversary, so delightful to him, with pony and whip prepared for him —what a day of confusion, distress, and wretchedness did it not recall to his elders? Anne could not choose but recall the time, as she sat alone in the window, looking out over the garden, the moon beginning to rise, and the sunset light still colouring the sky in the north-west, just as it had done when she returned home after the bonfire. The events of that sad morning had faded out of the foreground. The Oakshott family seemed to have resigned themselves to the mystery of Peregrine's fate. Only his mother had declined from the time of his disappearance. When it was ascertained that his uncle had died in Russia, and that nothing had been heard of him there, it seemed to bring on a fresh stage of her illness, and she had expired at last in Martha Browning's arms, her last words being a blessing not only to Robert, but to Peregrine, and a broken entreaty to her husband to forgive the boy, for he might have been better if they had used him well.

Martha was then found to hold out against the idea of his being dead. Little affection and scant civility as she had received from him, her dutiful heart had attached itself to her destined lord, and no doubt her imagination had been excited by his curious abilities, and her compassion by the persecution he suffered at home.   At any rate, when, after a proper interval, the Major tried to transfer her to his remaining son, she held out against it for a long interval, until at last, after full three years, the desolation and disorganisation of Oakwood without a mistress, a severe illness of the Major, and the distress of his son, so worked upon her feelings that she consented to the marriage with Robert, and had ever since been the ruling spirit at Oakwood, and a very different one from what had been expected — sensible, kindly, and beneficent, and allowing the young husband more liberty and indulgence than he had ever known before.

The remembrance of Peregrine seemed to have entirely passed away, and Anne had been troubled with no more apparitions, so that though she thought over the strange scene of that terrible morning, the rapid combat, the hasty concealment, the distracted face of the unhappy youth, it was with the thought that time had been a healer, and that Charles might surely now return home. And what then ?

She raised her eyes to the open window, and what did she behold in the moonlight streaming full upon the great tree-rose below ? It was the same face and figure that had three times startled her before, the figure dark and the face very white in the moonlight, but like nothing else, and with that odd, one-sided feather as of old. It had flitted ere she could point its place—gone in a single flash—but she was greatly startled! Had it come to protest against the scheme she had begun to indulge in on that very night of all nights, or had it merely been her imagination? For nothing was visible, though she leant from the window, no sound was to be heard, though when she tried to complete her work, her hands trembled and the paper rustled, so that Philip showed symptoms of wakening, and she had to defer her task till early morning.

She said nothing of her strange sight, and Phil had a happy, successful birthday, flying the kite with a propitious wind, and riding into Portsmouth on his new pony with grand-papa. But there was one strange event. The servants had a holiday, and some of them went into Portsmouth, Black Hans, who never returned, being one. The others had lost sight of him, but had not been uneasy, knowing him to be perfectly well able to find his way home; but as he never appeared, the conclusion was that he must have been kidnapped by some ship's crew to serve as a cook. He had not been very happy among the servants at Fareham, who laughed at his black face and Dutch English, and he would probably have gone willingly with Dutchmen; but Anne and her uncle were grieved, and felt as if they had failed in the trust that poor Sir Peregrine had left them.

CHAPTER XXV

'He has more cause to be proud.   Where is he wounded?'
                                          Coriolanus.

IT was a wet autumn day, when the yellow leaves of the poplars in front of the house were floating down amid the misty rain; Dr. Woodford had gone two days before to consult a book in the Cathedral library, and was probably detained at Winchester by the weather; Lady Archfield was confined to her bed by a sharp attack of rheumatism; Sir Philip was taking his after-dinner doze in his arm-chair; and little Philip was standing by Anne, who was doing her best to keep him from awakening his grandfather, as she partly read, partly romanced, over the high-crowned hatted fishermen in the illustrations to Izaak Walton's *Complete Angler.*

He had just, caught by the musical sound, made her read to him a second time Marlowe's verses,

'Come live with me and be my love,'

and informed her that his Nana was his love, and that she was to watch him fish in the summer rivers, when the servant who had been sent to meet His Majesty's mail and extract the *Weekly Gazette* came in, bringing not only that, but a thick, sealed packet, the aspect of which made the boy dance and exclaim, 'A packet from my papa! Oh! will he have written an answer to my own letter to him?'

But Sir Philip, who had started up at the opening of the door, had no sooner glanced at the packet than he cried out, ''Tis not his hand!' and when he tried to break the heavy seals and loosen the string, his hands shook so much that he pushed it over to Anne, saying, 'You open it; tell me if my boy is dead.'

Anne's alarm took the course of speed. She tore off the wrapper, and after one glance said, ' No, no, it cannot be the worst; here is something from himself at the end. Here, sir.'

'I cannot! I cannot,' said the poor old man, as the tears dimmed his spectacles, and he could not adjust them. 'Read it, my dear wench, and let me know what I am to tell his poor mother.'

And he sank into a chair, holding between his knees his little grandson, who stood gazing with widely-opened blue eyes.

'He sends love, duty, blessing. Oh, he talks of coming home, so do not fear, sir!' cried Anne, a vivid colour on her cheeks.

'But what is it?' asked the father. 'Tell me first—the rest after.'

'It is in the side—the left side,' said Anne, gathering up in her agitation the sense of the crabbed writing as best she could. 'They have not extracted the bullet, but when they have, he will do well.'

'God grant it! Who writes?'

'Norman Graham of Glendhu—captain in his K. K. Regiment of Volunteer Dragoons. That's his great friend! Oh, sir, he has behaved so gallantly! He got his wound in saving the colours from the Turks, and kept his hands clutched over them as his men carried him out of the battle.'

Philip gave another little spring, and his grandfather bade Anne read the letter to him in detail.

It told how the Imperial forces had met a far superior number of Turks at Lippa, and had sustained a terrible defeat, with the loss of their General Veterani, how Captain Archfield had received a scimitar wound in the cheek while trying to save his commander, but had afterwards dashed forward among the enemy, recovered the colours of the regiment, and by a desperate charge of his fellow-soldiers, who were devotedly attached to him, had been borne off the field with a severe wound on the left side. Retreat had been immediately necessary, and he had been taken on an ammunition waggon along rough roads to the fortress called the Iron Gates of Transylvania, whence this letter was written, and sent by the messenger who was to summon the Elector of Saxony to the aid of the remnant of the army. It had not yet been possible to probe the wound, but Charles gave a personal message, begging his parents not to despond but to believe him recovering, so long as they did not see his servant return without him, and he added sundry tender and dutiful messages to his parents, and a blessing to his son, with thanks for the pretty letter he had not been able to answer (but which, his friend said, was lying spread on his pillow, not unstained with blood), and he also told his boy always to love and look up to her who had ever been as a mother to him.

Anne could hardly read this, and the scrap in feeble irregular lines she handed to Sir Philip.   It was—

With all my heart I entreat pardon for all the errors that have grieved you.   I leave you my child to comfort you, and mine own true love, whom you will cherish. She will cherish you as a daughter, as she will be, with your consent, if God spares me to come home.   The love of all my soul to her, my mother, sister, and you.

There was a scrawl for conclusion and signature, and Captain Graham added—

Writing and dictating have greatly exhausted him. He would have said more, but he says the lady can explain much, and he repeats his urgent entreaties that you will take her to your heart as a daughter, and that his son will love and honour her.

There was a final postscript——

The surgeon thinks him better for having disburthened his mind.

'My child,' said Sir Philip, with a long sigh, looking up at Anne, who had gathered the boy into her arms, and was hiding her face against his little awe-struck head, 'my child, have you read?'

'No,' faltered Anne.

'Read then.' And as she would have taken it, he suddenly drew her into his embrace and kissed her as the eyes of both overflowed. 'My poor girl!' he said, 'this is as hard to you as to us! Oh, my brave boy!' and he let her lay her head on his shoulder and held her hand as they wept together, while little Phil stared for a moment or two at so strange a sight and then burst out with a great cry—

'You shall not cry! you shall not! my papa is not dead!' and he stamped his little foot. 'No, he isn't. He will get well; the letter said so, and I will go and tell grandmamma.'

The need of stopping this roused them both; Sir Philip, heavily groaning, went away to break the tidings to his wife, and Anne went down on her knees on the hearth to caress the boy, and help him to understand his father's state and realise the valorous deeds that would always be a crown to him, and which already made the little fellow's eye flash and his fair head go higher.

By and by she was sent for to Lady Archfield's room, and there she had again to share the grief and the fears and try to dwell on the glory and the hopes. When in a calmer moment the parents interrogated her on what had passed with Charles, it was not in the spirit of doubt and censure, but rather as dwelling on all that was to be told of one whom alike they loved, and finally Sir Philip said, ' I see, dear child, I would not believe how far it had gone before, though you tried to tell me. Whatever betide, you have won a daughter's place.'

It was true that naturally a far more distinguished match would have been sought for the heir, and he could hardly have carried out his purpose without more opposition than under their present feelings his parents supposed themselves likely to make, but they really loved Anne enough to have yielded at last; and Lady Nutley, coming home with a fuller knowledge of her brother's heart, prevented any reaction, and Anne was allowed full sympathies as a betrothed maiden, in the wearing anxiety that continued in the absence of all intelligence. On the principle of doing everything to please him, she was even encouraged to write to Charles in the packet in which he was almost implored to recover, though all felt doubts whether he were alive even while the letters were in hand, and this doubt lasted long and long. It was all very well to say that as long as the servant did not return his master must be safe—perhaps himself on the way home; but the journey from Transylvania was so long, and there were so many difficulties in the way of an Englishman, that there was little security in this assurance. And so the winter set in while the suspense lasted; and still Dr. Woodford spoke Charles's name in the intercessions in the panelled household chapel, and his mother and Anne prayed together and separately, and his little son morning and evening entreated God to 'Bless papa, and make him well, and bring him home.'

Thus passed more than six weeks, during which Sir Philip's attention was somewhat

diverted from domestic anxieties by an unin-
vited visit to Portchester from Mr. Charnock,
who had once been a college mate of Mr.
Fellowes, and came professing anxiety, after
all these years, to renew the friendship which
had been broken when they took different
sides on the election of Dr. Hough to the
Presidency of Magdalen College. From his
quarters at the Rectory Mr. Charnock had
gone over to Fareham, and sounded Sir
Philip on the practicability of a Jacobite
rising, and whether he and his people would
join it. The old gentleman was much distressed, his age would not permit him to
exert himself in either cause, and he had
been too much disturbed by James's proceed-
ings to feel desirous of his restoration, though
his loyal heart would not permit of his opposing it, and he had never overtly acknowledged
William of Orange as his sovereign.

He could only reply that in the present
state of his family he neither could nor would
undertake anything, and he urgently pleaded
against any insurrection that could occasion
a civil war.

There was reason to think that Sedley

had no hesitation in promising to use all his influence over his uncle's tenants, and considerably magnifying their extremely small regard to him—nay, probably, dwelling on his own expectations.

At any rate, even when Charnock was gone, Sedley continued to talk big of the coming changes and his own distinguished part in them.   Indeed one very trying effect of the continued alarm about Charles was that he took to haunting the place, and report declared that he had talked loudly and coarsely of his cousin's death and his uncle's dotage, and of his soon being called in to manage the property for the little heir—insomuch that Sir Edmund Nutley thought it expedient to let him know that Charles, on going on active service soon after he had come of age, had sent home a will, making his son, who was a young gentleman of very considerable property on his mother's side, ward to his grandfather first, and then to Sir Edmund Nutley himself and to Dr. Woodford.

CHAPTER XXVI

THE LEGEND OF PENNY GRIM

> ' O dearest Marjorie, stay at hame,
> For dark's the gate ye have to go,
> For there's a maike down yonder glen
> Hath frightened me and many mo.'
>
> HOGG.

'NANA,' said little Philip in a meditative voice, as he looked into the glowing embers of the hall fire, 'when do fairies leave off stealing little boys?'

'I do not believe they ever steal them, Phil.'

'Oh yes, they do;' and he came and stood by her with his great limpid blue eyes wide open. 'Goody Dearlove says they stole a little boy, and his name was Penny Grim.'

'Goody Dearlove is a silly old body to tell my boy such stories,' said Anne, disguising how much she was startled.

'Oh, but Ralph Huntsman says 'tis true, and he knew him.'

'How could he know him when he was stolen?'

'They put another instead,' said the boy, a little puzzled, but too young to make his story consistent. 'And he was an elf—a cross spiteful elf, that was always vexing folk. And they stole him again every seven years. Yes—that was it—they stole him every seven years.'

'Whom, Phil; I don't understand—the boy or the elf?' she said, half-diverted, even while shocked at the old story coming up in such a form. ^

'The elf, I think,' he said, bending his brows; 'he comes back, and then they steal him again. Yes; and at last they stole him quite—quite away—but it is seven years, and Goody Dearlove says he is to be seen again!'

'No!' exclaimed Anne, with an irrepressible start of dismay. 'Has any one seen him, or fancied so?' she added, though feeling that her chance of maintaining her rational incredulity was gone.

'Goody Dearlove's Jenny did,' was the answer. 'She saw him stand out on the beach at night by moonlight, and when she screamed out, he was gone like the snuff of a candle.'

'Saw him? What was he like?' said Anne, struggling for the dispassionate tone of the governess, and recollecting that Jenny Dearlove was a maid at Portchester Rectory.

'A little bit of a man, all twisty on one side, and a feather sticking out. Ralph said they always were like that;' and Phil's imitation, with his lithe, graceful little figure, of Ralph's clumsy mimicry was sufficient to show that there was some foundation for this story, and she did not answer at once, so that he added, 'I am seven, Nana; do you think they will get me?'

'Oh no, no, Phil, there's no fear at all of that. I don't believe fairies steal anybody, but even old women like Goody Dearlove only say they steal little tiny babies if they are left alone before they are christened.'

The boy drew a long breath, but still asked, 'Was Penny Grim a little baby?'

'So they said,' returned Anne, by no

means interfering with the name, and with a quailing heart as she thought of the child's ever knowing what concern his father had in that disappearance.   She was by no means sorry to have the conversation broken off by Sir Philip's appearance, booted and buskined, prepared for an expedition to visit a flock of sheep and their lambs under the shelter of Portsdown Hill, and in a moment his little namesake was frisking round eager to go with grandpapa.

'Well, 'tis a brisk frost.   Is it too far for him, think you, Mistress Anne?'

'Oh no, sir; he is a strong little man and a walk will only be good for him, if he does not stand still too long and get chilled. Run, Phil, and ask nurse for your thick coat and stout shoes and leggings.'

'His grandmother only half trusts me with him,' said Sir Philip, laughing.   'I tell her she was not nearly so careful of his father. I remember him coming in crusted all over with ice, so that he could hardly get his clothes off, but she fancies the boy may have some of his poor mother's weakliness about him.'

' I see no tokens of it, sir.'

' Grand-dames will be anxious, specially over one chick. Heigho! Winter travelling must be hard in Germany, and posts do not come. How now, my man! Are you rolled up like a very Russian bear? The poor ewes will think you are come to eat up their lambs.'

' I'll growl at them,' said Master Philip, uttering a sound sufficient to disturb the nerves of any sheep if he were permitted to make it, and off went grandfather and grandson together, Sir Philip only pausing at the door to say—

' My lady wants you, Anne, she is fretting over the delay, I fear, though I tell her it bodes well.'

Anne watched for a moment the hale old gentleman briskly walking on, the merry child frolicking hither and thither round him, and the sturdy body-servant Ralph, without whom he never stirred, plodding after, while Keeper, the only dog allowed to follow to the sheepfolds, marched decorously along, proud of the distinction. Then she went up to Lady Archfield, who could not be perfectly easy as to the precious grandchild being left to his own devices in the cold, while Sir Philip was sure to run into a discussion with the shepherd over the turnips, which were too much of a novelty to be approved by the Hampshire mind. It was quite true that she could not watch that little adventurous spirit with the same absence of anxiety as she had felt for her own son in her younger days, and Anne had to devote herself to soothing and diverting her mind, till Dr. Woodford knocked at the door to read and converse with her.

The one o'clock dinner waited for the grandfather and grandson, and when they came at last, little Philip looked somewhat blue with cold and more subdued than usual, and his grandfather observed severely that he had been a naughty boy, running into dangerous places, sliding where he ought not, and then muttered under his breath that Sedley ought to have known better than to have let him go there.

Discipline did not permit even a darling like little Phil to speak at dinner-time; but he fidgeted, and the tears came into his eyes, and Anne hearing a little grunt behind Sir Philip's chair, looked up, and was aware that old Ralph was mumbling what to her ears sounded like: 'Knew too well.' But his master, being slightly deaf, did not hear, and went on to talk of his lambs and of how Sedley had joined them on the road, but had not come back to dinner.

Phil was certainly quieter than usual that afternoon, and sat at Anne's feet by the fire, filling little sacks with bran to be loaded on his toy cart to go to the mill, but not chattering as usual. She thought him tired, and hearing a sort of sigh took him on her knee, when he rested his fair little head on her shoulder, and presently said in a low voice—

'I've seen him.'

'Who? Not your father? Oh, my child!' cried Anne, in a sudden horror.

'Oh no—the Penny Grim thing.'

'What? Tell me, Phil dear, how or where?'

'By the end of the great big pond; and he threw up his arms, and made a horrid grin.' The boy trembled and hid his face against her.

'But go on, Phil. He can't hurt you, you know. Do tell me. Where were you?'

'I was sliding on the ice. Grandpapa was ever so long talking to Bill Shepherd, and looking at the men cutting turnips, and I got cold and tired, and ran about with Cousin Sedley till we got to the big pond, and we began to slide, and the ice was so nice and hard—you can't think. He showed me how to take a good long slide, and said I might go out to the other end of the pond by the copse, by the great old tree. And I set off, but before I got there, out it jumped, out of the copse, and waved its arms, and made *that* face.'

He cowered into her bosom again and almost cried. Anne knew the place, and was ready to start with dismay in her turn. It was such a pool as is frequent in chalk districts —shallow at one end, but deep and dangerous with springs at the other.

'But, Phil dear,' she said, 'it was well you were stopped ; the ice most likely would have broken at that end, and then where would Nana's little man have been ?'

'Cousin Sedley never told me not,' said

the boy in self-defence; 'he was whistling
to me to go on.   But when I tumbled down
Ralph and grandpapa and all *did* scold me so
—and Cousin Sedley was gone.   Why did
they scold me, Nana?   I thought it was
brave not to mind danger—like papa.'

'It is brave when one can do any good by
it, but not to slide on bad ice, when one must
be drowned,' said Anne.   'Oh, my dear, dear
little fellow, it was a blessed thing you saw
that, whatever it was!   But why do you call
it Pere—Penny Grim?'

'It was, Nana!   It was a little man—
rather.   And one-sided looking, with a bit of
hair sticking out, just like the picture of
Riquet-with-a-tuft in your French fairy-book.'

This last was convincing to Anne that the
child must have seen the phantom of seven
years ago, since he was not repeating the
popular description he had given her in the
morning, but one quite as individual.   She
asked if grandpapa had seen it.

'Oh no; he was in the shed, and only
came out when he heard Ralph scolding me.
Was it a wicked urchin come to steal me,
Nana?'

'No, I think not,' she answered. 'Whatever it was, I think it came because God was taking care of His child, and warning him from sliding into the deep pool. We will thank him, Phil. "He shall give his angels charge over thee, to keep thee in all thy ways."' And to that verse she soothed the tired child till he fell asleep, and she could lay him on the settle, and cover him with a cloak, musing the while on the strange story, until presently she started up and repaired to the buttery in search of the old servant.

'Ralph, what is this Master Philip tells me?' she asked. 'What has he seen?'

'Well, Mistress Anne, that is what I can't tell—no, not I; but I knows this, that the child has had a narrow escape of his precious life, and I'd never trust him again with that there Sedley—no, not for hundreds of pounds.'

'You *really* think, Ralph——?'

'What can I think, ma'am? When I finds he's been a-setting that there child to slide up to where he'd be drownded as sure as he's alive, and you see, if we gets ill news of Master Archfield (which God forbid), there's naught but the boy atween him and this here place—and he over head and ears in debt. Be it what it might that the child saw, it saved the life of him.'

' Did you see it ?'

' No, Mistress Anne ; I can't say as I did. I only heard the little master cry out as he fell. I was in the shed, you see, taking a pipe to keep me warm. And when I took him up, he cried out like one dazed. "'Twas Penny Grim, Ralph ! Keep me. He is come to steal me." But Sir Philip wouldn't hear nothing of it, only blamed Master Phil for being foolhardy, and for crying for the fall, and me for letting him out of sight.'

' And Mr. Sedley—did he see it ?'

' Well, mayhap he did, for I saw him as white as a sheet and his eyes staring out of his head ; but that might have been his evil conscience.'

' What became of him ?'

' To say the truth, ma'am, I believe he be at the Brocas Arms, a-drowning of his fright —if fright it were, with Master Harling's strong waters.'

' But this apparition, this shape—or whatever it is ?   What put it into Master Philip's head ?   What has been heard of it ?'

Ralph looked unwilling.   ' Bless you, Mistress Anne, there's been some idle talk among the women folk, as how that there crooked slip of Major Oakshott's, as they called Master Perry or Penny, and said was a changeling, has been seen once and again. Some says as the fairies have got him, and 'tis the seven year for him to come back again.   And some says that he met with foul play, and 'tis the ghost of him, but I holds it all mere tales, and I be sure 'twere nothing bad as stopped little master on that there pond.   So I be.'

Anne could not but be of the same mind, but her confusion, alarm, and perplexity were great.   It seemed strange, granting that this were either spirit or elf connected with Peregrine Oakshott, that it should interfere on behalf of Charles Archfield's child, and on the sweet hypothesis that a guardian angel had come to save the child, it was in a most unaccountable form.

And more pressing than any such mysterious idea was the tangible horror of Ralph's suggestion, too well borne out by the boy's own unconscious account of the adventure. It was too dreadful, too real a peril to be kept to herself, and she carried the story to her uncle on his return, but without speaking of the spectral warning. Not only did she know that he would not attend to it, but the hint, heard for the first time, that Peregrine was supposed to have met with foul play, sealed her lips, just when she still was hoping against hope that Charles might be on the way home. But that Ralph believed, and little Philip's own account confirmed, that his cousin had incited the little heir to the slide that would have been fatal save for his fall, she told with detail, and entreated that the grandfather might be warned, and some means be found of ensuring the safety of her darling, the motherless child!

To her disappointment Dr. Woodford was not willing to take alarm. He did not think so ill of Sedley as to believe him capable of such a secret act of murder, and he had no great faith in Ralph's sagacity, besides that he thought his niece's nerves too much strained by the long suspense to be able to judge fairly. He thought it would be cruel to the grandparents, and unjust to Sedley, to make such a frightful suggestion without further grounds during their present state of anxiety, and as to the boy's safety, which Anne pleaded with an uncontrollable passion of tears, he believed that it was provided for by watchfulness on the part of his two constant guardians, as well as himself, since, even supposing the shocking accusation to be true, Sedley would not involve himself in danger of suspicion, and it was already understood that he was not a fit companion for his little cousin to be trusted with. Philip had already brought home words and asked questions that distressed his grandmother, and nobody was willing to leave him alone with the ex-lieutenant. So again the poor maiden had to hold her peace under an added burthen of anxiety and many a prayer.

When the country was ringing with the tidings of Sir George Barclay's conspiracy for the assassination of William III, it was impossible not to hope that Sedley's boastful tongue might have brought him sufficiently under suspicion to be kept for a while under lock and key ; but though he did not appear at Fareham, there was reason to suppose that he was as usual haunting the taverns and cockpits of Portsmouth.

No one went much abroad that winter. Sir Philip, perhaps from anxiety and fretting, had a fit of the gout, and Anne kept herself and her charge within the garden or the street of the town.   In fact there was a good deal of danger on the roads.   The neighbourhood of the seaport was always lawless, and had become more so since Sir Philip had ceased to act as Justice of the Peace, and there were reports of highway robberies of an audacious kind, said to be perpetrated by a band calling themselves the Black Gang, under a leader known as Piers Pigwiggin, who were alleged to be half smuggler, half Jacobite, and to have their headquarters somewhere in the back of the Isle of Wight, in spite of the Governor, the terrible Salamander, Lord Cutts, who was, indeed, generally absent with the army.

CHAPTER XXVII

THE VAULT

'Heaven awards the vengeance due.'
COWPER.

THE weary days had begun to lengthen before the door of the hall was flung open, and little Phil, forgetting his bow at the door, rushed in, 'Here's a big packet from foreign parts! Harry had to pay ever so much for it.'

'I have wellnigh left off hoping,' sighed the poor mother. 'Tell me the worst at once.'

'No fear, my lady,' said her husband. 'Thank God! 'Tis our son's hand.'

There was the silence for a moment of intense relief, and then the little boy was called to cut the silk and break the seals.

Joy ineffable! There were three letters

—for Master Philip Archfield, for Mistress Anne Jacobina Woodford, and for Sir Philip himself.   The old gentleman glanced over it, caught the words 'better,' and 'coming home,' then failed to read through tears of joy as before through tears of sorrow, and was fain to hand the sheet to his old friend to be read aloud, while little Philip, handling as a treasure the first letter he had ever received, though as yet he was unable to decipher it, stood between his grandfather's knees listening as Dr. Woodford read—

DEAR AND HONOURED SIR—I must ask your pardon for leaving you without tidings so long, but while my recovery still hung in doubt I thought it would only distress you to hear of the fluctuations that I went through, and the pain to which the surgeons put me for a long time in vain.   Indeed, frequently I had no power either to think or speak, until at last with much difficulty, and little knowledge or volition of my own, my inestimable friend Graham brought me to Vienna, where I have at length been relieved from my troublesome companion, and am enjoying the utmost care and kindness from my friend's mother, a near kinswoman, as indeed he is himself, of the brave and lamented Viscount Dundee.   My wound is healing finally, as I hope, and though I have not yet left my bed, my friends assure me that I am on the way to full and complete recovery, for which I am more thankful to the Almighty than I could have been before I knew what suffering and illness meant. As soon as I can ride again, which they tell me will be in a fortnight or three weeks, I mean to set forth on my way home. I cannot describe to you how I am longing after the sight of you all, nor how home-sick I have become. I never had time for it before, but I have lain for hours bringing all your faces before me, my father's and mother's, my sister's, and that of her whom I hope to call my own; and figuring to myself that of the little one. I have thought much over my past life, and become sensible of much that was amiss, and while earnestly entreating your forgiveness, especially for having absented myself all these years, I hope to return so as to be more of a comfort than I was in the days of my rash and inconsiderate youth. I am of course at present invalided, but I want to consult you, honoured sir, before deciding whether it be expedient for me to resign my commission. How I thank and bless you for the permission you have given me, and the love you bear to my own heart's joy, no words can tell. It shall be the study of my life to be worthy of her and of you.— And so no more from your loving and dutiful son,

CHARLES ARCHFIELD.

Having drunk in these words with her ears, Anne left Phil to have his note interpreted by his grandparents, and fled away to enjoy her own in her chamber, yet it was as short as could be and as sweet.

Mine own, mine own sweet Anne, sweetheart of good old days, your letter gave me strength to go through with it. The doctors could not guess why I was so much

better and smiled through all their torments.   These
are our first, I hope our last letters, for I shall soon
follow them home, and mine own darling will be mine.—
Thine own,   C. A.

She had but short time to dwell on it and
kiss it, for little Philip was upon her, waving
his letter, which he already knew by heart;
and galloping all over the house to proclaim
the good news to the old servants, who came
crowding into the hall, trembling with joy, to
ask if there were indeed tidings of Mr. Archfield's return, whereupon the glad father
caused his grandson to carry each a full
glass of wine to drink to the health of the
young master.

Anne had at first felt only the surpassing
rapture of the restoration of Charles, but
there ensued another delight in the security
his recovery gave to the life of his son.
Sedley Archfield would not be likely to renew
his attempt, and if only on that account the
good news should be spread as widely as
possible.   She was the first to suggest the
relief it would be to Mr. Fellowes, who had
never divested himself of the feeling that he
ought to have divined his pupil's intention.

Dr. Woodford offered to ride to Portchester with the news, and Sir Philip, in the gladness of his heart, proposed that Anne should go with him and see her friend.

Shall it be told how on the way Anne's mind was assailed by feminine misgivings whether three and twenty could be as fair in her soldier's eyes as seventeen had been? Old maidenhood came earlier then than in these days, and Anne knew that she was looked upon as an old waiting-gentlewoman or governess by the belles of Winchester. Her glass might tell her that her eyes were as softly brown, her hair as abundant, her cheek as clear and delicately moulded as ever, but there was no one to assure her that the early bloom had not passed away, and that she had not rather gained than lost in dignity of bearing and the stately poise of the head, which the jealous damsels called Court airs. 'And should he be disappointed, I shall see it in his eyes,' she said to herself, 'and then his promise shall not bind him, though it will break my heart, and oh! how hard to resign my Phil to a strange stepmother.' Still her heart was lighter than for many a long year, as she cantered along in the brisk March air, while the drops left by the departing frost glistened in the sunshine, and the sea lay stretched in a delicate gray haze. The old castle rose before her in its familiar home-like massiveness as they turned towards the Rectory, where in that sheltered spot the well-known clusters of crocuses were opening their golden hearts to the sunshine, and re-calling the days when Anne was as sunny-hearted as they, and she felt as if she could be as bright again.

In Mrs. Fellowes's parlour they found an unexpected guest, no other than Mrs. Oak-shott.

'Gadding about' not being the fashion of the Archfield household, Anne had not seen the lady for several years, and was agreeably surprised by her appearance. Perhaps the marks of smallpox had faded, perhaps mother-hood had given expression, and what had been gaunt ungainliness in the maiden had rounded into a certain importance in the matron, nor had her dress, though quiet, any of the Puritan rigid ugliness that had been complained of, and though certainly not beautiful, she was a person to inspire respect.

It was explained that she was waiting for her husband, who was gone with Mr. Fellowes to speak to the officer in command of the soldiers at the castle. 'For,' said she, 'I am quite convinced that there is something that ought to be brought to light, and it may be in that vault.'

Anne's heart gave such a throb as almost choked her.

Dr. Woodford asked what the lady meant.

'Well, sir, when spirits and things 'tis not well to talk of are starting up and about here, there, and everywhere, 'tis plain there must be cause for it.'

'I do not quite take your meaning, madam.'

'Ah, well! you gentlemen, reverend ones especially, are the last to hear such things. There's the poor old Major, he won't believe a word of it, but you know, Mistress Wood- ford. I see it in your face. Have you seen anything?'

'Not here, not now,' faltered Anne. 'You have, Mrs. Fellowes?'

'I have heard of some foolish fright of the maids,' said Naomi, 'partly their own fancy, or perhaps caught from the sentry. There is no keeping those giddy girls from running after the soldiers.'

Perhaps Naomi hoped by throwing out this hint to conduct her visitors off into the safer topic of domestic delinquencies, but Mrs. Oakshott was far too earnest to be thus diverted, and she exclaimed, 'Ah, they saw him, I'll warrant!'

'Him?' the Doctor asked innocently.

'Him or his likeness,' said Mrs. Oakshott, 'my poor brother-in-law, Peregrine Oakshott; you remember him, sir? He always said, poor lad, that you and Mrs. Woodford were kinder to him than his own flesh and blood, except his uncle, Sir Peregrine. For my part, I never did give in to all the nonsense folk talked about his being a changeling or at best a limb of Satan. He had more spirit and sense than the rest of them, and they led him the life of a dog, though they knew no better. If I had had him at Emsworth, I would have shown them what he was;' and she sighed heavily. 'Well, I did not so

much wonder when he disappeared, I made
sure that he could bear it no longer and had
run away. I waited as long as there was
any reason, till there should be tidings of
him, and only took his brother at last because
I found they could not do without me at
home.'

Remarkable frankness! but it struck both
the Doctor and Anne that if Peregrine could
have submitted, his life might have been freer
and less unhappy than he had expected,
though Mrs. Martha spoke the broadest
Hampshire.

Naomi asked, ' Then you no longer think
that he ran away?'

' No, madam; I am certain there was
worse than that. You remember the night
of the bonfire for the Bishops' acquittal, Miss
Woodford?'

' Indeed I do.'

' Well, he was never seen again after that,
as you know. The place was full of wild
folk. There was brawling right and left.'

' Were you there?' asked Anne surprised.

' Yes; in my coach with my uncle and
aunt that lived with me, though, except

Robin, none of the young sparks would come near me, except some that I knew were after my pockets,' said Martha, with a good-humoured laugh. 'Properly frightened we were too by the brawling sailors ere we got home! Now, what could be more likely than that some of them got hold of poor Perry? You know he always would go about with the rapier he brought from Germany, with amber set in the hilt, and the mosaic snuff-box he got in Italy, and what could be looked for but that the poor dear lad should be put out of the way for the sake of these gew-gaws?'

This supposition was gratifying to Anne, but her uncle must needs ask why Mrs. Oakshott thought so more than before.

'Because,' she said impressively, 'there is no doubt but that he has been seen, and not in the flesh, once and again, and always about these ruins.'

'By whom, madam, may I ask?'

'Mrs. Fellowes's maids, as she knows, saw him once on the beach at night, just there. The sentry, who is Tom Hart, from our parish, saw a shape at the opening of the old vault before the keep and challenged him, when he vanished out of sight ere there was time to present a musket. There was once more, when one moonlight night our sexton, looking out of his cottage window, saw what he declares was none other than Master Perry standing among the graves of our family, as if, poor youth, he were asking why he was not among them. When I heard that, I said to my husband, " Depend upon it," says I, " he met with his death that night, and was thrown into some hole, and that's the reason he cannot rest. If I pay a hundred pounds for it, I'll not give up till his poor corpse is found to have Christian burial, and I'll begin with the old vault at Portchester!" My good father, the Major, would not hear of it at first, nor my husband either, but 'tis my money, and I know how to tackle Robin.'

It was with strangely mingled feelings that Anne listened. That search in the vault, inaugurated by faithful Martha, was what she had always felt ought to be made, and she had even promised to attempt it if the apparitions recurred. The notion of the deed being attributed to lawless sailors and

smugglers or highwaymen, who were known
to swarm in the neighbourhood, seemed to
remove all danger of suspicion.   Yet she
could not divest herself of a vague sense of
alarm at this stirring up of what had slept for
seven years.   Neither she nor her uncle
deemed it needful to mention the appearance
seen by little Philip, but to her surprise
Naomi slowly and hesitatingly said it was
very remarkable, that her husband having
occasion to be at the church at dusk one
evening just after Midsummer, had certainly
seen a figure close to Mrs. Woodford's grave,
and lost sight of it before he could speak of
it.   He thought nothing more of it till these
reports began to be spread, but he had then
recollected that it answered the descriptions
given of the phantom.

Here the ladies were interrupted by the
appearance of Mr. Fellowes and Robert
Oakshott, now grown into a somewhat heavy
but by no means foolish-looking young man.

'Well, madam,' said he, in Hampshire as
broad as his wife's, 'you will have your will.
Not that Captain Henslowe believes a word
of your ghosts—not he; but he took fire

when he heard of queer sights about the castle. He sent for the chap who stood sentry, and was downright sharp on him for not reporting what he had seen, and he is ordering out a sergeant's party to open the vault, so you may come and see, if you have any stomach for it.'

' I could not but come!' said Madam Oakshott, who certainly did not look squeamish, but who was far more in earnest than her husband, and perhaps doubted whether without her presence the quest would be thorough. Anne was full of dread, and almost sick at the thought of what she might see, but she was far too anxious to stay away. Mrs. Fellowes made some excuse about the children for not accompanying them.

It always thrilled Anne to enter that old castle court, the familiar and beloved play-place of her childhood, full of memories of Charles and of Lucy, and containing in its wide precincts the churchyard where her mother lay. She moved along in a kind of dream, glad to be let alone, since Mr. Fellowes naturally attended Mrs. Oakshott, and Robert was fully occupied in explaining to the Doctor that he only gave in to this affair for the sake of pacifying madam, since women folk would have their little megrims. Assuredly that tall, solid, resolute figure stalking on in front, looked as little subject to megrims as any of her sex. Her determination had brought her husband thither, and her determination further carried the day, when the captain, after staring at the solid-looking turf, stamping on the one stone that was visible, and trampling down the bunch of nettles beside it, declared that the entrance had been so thoroughly stopped that it was of no use to dig farther. It was Madam Martha who demanded permission to offer the four soldiers a crown apiece if they opened the vault, a guinea each if they found anything. The captain could not choose but grant it, though with something of a sneer, and the work was begun. He walked up and down with Robert, joining in hopes that the lady would be satisfied before dinnertime. The two clergymen likewise walked together, arguing, as was their wont, on the credibility of apparitions. The two ladies stood in almost breathless watch, as the bricks that had covered in the opening were removed, and the dark hole brought to light. Contrary to expectation, when the opening had been enlarged, it was found that there were several steps of stone, and where they were broken away, there was a rude ladder.

A lantern was fetched from the guard-room in the bailey, and after much shaking and trying of the ladder, one of the soldiers descended, finding the place less deep than was commonly supposed, and soon calling out that he was at the bottom. Another followed him, and presently there was a shout. Something was found! 'A rusty old chain, no doubt,' grumbled Robert; but his wife shrieked. It was a sword in its sheath, the belt rotted, the clasp tarnished, but of silver. Mrs. Oakshott seized it at once, rubbed away the dust from the handle, and brought to light a glistening yellow piece of amber, which she mutely held up, and another touch of her handkerchief disclosed on a silver plate in the scabbard an oak-tree, the family crest, and the twisted cypher P. O. Her eyes were full of tears, and she did not speak. Anne, white and trembling, was forced to sink down on the stone, unnoticed by all, while Robert Oakshott, convinced indeed, hastily went down himself. The sword had been hidden in a sort of hollow under the remains of the broken stair. Thence likewise came to light the mouldy remnant of a broad hat and the quill of its plume, and what had once been a coat, even in its present state showing that it had been soaked through and through with blood, the same stains visible on the watch and the mosaic snuff-box. That was all; there was no purse, and no other garments, though, considering the condition of the coat, they might have been entirely destroyed by the rats and mice. There was indeed a fragment of a handkerchief, with the cypher worked on it, which Mrs. Oakshott showed to Anne with the tears in her eyes: 'There! I worked that, though he never knew it. No! I know he did not like me! But I would have made him do so at last. I would have been so good to him. Poor fellow, that he should have been lying there all this time!'

Lying there; but where, then, was he? No signs of any corpse were to be found, though one after another all the gentlemen descended to look, and Mrs. Oakshott was only withheld by her husband's urgent representations, and promise to superintend a diligent digging in the ground, so as to ascertain whether there had been a hasty burial there.

Altogether, Anne was so much astonished and appalled that she could hardly restrain herself, and her mind reverted to Bishop Ken's theory that Peregrine still lived; but this was contradicted by the appearance at Douai, which did not rest on the evidence of her single perceptions.

Mrs. Fellowes sent out an entreaty that they would come to dinner, and the gentlemen were actually base enough to wish to comply, so that the two ladies had no choice save to come with them, especially as the soldiers were unwilling to work on without their meal. Neither Mrs. Oakshott nor Anne felt as if they could swallow, and the polite pressure to eat was only preferable in Anne's eyes to the conversation on the discoveries that had been made, especially the conclusion arrived at by all, that though the purse and rings had not been found, the presence of the watch and snuff-box precluded the idea of robbery.

'These would be found on the body,' said Mr. Oakshott. 'I could swear to the purse. You remember, madam, your uncle bantering him about French ladies and their finery, asking whose token it was, and how black my father looked? Poor Perry, if my father could have had a little patience with him, he would not have gone roaming about and getting into brawls, and we need not be looking for him in yonder black pit.'

'You'll never find him there, Master Robert,' spoke out the old Oakwood servant, behind Mrs. Oakshott's chair, free and easy after the manner of the time.

'And wherefore not, Jonadab?' demanded his mistress, by no means surprised at the liberty.

'Why, ma'am, 'twas the seven years, you sees, and in course when them you wot of had power to carry him off, they could not take his sword, nor his hat, not they couldn't.'

'How about his purse, then?' put in Dr. Woodford.

'I'll be bound you will find it yet, sir,' responded Jonadab, by no means disconcerted, 'leastways unless some two-legged fairies have got it.'

At this some of the party found it impossible not to laugh, and this so upset poor Martha's composure that she was obliged to leave the table, and Anne was not sorry for the excuse of attending her, although there were stings of pain in all her rambling lamentations and conjectures.

Very tardily, according to the feelings of the anxious women, was the dinner finished, and their companions ready to take them out again. Indeed, Madam Oakshott at last repaired to the dining-parlour, and roused her husband from his glass of Spanish wine to renew the search. She would not listen to Mrs. Fellowes's advice not to go out again, and Anne could not abstain either from watching for what could not be other than grievous and mournful to behold.

The soldiers were called out again by their captain, and reinforced by the Rectory servant and Jonadab.

There was an interval of anxious prowling

round the opening. Mr. Oakshott and the
captain had gone down again, and found,
what the military man was anxious about,
that if there were passages to the outer air,
they had been well blocked up and not
reopened.

Meantime the digging proceeded.

It was just at twilight that a voice below
uttered an exclamation.   Then came a pause.
The old sergeant's voice ordered care and a
pause, somewhere below the opening with,
'Sir, the spades have hit upon a skull.'

There was a shuddering pause. All the
gentlemen except Dr. Woodford, who feared
the chill, descended again.   Mrs. Oakshott
and Anne held each other's hands and
trembled.

By and by Mr. Fellowes came up first.
'We have found,' he said, looking pale and
grave, 'a skeleton. Yes, a perfect skeleton,
but no more — no remains except a fine
dust.'

And Robert Oakshott following, awe-struck
and sorrowful, added, 'Yes, there he is, poor
Perry—all that is left of him—only his bones.
No, madam, we must leave him there for the

present ; we cannot bring it up without preparation.'

'You need not fear meddling curiosity, madam,' said the captain. 'I will post a sentry here to bar all entrance.'

'Thanks, sir,' said Robert. 'That will be well till I can bury the poor fellow with all due respect by my mother and Oliver.'

'And then I trust his spirit will have rest,' said Martha Oakshott fervently. 'And now home to your father. How will he bear it, sir ?'

'I verily believe he will sleep the quieter for knowing for a certainty what has become of poor Peregrine,' said her husband.

And Anne felt as if half her burthen of secrecy was gone when they all parted, starting early because the Black Gang rendered all the roads unsafe after dark.

CHAPTER XXVIII

THE DISCLOSURE

' He looked about as one betrayed,
What hath he done, what promise made ?
Oh ! weak, weak moment, to what end
Can such a vain oblation tend ? '
WORDSWORTH.

FOR the most part Anne was able to hold her peace and keep out of sight while Dr. Woodford related the strange revelations of the vault with all the circumstantiality that was desired by two old people living a secluded life and concerned about a neighbour of many years, whom they had come to esteem by force of a certain sympathy in honest opposition. The mystery occupied them entirely, for though the murder was naturally ascribed to some of the lawless coast population, the valuables remaining with the clothes made a strange feature in the case.

It was known that there was to be an inquest held on the remains before their removal, and Dr. Woodford, both from his own interest in the question, and as family intelligencer, rode to the castle. Sir Philip longed to go, but it was a cold wet day, and he had threatenings of gout, so that he was persuaded to remain by the fireside. Inquests were then always held where the body lay, and the court of Portchester Castle was no place for him on such a day.

Dr. Woodford came home just before twilight, looking grave and troubled, and, much to Anne's alarm, desired to speak to Sir Philip privately in the gun-room. Lady Archfield took alarm, and much distressed her by continually asking what could be the meaning of the interview, and making all sorts of guesses.

When at last they came together into the parlour the poor lady looked so anxious and frightened that her husband went up to her and said, 'Do not be alarmed, sweetheart. We shall clear him; but those foolish fellows have let suspicion fall on poor Sedley.'

Nobody looked at Anne, or her deadly

paleness must have been remarked, and the trembling which she could hardly control by clasping her hands tightly together, keeping her feet hard on the floor, and setting her teeth.

Lady Archfield was perhaps less fond of the scapegrace nephew than was her husband, and she felt the matter chiefly as it affected him, so that she heard with more equanimity than he had done ; and as they sat round the fire in the half-light, for which Anne was thankful, the Doctor gave his narration in order.

'I found a large company assembled in the castle court, waiting for the coroner from Portsmouth, though the sentry on guard would allow no one to go down, in spite of some, even ladies, I am ashamed to say, who offered him bribes for the permission. Everything, I heard, had been replaced as we found it. The poor Major himself was there, looking sadly broken, and much needing the help of his son's arm. " To think that I was blaming my poor son as a mere reprobate, and praying for his conversion," says he, " when he was lying here, cut off without a moment for repentance." There was your nephew, suspecting nothing, Squire Brocas, Mr. Eyre, of Botley Grange, Mr. Biden, Mr. Larcom, and Mr. Bargus, and a good many more, besides Dr. James Yonge, the naval doctor, and the Mayor of Portsmouth, and more than I can tell you. When the coroner came, and the jury had been sworn in, they went down and viewed the spot, and all that was there. The soldiers had put candles round, and a huge place it is, all built up with large stones. Then, as it was raining hard, they adjourned to the great room in the keep and took the evidence. Robert Oakshott identified the clothes and the watch clearly enough, and said he had no doubt that the other remains were Peregrine's; but as to swearing to a brother's bones, no one could do that; and Dr. Yonge said in my ear that if the deceased were so small a man as folks said, the skeleton could scarce be his, for he thought it had belonged to a large-framed person. That struck no one else, for naturally it is only a chirurgeon who is used to reckon the proportion that the bones bear to the body, and I also asked him whether in seven years the other parts would be so entirely consumed, to which he answered that so much would depend on the nature of the soil that there was no telling. However, jury and coroner seemed to feel no doubt, and that old seafaring man, Tom Block, declared that poor Master Peregrine had been hand and glove with a lot of wild chaps, and that the vault had been well known to them before the gentlemen had had it blocked up. Then it was asked who had seen him last, and Robert Oakshott spoke of having parted with him at the bonfire, and never seen him again. There, I fancy, it would have ended in a verdict of wilful murder against some person or persons unknown, but Robert Oakshott must needs say, " I would give a hundred pounds to know who the villain was." And then who should get up but George Rackstone, with " Please your Honour, I could tell summat." The coroner bade swear him, and he deposed to having seen Master Peregrine going down towards the castle somewhere about four o'clock that morning after the bonfire when he was getting up to go to his mowing. But that was not all. You remember, Anne, that his father's cottage stands on the road towards Portsmouth. Well, he brought up the story of your running in there, frightened, the day before the bonfire, when I was praying with his sick mother, calling on me to stop a fray between Peregrine and young Sedley, and I had to get up and tell of Sedley's rudeness to you, child.'

'What was that?' hastily asked Lady Archfield.

'The old story, my lady. The young officer's swaggering attempt to kiss the girl he meets on the road. I doubt even if he knew at the moment that it was my niece. Peregrine was coming by at the moment, and interfered to protect her, and swords were drawn. I could not deny it, nor that there was ill blood between the lads; and then young Brocas, who was later on Portsdown than we were, remembered high words, and had thought to himself that there would be a challenge. And next old Goody Spore recollects seeing Master Sedley and another soldier officer out on the Portsmouth road early that morning. The hay was making in

the court then, and Jenny Light remembered
that when the haymakers came she raked up
something that looked like a bloody spot, and
showed it to one of the others, but they told
her that most likely a rabbit or a hare had
been killed there, and she had best take no
heed.   Probably there was dread of getting
into trouble about a smugglers' fray.   Well,
every one was looking askance at Master
Sedley by this time, and the coroner asked
him if he had anything to say.   He spoke
out boldly enough.   He owned to the dispute
with Peregrine Oakshott, and to having parted
with him that night on terms which would
only admit of a challenge.   He wrote a cartel
that night, and sent it by his friend Lieutenant
Ainslie, but doubting whether Major Oakshott
might not prevent its delivery, he charged him
to try to find Peregrine outside the house, and
arrange with him a meeting on the hill, where
you know the duellists of the garrison are
wont to transact such encounters.   Sedley
himself walked out part of the way with his
friend, but neither of them saw Peregrine, nor
heard anything of him.   So he avers, but
when asked for his witness to corroborate the

story, he says that Ainslie, I fear the only person who could have proved an *alibi*—if so it were—was killed at Landen ; but, he added, certainly with too much of his rough way, it was a mere absurdity to charge it upon him. What should a gentleman have to do with private murders and robberies ?   Nor did he believe the bones to be Perry Oakshott's at all.   It was all a bit of Whiggish spite !   He worked himself into a passion, which only added to the impression against him ; and I own I cannot wonder that the verdict has sent him to Winchester to take his trial.   Why, Anne, child, how now ?'

'' Tis a terrible story.   Take my essences, child,' said Lady Archfield, tottering across, and Anne, just saving herself from fainting by a long gasp at them, let herself be led from the room.

The maids buzzed about her, and for some time she was sensible of nothing but a longing to get rid of them, and to be left alone to face the grievous state of things which she did not yet understand.   At last, with kind good-nights from Lady Archfield, such as she could hardly return, she was left by herself in the darkness to recover from the stunned helpless feeling of the first moment.

Sedley accused! Charles to be sacrificed to save his worthless cousin, the would-be murderer of his innocent child, who morally thus deserved to suffer! Never, never! She could not do so. It would be treason to her benefactors, nay, absolute injustice, for Charles had struck in generous defence of herself; but Sedley had tried to allure the boy to his death merely for his own advantage. Should she not be justified in simply keeping silence? Yet there was, like an arrow in her heart, the sense of guilt in so doing, guilt towards God and truth, guilt towards man and justice. She should die under the load, and it would be for Charles. Might it only be before he came home, then he would know that she had perished under his secret to save him. Nay, but would he be thankful at being saved at the expense of his cousin's life? If he came, how should she meet him?

The sense of the certain indignation of a good and noble human spirit often awakes the full perception of what an action would be in the sight of Heaven, and Anne began to realise the sin more than at first, and to feel the compulsion of truth.   If only Charles were not coming home she could write to him and warn him, but the thought that he might be already on the way had turned from joy to agony.   'And to think,' she said to herself, 'that I was fretting as to whether he would think me pretty!'

She tossed about in misery, every now and then rising on her knees to pray—at first for Charles's safety—for she shrank from asking for Divine protection, knowing only too well what that would be.   Gradually, however, a shudder came over her at the thought that if she would not commit her way unto the Lord, she might indeed be the undoing of her lover, and then once more the higher sense of duty rose on her.   She prayed for forgiveness for the thought, and that it might not be visited upon him ; she prayed for strength to do what must be her duty, for safety for him, and comfort to his parents, and so, in passing gusts of misery and apprehension, of failing heart and recovered resolution, of anguish and of prayer, the long night at length passed, and with the first dawn she arose, shaken and weak, but resolved to act on her terrible resolution before it again failed her.

Sir Philip was always an early riser, and she heard his foot on the stairs before seven o'clock. She came out on the staircase, which met the flight which he was descending, and tried to speak, but her lips seemed too dry to part.

'Child! child! you are ill,' said the old gentleman, as he saw her blanched cheek; 'you should be in bed this chilly morning. Go back to your chamber.'

'No, no, sir, I cannot. Pray, your Honour, come here, I have something to say;' and she drew him to the open door of his justice-room, called the gun-room.

'Bless me,' he muttered, 'the wench does not mean that she has got smitten with that poor rogue my nephew!'

'Oh! no, no,' said Anne, almost ready for a hysterical laugh, yet letting the old man seat himself, and then dropping on her knees before him, for she could hardly stand, 'it is worse than that, sir; I know who it was who did that thing.'

'Well, who?' he said hastily; 'why have

you kept it back so long and let an innocent man get into trouble?'

'O Sir Philip! I could not help it.   Forgive me;' and with clasped hands, she brought out the words, 'It was your son, Mr. Archfield;' and then she almost collapsed again.

'Child! child! you are ill; you do not know what you are saying.   We must have you to bed again.   I will call your uncle.'

'Ah! sir, it is only too true;' but she let him fetch her uncle, who was sure to be at his devotions in a kind of oratory on the farther side of the hall.   She had not gone to him first, from the old desire to keep him clear of the knowledge, but she longed for such support as he might give her, or at least to know whether he were very angry with her.

The two old men quickly came back together, and Dr. Woodford began, 'How now, niece, are you telling us dreams?' but he broke off as he saw the sad earnest of her face.

'Sir, it is too true.   He charged me to speak out if any one else were brought into danger.'

'Come,' said Sir Philip testily; 'don't crouch grovelling on the floor there. Get up and let us know the meaning of this. Good heavens! the lad may be here any day.'

Anne had much rather have knelt where she was, but her uncle raised her, and placed her in a chair, saying, 'Try to compose yourself, and tell us what you mean, and why it has been kept back so long.'

'Indeed he did not intend it,' pleaded Anne; 'it was almost an accident—to protect me—Peregrine was—pursuing me.'

'Upon my word, young mistress,' burst out the father, 'you seem to have been setting all the young fellows together by the ears.'

'I doubt if she could help it,' said the Doctor. 'She tried to be discreet, but it was the reason her mother——'

'Well, go on,' interrupted poor Sir Philip, too unhappy to remember manners or listen to the defence; 'what was it? when was it?'

Anne was allowed then to proceed. 'It was the morning I went to London. I went out to gather some mouse-ear.'

'Mouse-ear! mouse-ear!' growled he. 'Some one else's ear.'

'It was for Lady Oglethorpe.'

'It was,' said her uncle, 'a specific, it seems, for whooping-cough. I saw the letter, and knew——'

'Umph! let us hear,' said Sir Philip, evidently with the idea of a tryst in his mind. 'No wonder mischief comes of maidens running about at such hours. What next?'

The poor girl struggled on : 'I saw Peregrine coming, and hoping he would not see me, I ran into the keep, meaning to get home by the battlements out of his sight, but when I looked down he and Mr. Archfield were fighting. I screamed, but I don't think they heard me, and I ran down ; but I had fastened all the doors, and I was a long time getting out, and by that time Mr. Archfield had dragged him to the vault and thrown him in. He was like one distracted, and said it must be hidden, or it would be the death of his wife and his mother, and what could I do?'

'Is that all the truth?' said Sir Philip

sternly. 'What brought them there—either of them?'

'Mr. Archfield came to bring me a pattern of sarcenet to match for poor young Madam in London.'

No doubt Sir Philip recollected the petulant anger that this had been forgotten, but he was hardly appeased. 'And the other fellow? Why, he was brawling with my nephew Sedley about you the day before!'

'I do not think she was to blame there,' said Dr. Woodford. 'The unhappy youth was set against marrying Mistress Browning, and had talked wildly to my sister and me about wedding my niece.'

'But why should she run away as if he had the plague, and set the foolish lads to fight?'

'Sir, I must tell you,' Anne owned, 'he had beset me, and talked so desperately that I was afraid of what he might do in that lonely place and at such an hour in the morning. I hoped he had not seen me.'

'Umph!' said Sir Philip, much as if he thought a silly girl's imagination had caused all the mischief.

'When did he thus speak to you, Anne?' asked her uncle, not unkindly.

'At the inn at Portsmouth, sir,' said Anne. 'He came while you were with Mr. Stanbury and the rest, and wanted me to marry him and flee to France, or I know not where, or at any rate marry him secretly so as to save him from poor Mistress Browning. I could not choose but fear and avoid him, but oh! I would have faced him ten times over rather than have brought this on—us all. And now what shall I do? He, Mr. Archfield, when I saw him in France, said as long as no one was suspected, it would only give more pain to say what I knew, but that if suspicion fell on any one——' and her voice died away.

'He could not say otherwise,' returned Sir Philip, with a groan.

'And now what shall I do? what shall I do?' sighed the poor girl. 'I must speak truth.'

'I never bade you perjure yourself,' said Sir Philip sharply, but hiding his face in his hands, and groaning out, 'Oh, my son! my son!'

Seeing that his distress so overcame poor

Anne that she could scarcely contain herself, Dr. Woodford thought it best to take her from the room, promising to come again to her. She could do nothing but lie on her bed and weep in a quiet heart-broken way. Sir Philip's anger seemed to fill up the measure, by throwing the guilt back upon her and rousing a bitter sense of injustice, and then she wept again at her cruel selfishness in blaming the broken-hearted old man.

She could hardly have come down to breakfast, so heavy were her limbs and so sick and faint did every movement render her, and she further bethought herself that the poor old father might not brook the sight of her under the circumstances. It was a pang to hear little Philip prancing about the house, and when he had come to her to say his prayers, she sent him down with a message that she was not well enough to come downstairs, and that she wanted nothing, only to be quiet.

The little fellow was very pitiful, and made her cry again by wanting to know whether she had gout like grandpapa or rheumatics like grandmamma, and then stroking her face, calling her his dear Nana, and telling her of the salad in his garden that his papa was to eat the very first day he came home.

By and by Dr. Woodford knocked at her door. He had had a long conversation with poor old Sir Philip, who was calmer now than under the first blow, and somewhat less inclined to anger with the girl, who might indeed be the cause, but surely the innocent cause, of all. The Doctor had done his best to show that her going out had no connection with any of the youths, and he thought Sir Philip would believe it on quieter reflection. He had remembered too signs of self-reproach mixed with his son's grief for his wife, and his extreme relief at the plan for going abroad, recollecting likewise that Charles had strongly disliked poor Peregrine, and had much resented the liking which young Madam had shown for one whose attentions might have been partly intended to tease the young husband.

'Of course,' said Dr. Woodford, 'the unhappy deed was no more than an unfortunate accident, and if all had been known at first, probably it would so have been treated. The concealment was an error, but it is impossible to blame either of you for it.'

'Oh never mind that, dear uncle! Only tell me! Must he—must Charles suffer to save that man? You know what he is, real murderer in heart! Oh I know. The right must be done! But it is dreadful!'

'The right must be done and the truth spoken at all costs. No one knows that better than our good old patron,' said the Doctor; 'but, my dear child, you are not called on to denounce this young man as you seem to imagine, unless there should be no other means of saving his cousin, or unless you are so questioned that you cannot help replying for truth's sake. Knowing nothing of all this, it struck others besides myself at the inquest that the evidence against Sedley was utterly insufficient for a conviction, and if he should be acquitted, matters will only be as they were before.'

'Then you think I am not bound to speak —The truth, the whole truth, nothing but the truth,' she murmured in exceeding grief, yet firmly.

'You certainly may, nay, *must* keep your former silence till the trial, at the Lent Assizes. I trust you may not be called on as a witness to the fray with Sedley, but that I may be sufficient testimony to that. I could testify to nothing else. Remember, if you are called, you have only to answer what you are asked, nor is it likely, unless Sedley have any suspicion of the truth, that you will be asked any question that will implicate Mr. Archfield. If so, God give you strength my poor child, to be true to Him. But the point of the trial is to prove Sedley guilty or not guilty; and if the latter, there is no more to be said. God grant it.'

'But he—Mr. Archfield?'

'His father is already taking measures to send to all the ports to stop him on his way till the trial is over. Thus there will be no actual danger, though it is a sore disappointment, and these wicked attempts of Charnock and Barclay put us in bad odour, so that it may be less easy to procure a pardon than it once would have been. So, my dear child, I do not think you need be in terror for his life, even if you are obliged to speak out plainly.'

And then the good old man knelt with Anne to pray for pardon, direction, and firmness, and protection for Charles. She made an entreaty after they rose that her uncle would take her away—her presence must be so painful to their kind hosts. He agreed with her, and made the proposition, but Sir Philip would not hear of it. Perhaps he was afraid of any change bringing suspicion of the facts, and he might have his fears of Anne being questioned into dangerous admissions, besides which, he hoped to keep his poor old wife in ignorance to the last. So Anne was to remain at Fareham, and after that one day's seclusion she gathered strength to be with the family as usual. Poor old Sir Philip treated her with a studied but icy courtesy which cut her to the heart ; but Lady Archfield's hopes of seeing her son were almost worse, together with her regrets at her husband's dejection at the situation of his nephew and the family disgrace. As to little Philip, his curious inquiries about Cousin Sedley being in jail for murdering Penny

Grim had to be summarily hushed by the assurance that such things were not to be spoken about.   But why did Nana cry when he talked of papa's coming home ?

All the neighbourhood was invited to the funeral in Havant Churchyard, the burial-place of the Oakshotts.   Major Oakshott himself wrote to Dr. Woodford, as having been one of the kindest friends of his poor son, adding that he could not ask Sir Philip Archfield, although he knew him to be no partner in the guilt of his unhappy nephew, who so fully exemplified that Divine justice may be slow, but is sure.

Dr. Woodford decided on accepting the invitation, not only for Peregrine's sake, but to see how the land lay.   Scarcely anything remarkable, however, occurred, except that it was painful to perceive the lightness of the coffin.   A funeral sermon was previously preached by a young Nonconformist minister in his own chapel, on the text, 'Whoso sheddeth man's blood, by man shall his blood be shed ;' and then the burial took place, watched by a huge crowd of people.   But just as the procession was starting from the chapel for the churchyard, over the wall there came a strange peal of wild laughter.

'Oh, would not the unquiet spirit be at rest till it was avenged?' thought Anne when she was told of it.

CHAPTER XXIX

THE ASSIZE COURT

' O terror ! what hath she perceived ? O joy,
What doth she look on ? whom hath she perceived ? '
WORDSWORTH.

TIME wore away, and the Lent Assizes at
Winchester had come. Sir Philip had procured the best legal assistance for his nephew,
but in criminal cases, though the prisoner was
allowed the advice of counsel, the onus of
defence rested upon himself. To poor Anne's
dismay, a subpœna was sent to her, as well
as to her uncle, to attend as a witness at
the trial. Sir Philip was too anxious to
endure to remain at a distance from Winchester, and they travelled in his coach, Sir
Edmund Nutley escorting them on horseback,
while Lucy was left with her mother, both
still in blissful ignorance. They took rooms

at the George Inn. That night was a
strange and grievous one to Anne, trying
hard to sleep so as to be physically capable of composure and presence of mind,
yet continually wakened by ghastly dreams,
and then recollecting that the sense of
something terrible was by no means all a
dream.

Very white, very silent, but very composed,
she came to the sitting-room, and was con-
strained by her uncle and Sir Philip to eat,
much as it went against her. On this morning Sir Philip had dropped his sternness
towards her, and finding a moment when his
son-in-law was absent, he said, ' Child, I know
that this is wellnigh, nay, quite as hard for
you as for me. I can only say, Let no
earthly regards hold you back from whatever
is your duty to God and man. Speak the
truth whatever betide, and leave the rest to
the God of truth. God bless you, however
it may be ; ' and he kissed her brow.

The intelligence that the trial was coming
on was brought by Sedley's counsel, Mr.
Simon Harcourt. They set forth for the
County Hall up the sharply-rising street,

thronged with people, who growled and murmured at the murderer savagely, Sir Philip, under the care of his son-in-law, and Anne with her uncle. Mr. Harcourt was very hopeful ; he said the case for the prosecution had not a leg to stand on, and that the prisoner himself was so intelligent, and had so readily understood the line of defence to take, that he ought to have been a lawyer. There would be no fear except that it might be made a party case, and no stone was likely to be left unturned against a gentleman of good loyal family. Moreover, Mr. William Cowper, whom Robert Oakshott, or rather his wife, had engaged at great expense for the prosecution, was one of the most rising of barristers, noted for his persuasive eloquence, and unfortunately Mr. Harcourt had not the right of reply.

The melancholy party were conducted into court, Sir Philip and Sir Edmund to the seats disposed of by the sheriff, beside the judge, strangely enough only divided by him from Major Oakshott. The judge was Mr. Baron Hatsel, a somewhat weak-looking man, in spite of his red robes and flowing wig, as he sat under his canopy beneath King Arthur's Round Table. Sedley, perhaps a little thinner since his imprisonment, but with the purple-red on his face, and his prominent eyes so hard and bold that it was galling to know that this was really the confidence of innocence.

Mr. Cowper was with great ability putting the case. Here were two families in immediate neighbourhood, divided from the first by political opinions of the strongest complexion ; and he put the Oakshott views upon liberty, civil and religious, in the most popular light. The unfortunate deceased he described as having been a highly promising member of the suite of the distinguished Envoy, Sir Peregrine Oakshott, whose name he bore. On the death of the eldest brother he had been recalled, and his accomplishments and foreign air had, it appeared, excited the spleen of the young gentlemen of the county belonging to the Tory party, then in the ascendant, above all of the prisoner. There was then little or no etiquette as to irrelevant matter, so that Mr. Cowper could dwell at length on Sedley's antecedents, as abusing the bounty of his uncle, a known bully expelled for misconduct from Winchester College, then acting as a suitable instrument in those violences in Scotland which had driven the nation finally to extremity, noted for his debaucheries when in garrison, and finally broken for insubordination in Ireland.

After this unflattering portrait, which Sedley's looks certainly did not belie, the counsel went back to 1688, proceeded to mention several disputes which had taken place when Peregrine had met Lieutenant Archfield at Portsmouth ; but, he added with a smile, that no dart of malice was ever thoroughly winged till Cupid had added his feather ; and he went on to describe in strong colours the insult to a young gentlewoman, and the interference of the other young man in her behalf, so that swords were drawn before the appearance of the reverend gentleman her uncle.   Still, he said, there was further venom to be added to the bolt, and he showed that the two had parted after the rejoicings on Portsdown Hill with a challenge all but uttered between them, the Whig upholding religious liberty, the Tory hotly defending such honour as the King possessed, and both parting in anger.

Young Mr. Oakshott was never again seen alive, though his family long hoped against hope. There was no need to dwell on the strange appearances that had incited them to the search. Certain it was, that after seven years' silence, the grave had yielded up its secrets. Then came the description of the discovery of the bones, and of the garments and sword, followed by the mention of the evidence as to the blood on the grass, and the prisoner having been seen in the neighbourhood of the castle at that strange hour. He was observed to have an amount of money unusual with him soon after, and, what was still more suspicious, after having gambled this away, he had sold to a goldsmith at Southampton a ruby ring, which both Mr. and Mrs. Oakshott could swear to have belonged to the deceased. In fact, when Mr. Cowper marshalled the facts, and even described the passionate encounter taking place hastily and without witnesses, and the subsequent concealment of guilt in the vault, the purse taken, and whatever could again be identified hidden, while providentially the blocking up of the vault preserved the evidence of the crime so long undetected and unavenged, it was hardly possible to believe the prisoner innocent.

When the examination of the witnesses began, however, Sedley showed himself equal to his own defence.   He made no sign when Robert Oakshott identified the clothes, sword, and other things, and their condition was described ; but he demanded of him sharply how he knew the human remains to be those of his brother.

'Of course they were,' said Robert.

'Were there any remains of clothes with them ?'

'No.'

'Can you swear to them ?   Did you ever before see your brother's bones ?'

At which, and at the witness's hesitating, 'No, but——' the court began to laugh.

'What was the height of the deceased ?'

'He reached about up to my ear,' said the witness with some hesitation.

'What was the length of the skeleton ?'

'Quite small.   It looked like a child's.'

'My lord,' said Sedley, 'I have a witness here, a surgeon, whom I request may be called to certify the proportion of a skeleton to the size of a living man.'

Though this was done, the whole matter of size was so vague that there was nothing proved, either as to the inches of Peregrine or those of the skeleton, but still Sedley made his point that the identity of the body was unproved at least in some minds. Still, there remained the other articles, about which there was no doubt.

Mr. Cowper proceeded with his examination as to the disputes at Portsmouth, but again the prisoner scored a point by proving that Peregrine had staked the ring against him at a cock-fight at Southampton, and had lost it.

Dr. Woodford was called, and his evidence could not choose but to be most damaging as to the conflict on the road at Portsmouth ; but as he had not seen the beginning, 'Mistress Anne Jacobina Woodford' was called for.

There she stood, tall and stately, almost majestic in the stiffness of intense self-restraint.

in her simple gray dress, her black silk hood somewhat back, her brown curls round her face, a red spot in each cheek, her earnest brown eyes fixed on the clerk as he gabbled out the words so awful to her, ' The truth, the whole truth, and nothing but the truth ; ' and her soul re-echoed the words, ' So help you God.'

Mr. Cowper was courteous ; he was a gentleman, and he saw she was no light-minded girl.   He asked her the few questions needful as to the attack made on her, and the defence ; but something moved him to go on and ask whether she had been on Portsdown Hill, and to obtain from her the account of the high words between the young men. She answered each question in a clear low voice, which still was audible to all.   Was it over, or would Sedley begin to torture her, when so much was in his favour ?   No ! Mr. Cowper—oh ! why would he ? was asking in an affirmative tone, as if to clench the former evidence, ' And did you ever see the deceased again ? '

' Yes.'   The answer was at first almost choked, then cleared into sharpness, and

every eye turned in surprise on the face
that had become as white as her collar.

'Indeed!   And when?'

'The next morning,' in a voice as if pro-
nouncing her own doom, and with hands
clinging tight to the front of the witness-box
as though in anguish.

'Where?' said the counsel, like inexorable
fate.

'I will save the gentlewoman from replying
to that question, sir;' and a gentleman with
long brown hair, in a rich white and gold
uniform, rose from among the spectators.
'Perhaps I may be allowed to answer for
her, when I say that it was at Portchester
Castle, at five in the morning, that she saw
Peregrine Oakshott slain by my hand, and
thrown into the vault.'

There was a moment of breathless amaze-
ment in the court, and the judge was the first
to speak.   'Very extraordinary, sir!   What
is your name?'

'Charles Archfield,' said the clear, resolute
voice.

Then came a general movement and
sensation, and Anne, still holding fast to the

support, saw the newcomer start forward with a cry, 'My father!' and with two or three bounds reach the side of Sir Philip, who had sunk back in his seat for a moment, but recovered himself as he felt his son's arm round him.

There was a general buzz, and a cry of order, and in the silence thus produced the judge addressed the witness :—

'Is what this gentleman says the truth ?'

And on Anne's reply, 'Yes, my Lord,' spoken with the clear ring of anguish, the judge added—

'Was the prisoner present ?'

'No, my Lord; he had nothing to do with it.'

'Then, brother Cowper, do you wish to proceed with the case ?'

Mr. Cowper replied in the negative, and the judge then made a brief summing-up, and the jury, without retiring, returned a verdict of 'Not guilty.'

In the meantime Anne had been led like one blinded from the witness-box, and almost dropped into her uncle's arms. 'Cheer up, cheer up, my child,' he said. 'You have done your part bravely, and after so upright a confession no one can deal hardly with the young man. God will surely protect him.'

The acquittal had been followed by a few words from Baron Hatsel, congratulating the late prisoner on his deliverance through this gentleman's generous confession. Then there was a moment's hesitation, ended by the sheriff asking Charles, who stood up by his old father, one arm supporting the trembling form, and the other hand clasped in the two aged ones, 'Then, sir, do you surrender to take your trial?'

'Certainly, sir,' said Charles. 'I ought to have done so long ago, but in the first shock——'

Mr. Harcourt here cautioned him not to say anything that could be used against him, adding in a low tone, much to Sir Philip's relief, 'It may be brought in manslaughter, sir.'

'He should be committed,' another authority said. 'Is there a Hampshire magistrate here to sign a warrant?'

Of these there were plenty; and as the

clerk asked for his description, all eyes turned on the tall and robust form in the prime of manhood, with the noble resolute expression on his fine features and steadfast eyes, except when, as he looked at his father, they were full of infinite pity. The brown hair hung over the rich gold-laced white coat, faced with black, and with a broad gold-coloured sash fringed with black over his shoulder, and there was a look of distinction about him that made his answer only natural. 'Charles Archfield, of Archfield House, Fareham, Lieutenant-Colonel of his Imperial Majesty's Light Dragoons, Knight of the Holy Roman Empire. Must I give up my sword like a prisoner of war?' he asked, with a smile.

Sir Philip rose to his feet with an earnest trembling entreaty that bail might be taken for him, and many voices of gentlemen and men of substance made offers of it. There was a little consultation, and it was ruled that bail might be accepted under the circumstances, and Charles bowed his thanks to the distant and gave his hand to the nearer, while Mr. Eyre of Botley Grange, and Mr. Brocas of Roche Court, were accepted as sureties.

The gentle old face of Mr. Cromwell of
Hursley was raised to poor old Sir Philip's
with the words, spoken with a remnant of
the authority of the Protector: 'Your son
has spoken like a brave man, sir ; God bless
you, and bring you well through it.'

Charles was then asked whether he wished
for time to collect witnesses. 'No, my lord,'
he said. 'I thank you heartily, but I have
no one to call, and the sooner this is over the
better for all.'

After a little consultation it was found that
the Grand Jury had not been dismissed, and
could find a true bill against him ; and it was
decided that the trial should take place
after the rest of the criminal cases were
disposed of.

This settled, the sorrowful party with the
strangely welcomed son were free to return
to their quarters at the George. Mr. Cromwell pressed forward to beg that they would
make use of his coach. It was a kind thought,
for Sir Philip hung feebly on his son's arm,
and to pass through the curious throng would
have been distressing. After helping him in,
Charles turned and demanded—

'Where is she, the young gentlewoman, Miss Woodford?'

She was just within, her uncle waiting to take her out till the crowd's attention should be called off. Charles lifted her in, and Sir Edmund and Dr. Woodford followed him, for there was plenty of room in the capacious vehicle.

Nobody spoke in the very short interval the four horses took in getting themselves out of the space in front of the County Hall and down the hill to the George. Only Charles had leant forward, taken Anne's hand, drawn it to his lips, and then kept fast hold of it.

They were all in the room at the inn at last, they hardly knew how; indeed, as Charles was about to shut the door there was a smack on his back, and there stood Sedley holding out his hand.

'So, Charley, old fellow, you were the sad dog after all. You got me out of it, and I owe you my thanks, but you need not have put your neck into the noose. I should have come off with flying colours, and made them all make fools of themselves, if you had only waited.'

' Do you think I could sit still and see *her* put to the torture ? ' said Charles.

' Torture ?   You are thinking of your barbarous countries.   No fear of the boot here, nor even in Scotland nowadays.'

' That's all the torture you understand,' muttered Sir Edmund Nutley.

' Not but what I am much beholden to you all the same,' went on Sedley.   ' And look here, sir,' turning to his uncle, ' if you wish to get him let off cheap you had better send up another special retainer to Harcourt, without loss of time, as he may be off.'

Sir Edmund Nutley concurred in the advice, and they hurried off together in search of the family attorney, through whom the great man had to be approached.

The four left together could breathe more freely.   Indeed Dr. Woodford would have taken his niece away, but that Charles already had her in his arms in a most fervent embrace, as he said, ' My brave, my true maid ! '

She could not speak, but she lifted up her eyes, with infinite relief in all her sorrow, as for a moment she rested against him ; but they had to move apart, for a servant came up with some wine, and Charles, putting her into a chair, began to wait on her and on his father.

'I have not quite forgotten my manners,' he said lightly, as if to relieve the tension of feeling, 'though in Germany the ladies serve the gentlemen.'

It was very hard not to burst into tears at these words, but Anne knew that would be the way to distress her companions and to have to leave the room and lose these precious moments. Sir Philip, after swallowing the wine, succeeded in saying, 'Have you been at home ?'

Charles explained that he had landed at Gravesend, and had ridden thence, sleeping at Basingstoke, and taking the road through Winchester in case his parents should be wintering there, and on arriving a couple of hours previously and inquiring for them, he had heard the tidings that Sir Philip Archfield was indeed there, for his nephew was being tried for his life for the wilful murder of Major Oakshott's son seven years ago.

'And you had none of my warnings ?   I

wrote to all the ports,' said his father, 'to warn you to wait till all this was over.'

No; he had crossed from Sluys, and had met no letter. 'I suppose,' he said, 'that I must not ride home to-morrow. It might make my sureties uneasy; but I would fain see them all.'

'It would kill your mother to be here,' said Sir Philip. 'She knows nothing of what Anne told me on Sedley's arrest. She is grown very feeble;' and he groaned. 'But we might send for your sister, if she can leave her, and the boy.'

'I should like my boy to be fetched,' said Charles. 'I should wish him to remember his father—not as a felon convicted!' Then putting a knee to the ground before Sir Philip, he said, 'Sir, I ask your blessing and forgiveness. I never before thoroughly understood my errors towards you, especially in hiding this miserable matter, and leaving all this to come on you, while my poor Anne there was left to bear all the load. It was a cowardly and selfish act, and I ask your pardon.'

The old man sobbed with his hand on his

son's head. 'My dear boy! my poor boy! you were distraught.'

'I was then. I did it, as I thought, for my poor Alice's sake at first, and as it proved, it was all in vain ; but at the year's end, when I was older, it was folly and wrong. I ought to have laid all before you, and allowed you to judge, and I sincerely repent the not having so done. And Anne, my sweetest Anne, has borne the burthen all this time,' he added, going back to her. 'Let no one say a woman cannot keep secrets, though I ought never to have laid this on her.'

'Ah! it might have gone better for you then,' sighed Sir Philip. 'No one would have visited a young lad's mischance hardly on a loyal house in those days. What is to be done, my son?'

'That we will discuss when the lawyer fellow comes. Is it old Lee? Meantime let us enjoy our meeting. So that is Lucy's husband. Sober and staid, eh? And my mother is feeble, you say. Has she been ill?'

Charles was comporting himself with the cheerfulness that had become habitual to him as a soldier, always in possible danger, but it was very hard to the others to chime in with his tone, and when a message was brought to ask whether his Honour would be served in private, the cheery greeting and shake of the hand broke down the composure of the old servant who brought it, and he cried, 'Oh, sir, to see you thus, and such a fine young gentleman!'

Charles, the only person who could speak, gave the orders, but they did not eat alone, for Sir Edmund Nutley and Sedley arrived with the legal advisers, and it was needful, perhaps even better, to have their company. The chief of the conversation was upon Hungarian and Transylvanian politics and the Turkish war. Mr. Harcourt seeming greatly to appreciate the information that Colonel Archfield was able to give him, and the anecdotes of the war, and descriptions of scenes therein actually brightened Sir Philip into interest, and into forgetting for a moment his son's situation in pride in his conduct, and at the distinction he had gained.

'We must save him,' said Mr. Harcourt to Sir Edmund. 'He is far too fine a fellow to be lost for a youthful mischance.'

The meal was a short one, and a consultation was to follow, while Sedley departed. Anne was about to withdraw, when Mr. Lee the attorney said, 'We shall need Mistress Woodford's evidence, sir, for the defence.'

'I do not see what defence there can be,' returned Charles. 'I can only plead guilty, and throw myself on the King's mercy, if he chooses to extend it to one of a Tory family.'

'Not so fast, sir,' said Mr. Harcourt; 'as far as I have gathered the facts, there is every reason to hope you may obtain a verdict of manslaughter, and a nominal penalty, although that rests with the judge.'

On this the discussion began in earnest. Charles, who had never heard the circumstances which led to the trial, was greatly astonished to hear what remains had been discovered. He said that he could only declare himself to have thrown in the body, full dressed, just as it was, and how it could have been stripped and buried he could not imagine. 'What made folks think of looking into the vault?' he asked.

'It was Mrs. Oakshott,' said Lee, 'the

young man's wife, she who was to have married the deceased. She took up some strange notion about stories of phantoms current among the vulgar, and insisted on having the vault searched, though it had been walled up for many years past.'

Charles and Anne looked at each other, and the former said, ' Again ?'

' Oh yes !' said Anne ; ' indeed there have been enough to make me remember what you bade me do, in case they recurred, only it was impossible.'

' Phantoms !' said Mr. Harcourt ; 'what does this mean ?'

' Mere vulgar superstitions, sir,' said the attorney.

' But very visible,' said Charles ; ' I have seen one myself, of which I am quite sure, besides many that may be laid to the account of the fever of my wound.'

' I must beg to hear,' said the barrister. ' Do I understand that these were apparitions of the deceased ?'

' Yes,' said Charles. ' Miss Woodford saw the first, I think.'

' May I beg you to describe it ?' said Mr.

Harcourt, taking a fresh piece of paper to make notes on.

Anne narrated the two appearances in London, and Charles added the story of the figure seen in the street at Douai, seen by both together, asking what more she knew of.

'Once at night last summer, at the very anniversary, I saw his face in the trees in the garden,' said Anne ; ' it was gone in a moment. That has been all I have seen ; but little Philip came to me full of stories of people having seen Penny Grim, as he calls it, and very strangely, once it rose before him at the great pond, and his fright saved him from sliding to the dangerous part.   What led Mrs. Oakshott to the examination was that it was seen once on the beach, once by the sentry at the vault itself, once by the sexton at Havant Churchyard, and once by my mother's grave.'

'Seven ?' said the counsel, reviewing the notes he jotted down.   'Colonel Archfield, I should recommend you pleading not guilty, and basing your defence, like your cousin, on the strong probability that this same youth is a living man.'

'Indeed!' said Charles, starting, 'I could have hoped it from these recent apparitions, but what I myself saw forbids the idea. If any sight were ever that of a spirit, it was what we saw at Douai; besides, how should he come thither, a born and bred Whig and Puritan?'

'There is no need to mention that; you can call witnesses to his having been seen within these few months. It would rest with the prosecution to disprove his existence in the body, especially as the bones in the vault cannot be identified.'

'Sir,' said Charles, 'the defence that would have served my innocent cousin cannot serve me, who know what I did to Oakshott. I am *now* aware that it is quite possible that the sword might not have killed him, but when I threw him into that vault I sealed his fate.'

'How deep is the vault?'

Mr. Lee and Dr. Woodford both averred that it was not above twenty or twenty-four feet deep, greatly to Charles's surprise, for as a lad he had thought it almost unfathomable; but then he owned his ideas of Winchester

High Street had been likewise far more magnificent than he found it. The fall need not necessarily have been fatal, especially to one insensible and opposing no resistance, but even supposing that death had not resulted, in those Draconian days, the intent to murder was equally subject with its full accomplishment to capital punishment. Still, as Colonel Archfield could plead with all his heart that he had left home with no evil intentions towards young Oakshott, the lawyers agreed that to prove that the death of the victim was uncertain would reduce the matter to a mere youthful brawl, which could not be heavily visited. Mr. Harcourt further asked whether it were possible to prove that the prisoner had been otherwise employed than in meddling with the body; but unfortunately it had been six hours before he came home.

'I was distracted,' said Charles; 'I rode I knew not whither, till I came to my senses on finding that my horse was ready to drop, when I led him into a shed at a wayside public-house, bade them feed him, took a drink, then I wandered out into the copse near, and lay on the ground there till I thought him rested, for how long I know not. I think it must have been near Bishops Waltham, but I cannot recollect.'

Mr. Lee decided on setting forth at peep of dawn the next morning to endeavour to collect witnesses of Peregrine's appearances. Sir Edmund Nutley intended to accompany him as far as Fareham to fetch little Philip and Lady Nutley, if the latter could leave her mother after the tidings had been broken to them, and also to try to trace whether Charles's arrival at any public-house were remembered.

To her dismay, Anne received another summons from the other party to act as witness.

'I hoped to have spared you this, my sweet,' said Charles, 'but never mind; you cannot say anything worse of me than I shall own of myself.'

The two were left to each other for a little while in the bay window. 'Oh, sir! can you endure me thus after all?' murmured Anne, as she felt his arm round her.

'Can you endure me after all I left you to bear?' he returned.

'It was not like what I brought on you,' she said.

But they could not talk much of the future; and Charles told how he had rested through all his campaigns in the knowledge that his Anne was watching and praying for him, and how his long illness had brought before him deeper thoughts than he had ever had before, and made him especially dwell on the wrong done to his parents by his long absence, and the lightness with which he had treated home duties and responsibilities, till he had resolved that if his life were then spared, he would neglect them no longer.

'And now,' he said, and paused, 'all I shall have done is to break their hearts. What is that saying, "Be sure your sin will find you out."'

'Oh, sir! they are sure not to deal hardly with you.'

'Perhaps the Emperor's Ambassador may claim me. If so, would you go into banishment with the felon, Anne, love? It would not be quite so mad as when I asked you before.'

'I would go to the ends of the world with

you ; and we would take little Phil. Do you know, he is growing a salad, and learning Latin, all for papa ? '

And so she told him of little Phil till his father was seen looking wistfully at him.

With Sir Philip, Charles was all cheerfulness and hope, taking such interest in all there was to hear about the family, estate, and neighbourhood, that the old gentleman was beguiled into feeling as if there were only a short ceremony to be gone through before he had his son at home, saving him ease and trouble.

But after Sir Philip had been persuaded to retire, worn out with the day's agitations, and Anne likewise had gone to her chamber to weep and pray, Charles made his arrangements with Mr. Lee for the future for all connected with him in case of the worst ; and after the lawyer's departure poured out his heart to Dr. Woodford in deep contrition, as he said he had longed to do when lying in expectation of death at the Iron Gates. ' However it may end,' he said, ' and I expect, as I deserve, the utmost, I am thankful for this opportunity, though unhappily it gives more pain to those about me than if I had died out there.   Tell them, when they need comfort, how much better it is for me.'

'My dear boy, I cannot believe you will have to suffer.'

'There is much against me, sir.   My foolish flight, the state of parties, and the recent conspiracy, which has made loyal families suspected and odious.   I saw something of that as I came down.   The crowd fancied my uniform French, and hooted and hissed me.   Unluckily I have no other clothes to wear.   Nor can I from my heart utterly disclaim all malice or ill will when I remember the thrill of pleasure in driving my sword home.   I have had to put an end to a Janissary or two more than once in the way of duty, but their black eyes never haunted me like those parti-coloured ones. Still I trust, as you tell me I may, that God forgives me, for our Blessed Lord's sake ; but I should like, if I could, to take the Holy Sacrament with my love while I am still thus far a free man.   I have not done so since the Easter before these troubles.'

'You shall, my dear boy, you shall.'

There were churches at which the custom freshly begun at the Restoration was not dropped.   The next was St Matthias's Day, and Anne and her uncle had already purposed to go to the quiet little church of St. Lawrence, at no great distance, in the very early morning.   They were joined on their way down the stair into the courtyard of the inn by a gentleman in a slouched hat and large dark cloak, who drew Anne's arm within his own.

Truly there was peace on that morning, and strength to the brave man beyond the physical courage that had often before made him bright in the face of danger, and Anne, though weeping, had a sense of respite and repose, if not of hope.

Late in the afternoon, little Philip was lifted down from riding before old Ralph into the arms of the splendid officer, whose appearance transcended all his visions.   He fumbled in his small pocket, and held out a handful of something green and limp.

' Here's my salad, papa.   I brought it all the way for you to eat.'

And Colonel Archfield ate every scrap of

it for supper, though it was much fitter for a
rabbit, and all the evening he held on his
knee the tired child, and responded to his
prattle about Nana and dogs and rabbits ;
nay, ministered to his delight and admiration
of the sheriff's coach, javelin men, and even
the judge, with a strange mixture of wonder,
delight, and with melancholy only in eyes and
undertones.

CHAPTER XXX

'I have hope to live, and am prepared to die.'
Measure for Measure.

RALPH was bidden to be ready to take his young master home early the next morning. At eight o'clock the boy, who had slept with his father, came down the stair, clinging to his father's hand, and Miss Woodford coming closely with him.

'Yes,' said Charles, as he held the little fair fellow in his arms, ere seating him on the horse, 'he knows all, Ralph. He knows that his father did an evil thing, and that what we do in our youth finds us out later, and must be paid for. He has promised me to be a comfort to the old people, and to look on this lady as a mother. Nay, no more, Ralph; 'tis not good-bye to any of you yet. There,

Phil, don't lug my head off, nor catch my hair in your buttons. Give my dutiful love to your grandmamma and to Aunt Nutley, and be a good boy to them.'

'And when I come to see you again I'll bring another salad,' quoth Philip, as he rode out of the court; and his father, by way of excusing a contortion of features, smoothed the entangled lock of hair, and muttered something about, ' This comes of not wearing a periwig.'   Then he said—

'And to think that I have wasted the company of such a boy as that, all his life except for this mere glimpse !'

'Oh! you will come back to him,' was all that could be said.

For it was time for Charles Archfield to surrender himself to take his trial.

He had been instructed over and over again as to the line of his defence, and cautioned against candour for himself and delicacy towards others, till he had more than once to declare that he had no intention of throwing his life away ; but the lawyers agreed in heartily deploring the rules that thus deprived the accused of the assistance of an advocate in examining witnesses and defending himself. All depended, as they knew and told Sir Edmund Nutley, on the judge and jury. Now Mr. Baron Hatsel had shown himself a well-meaning but weak and vacillating judge, whose summing-up was apt rather to confuse than to elucidate the evidence; and as to the jury, Mr. Lee scanned their stolid countenances somewhat ruefully when they were marshalled before the prisoner, to be challenged if desirable. A few words passed, into which the judge inquired.

'I am reminded, my Lord,' said Colonel Archfield, bowing, 'that I once incurred Mr. Holt's displeasure as a mischievous boy by throwing a stone which injured one of his poultry; but I cannot believe such a trifle would bias an honest man in a question of life and death.'

Nevertheless the judge put aside Mr. Holt.

'I like his spirit,' whispered Mr. Harcourt.

'But,' returned Lee, 'I doubt if he has done himself any good with those fellows by calling it a trifle to kill an old hen. I should like him to have challenged two or three more moody old whiggish rascals ; but he has been too long away from home to know how the land lies.'

'Too generous and high-spirited for this work,' sighed Sir Edmund, who sat with them.

The indictment was read, the first count being 'That of malice aforethought, by the temptation of the Devil, Charles Archfield did wilfully kill and slay Peregrine Oakshott,' etc. The second indictment was that 'By misadventure he had killed and slain the said Peregrine Oakshott.' To the first he pleaded 'Not guilty ;' to the second 'Guilty.'

Tall, well-made, manly, and soldierly, he stood, with a quiet, set face, while Mr. Cowper proceeded to open the prosecution, with a certain compliment to the prisoner and regret at having to push the case against one who had so generously come forward on behalf of a kinsman ; but he must unwillingly state the circumstances that made it doubtful, nay, more than doubtful, whether the prisoner's plea of mere misadventure could stand. The dislike to the unfortunate deceased existing among the young Tory country gentlemen of the county was, he should prove, intensified in the prisoner on account of not inexcusable jealousies, as well as of the youthful squabbles which sometimes lead to fatal results. On the evening of the 30th of June 1688 there had been angry words between the prisoner and the deceased on Portsdown Hill, respecting the prisoner's late lady. At four or five o'clock on the ensuing morning, the 1st of July, the one fell by the sword of the other in the then unfrequented court of Portchester Castle. It was alleged that the stroke was fatal only through the violence of youthful impetuosity; but was it consistent with that supposition that the young gentleman's time was unaccounted for afterwards, and that the body should have been disposed of in a manner that clearly proved the assistance of an accomplice, and with so much skill that no suspicion had arisen for seven years and a half, whilst the actual slayer was serving, not his own country, but a foreign prince, and had only returned at a most suspicious crisis?

The counsel then proceeded to construct a

plausible theory.   He reminded the jury that at that very time, the summer of 1688, messages and invitations were being despatched to his present Gracious Majesty to redress the wrongs of the Protestant Church, and protect the liberties of the English people. The father of the deceased was a member of a family of the country party, his uncle a distinguished diplomatist, to whose suite he had belonged.   What was more obvious than that he should be employed in the correspondence, and that his movements should be dogged by parties connected with the Stewart family? Already there was too much experience of how far even the most estimable and conscientious might be blinded by the sentiment that they dignified by the title of loyalty. The deceased had already been engaged in a struggle with one of the Archfield family, who had been acquitted of his actual slaughter; but considering the strangeness of the hour at which the two cousins were avowedly at or near Portchester, the condition of the clothes, stripped of papers, but not of valuables, and the connection of the principal witness with the pretended Prince of Wales, he could not help thinking that though personal animosity might have added an edge to the weapon, yet that there were deeper reasons, to prompt the assault and the concealment, than had yet been brought to light.

'He will make nothing of that,' whispered Mr. Lee. 'Poor Master Peregrine was no more a Whig than old Sir Philip there.'

''Twill prejudice the jury,' whispered back Mr. Harcourt, 'and discredit the lady's testimony.'

Mr. Cowper concluded by observing that half truths had come to light in the former trial, but whole truths would give a different aspect to the affair, and show the unfortunate deceased to have given offence, not only as a man of gallantry, but as a patriot, and to have fallen a victim to the younger bravoes of the so-called Tory party. To his (the counsel's) mind, it was plain that the prisoner, who had hoped that his crime was undiscovered and forgotten, had returned to take his share in the rising against Government so happily frustrated. He was certain that the traitor Charnock had been received at his father's house, and that Mr. Sedley Archfield had used seditious language on several occasions, so that the cause of the prisoner's return at this juncture was manifest, and only to the working of Providence could it be ascribed that the evidence of the aggravated murder should have at that very period been brought to light.

There was an evident sensation, and glances were cast at the upright, military figure, standing like a sentinel, as if the audience expected him to murder them all.

As before, the examination began with Robert Oakshott's identification of the clothes and sword, but Mr. Cowper avoided the subject of the skeleton, and went on to inquire about the terms on which the two young men had lived.

'Well,' said Robert, 'they quarrelled, but in a neighbourly sort of way.'

'What do you call a neighbourly way?'

'My poor brother used to be baited for being so queer.　But then we were as bad to him as the rest,' said Robert candidly.

'That is, when you were boys?'

'Yes.'

'And after his return from his travels?'

' It was the same then.   He was too fine a gentleman for any one's taste.'

' You speak generally.   Was there any especial animosity ?'

' My brother bought a horse that Archfield was after.'

' Was there any dispute over it ?'

' Not that I know of.'

' Can you give an instance of displeasure manifested by the prisoner at the deceased ?'

' I have seen him look black when my brother held a gate open for his wife.'

' Then there were gallant attentions towards Mrs. Archfield ?'

Charles's face flushed, and he made a step forward, but Robert gruffly answered : ' No more than civility ; but he had got Frenchified manners, and liked to tease Archfield.'

' Did they ever come to high words before you ?'

' No.   They knew better.'

' Thank you, Mr. Oakshott,' said the prisoner, as it was intimated that Mr. Cowper had finished. ' You bear witness that only the most innocent civility ever passed between your brother and my poor young wife ?'

'Certainly,' responded Robert.

'Nothing that could cause serious resentment, if it excited passing annoyance.'

'Nothing.'

'What were your brother's political opinions?'

'Well'—with some slow consideration—'he admired the Queen as was, and could not abide the Prince of Orange. My father was always *at him* for it.'

'Would you think him likely to be an emissary to Holland?'

'No one less likely.'

But Mr. Cowper started up. 'Sir, I believe you are the younger brother?'

'Yes.'

'How old were you at the time?'

'Nigh upon nineteen.'

'Oh!' as if that accounted for his ignorance.

The prisoner continued, and asked whether search was made when the deceased was missed.

'Hardly any.'

'Why not?'

'He was never content at home, and we believed he had gone to my uncle in Muscovy.'

'What led you to examine the vault?'

'My wife was disquieted by stories of my brother's ghost being seen.'

'Did you ever see this ghost?'

'No, never.'

That was all that was made of Robert Oakshott, and then again came Anne Woodford's turn, and Mr. Cowper was more satirical and less considerate than the day before. Still it was a less dreadful ordeal than previously, though she had to tell the worst, for she knew her ground better, and then there was throughout wonderful support in Charles's eyes, which told her, whenever she glanced towards him, that she was doing right and as he wished. As she had not heard the speech for the prosecution it was a shock, after identifying herself a niece to a 'non-swearing' clergyman, to be asked about the night of the bonfire, and to be forced to tell that Mrs. Archfield had insisted on getting out of the carriage and walking about with Mr. Oakshott.

'Was the prisoner present?'

'He came up after a time.'

'Did he show any displeasure?'

'He thought it bad for her health.'

'Did any words pass between him and the deceased?'

'Not that I remember.'

'And now, madam, will you be good enough to recur to the following morning, and continue the testimony in which you were interrupted the day before yesterday? What was the hour?'

'The church clock struck five just after.'

'May I ask what took a young gentlewoman out at such an untimely hour? Did you expect to meet any one?'

'No indeed, sir,' said Anne hotly. 'I had been asked to gather some herbs to carry to a friend.'

'Ah! And why at that time in the morning?'

'Because I was to leave home at seven, when the tide served.'

'Where were you going?'

'To London, sir.'

'And for what reason?'

'I had been appointed to be a rocker in the royal nursery.'

'I see. And your impending departure

may explain certain strange coincidences. May I ask what was this same herb?' in a mocking tone.

'Mouse-ear, sir,' said Anne, who would fain have called it by some less absurd title, but knew no other. 'A specific for the whooping-cough.'

'Oh! Not "Love in a mist." Are you sure?'

'My lord,' here Simon Harcourt ventured, 'may I ask, is this regular?'

The judge intimated that his learned brother had better keep to the point, and Mr. Cowper, thus called to order, desired the witness to continue, and demanded whether she was interrupted in her quest.

'I saw Mr. Peregrine Oakshott enter the castle court, and I hurried into the tower, hoping he had not seen me.'

'You said before he had protected you. Why did you run from him?'

She had foreseen this, and quietly answered, 'He had made me an offer of marriage which I had refused, and I did not wish to meet him.'

'Did you see any one else?'

'Not till I had reached the door opening on the battlements. Then I heard a clash, and saw Mr. Archfield and Mr. Oakshott fighting.'

'Mr. Archfield! The prisoner? Did he come to gather mouse-ear too?'

'No. His wife had sent him over with a pattern of sarcenet for me to match in London.'

'Early rising and prompt obedience.' And there ensued the inquiries that brought out the history of what she had seen of the encounter, of the throwing the body into the vault, full dressed, and of her promise of silence and its reason. Mr. Cowper did not molest her further except to make her say that she had been five months at the Court, and had accompanied the late Queen to France.

Then came the power of cross-examination on the part of the prisoner. He made no attempt to modify what had been said before, but asked in a gentle apologetic voice: 'Was that the last time you ever saw, or thought you saw, Peregrine Oakshott?'

'No.' And here every one in the court started and looked curious.

'When?'

'The 31st of October 1688, in the evening.'

'Where?'

'Looking from the window in the palace at Whitehall, I saw him, or his likeness, walking along in the light of the lantern over the great door.'

The appearance at Lambeth was then described, and that in the garden at Arch field House. This strange cross-examination was soon over, for Charles could not endure to subject her to the ordeal, while she equally longed to be able to say something that might not damage him, and dreaded every word she spoke. Moreover, Mr. Cowper looked exceedingly contemptuous, and made the mention of Whitehall and Lambeth a handle for impressing on the jury that the witness had been deep in the counsels of the late royal family, and that she was escorted from St. Germain by the prisoner just before he entered on foreign service.

One of the servants at Fareham was called upon to testify to the hour of his young master's return on the fatal day. It was long past dinner-time, he said. It must have been about three o'clock.

Charles put in an inquiry as to the condition of his horse. 'Hard ridden, sir, as I never knew your Honour bring home Black Bess in such a pickle before.'

After a couple of young men had been called who could speak to some outbreaks of dislike to poor Peregrine, in which all had shared, the case for the prosecution was completed. Cowper, in a speech that would be irregular now, but was permissible then, pointed out that the jealousy, dislike, and Jacobite proclivities of the Archfield family had been fully made out, that the coincidence of visits to the castle at that untimely hour had been insufficiently explained, that the condition of the remains in the vault was quite inconsistent with the evidence of the witness, Mistress Woodford, unless there were persons waiting below unknown to her, and that the prisoner had been absent from Fareham from four or five o'clock in the morning till nearly three in the afternoon. As to the strange story she had further told, he (Mr. Cowper) was neither superstitious nor philosophic, but the jury would decide whether conscience and the sense of an awful secret were not sufficient to conjure up such phantoms, if they were not indeed spiritual, occurring as they did in the very places and at the very times when the spirit of the unhappy young man, thus summarily dismissed from the world, his corpse left in an unblessed den, would be most likely to reappear, haunting those who felt themselves to be most account-able for his lamentable and untimely end.

The words evidently told, and it was at a disadvantage that the prisoner rose to speak in his own defence and to call his witnesses.

' My lord,' he said, ' and gentlemen of the jury, let me first say that I am deeply grieved and hurt that the name of my poor young wife has been brought into this matter. In justice to her who is gone, I must begin by saying that though she was flattered and gratified by the polite manners that I was too clownish and awkward to emulate, and though I may have sometimes manifested ill-humour, yet I never for a moment took serious offence nor felt bound to defend her honour or my own. If I showed displeasure it was because she was fatiguing herself against warning.   I can say with perfect truth, that when I left home on that unhappy morning, I bore no serious ill-will to any living creature.   I had no political purpose, and never dreamt of taking the life of any one.   I was a heedless youth of nineteen.   I shall be able to prove the commission of my wife's on which this learned gentleman has thought fit to cast a doubt. For the rest, Mistress Anne Woodford was my sister's friend and playfellow from early childhood.   When I entered the castle court I saw her hurrying into the keep, pursued by Oakshott, whom I knew her to dread and dislike.   I naturally stepped between.   Angry words passed.   He challenged my right to interfere, and in a passion drew upon me. Though I was the taller and stronger, I knew him to be proud of his skill in fencing, and perhaps I may therefore have pressed him the harder, and the dislike I acknowledge made me drive home my sword.   But I was free from all murderous intention up to that moment.   In my inexperience I had no doubt but that he was dead, and in a terror and confusion which I regret heartily, I threw him into the vault, and for the sake of my wife and mother bound Miss Woodford to secrecy. I mounted my horse, and scarcely knowing what I did, rode till I found it ready to drop. I asked for rest for it in the first wayside public-house I came to. I lay down meanwhile among some bushes adjoining, and there waited till my horse could take me home again. I believe it was at the White Horse, near Bishops Waltham, but the place has changed hands since that time, so that I can only prove my words, as you have heard, by the state of my horse when I came home. For the condition of the remains in the vault I cannot account; I never touched the poor fellow after throwing him there. My wife died a few hours after my return home, where I remained for a week, nor did I suggest flight, though I gladly availed myself of my father's suggestion of sending me abroad with a tutor. Let me add, to remove misconception, that I visited Paris because my tutor, the Reverend George Fellowes, one of the Fellows of Magdalen College expelled by the late King, and now Rector of Portchester, had been asked to provide for

Miss Woodford's return to her home, and he is here to testify that I never had any concern with politics. I did indeed accompany him to St. Germain, but merely to find the young gentlewoman, and in the absence of the late King and Queen, nor did I hold intercourse with any other person connected with their Court. After escorting her to Ostend, I went to Hungary to serve in the army of our ally, the Emperor, against the Turks, the enemies of all Christians. After a severe wound, I have come home, knowing nothing of conspiracies, and I was taken by surprise on arriving here at Winchester at finding that my cousin was on his trial for the unfortunate deed into which I was betrayed by haste and passion, but entirely without premeditation or intent to do more than to defend the young lady. So that I plead that my crime does not amount to murder from malicious intent; and likewise, that those who charge me with the actual death of Peregrine Oakshott should prove him to be dead.'

Charles's first witness was Mrs. Lang, his late wife's 'own woman,' who spared him many questions by garrulously declaring

'what a work' poor little Madam had made
about the rose-coloured sarcenet, causing the
pattern to be searched out as soon as she
came home from the bonfire, and how she
had 'gone on at' her husband till he promised
to give it to Mistress Anne, and how he had
been astir at four o'clock in the morning, and
had called to her (Mrs. Lang) to look to her
mistress, who might perhaps get some sleep
now that she had her will and hounded him
out to go over to Portchester about that
silk.

Nothing was asked of this witness by the
prosecution except the time of Mr. Archfield's
return.   The question of jealousy was passed
over.

Of the pond apparition nothing was said.
Anne had told Charles of it, but no one could
have proved its identity but Sedley, and his
share in it was too painful to be brought
forward.   Three other ghost seers were
brought forward : Mrs. Fellowes's maid, the
sentry, and the sexton ; but only the sexton
had ever seen Master Perry alive, and
he would not swear to more than that it
was something in his likeness ; the sentry

was already bound to declare it something unsubstantial ; and the maid was easily persuaded into declaring that she did not know what she had seen or whether she had seen anything.

There only remained Mr. Fellowes to bear witness of his pupil's entire innocence of political intrigues, together with a voluntary testimony addressed to the court, that the youth had always appeared to him a well-disposed but hitherto boyish lad, suddenly sobered and rendered thoughtful by a shock that had changed the tenor of his mind.

Mr. Baron Hatsel summed up in his dreary vacillating way. He told the gentlemen of the jury that young men would be young men, especially where pretty wenches were concerned, and that all knew that there was bitterness where Whig and Tory were living nigh together. Then he went over the evidence, at first in a tone favourable to the encounter having been almost accidental, and the stroke an act of passion. But he then added, it was strange, and he did not know what to think of these young sparks and the young gentlewoman all meeting in a lonely place when honest folks were abed, and the hiding in the vault, and the state of the clothes were strange matters scarce agreeing with what either prisoner or witness said. It looked only too like part of a plot of which some one should make a clean breast. On the other hand, the prisoner was a fine young gentleman, an only son, and had been fighting the Turks, though it would have been better to have fought the French among his own countrymen. He had come ingenuously forward to deliver his cousin, and a deliberate murderer was not wont to be so generous, though may be he expected to get off easily on this same plea of misadventure. If it was misadventure, why did he not try to do something for the deceased, or wait to see whether he breathed before throwing him into this same pit? though, to be sure, a lad might be inexperienced. For the rest, as to these same sights of the deceased or his likeness, he (the judge) was no believer in ghosts, though he would not say there were no such things, and the gentlemen of the jury must decide whether it was more likely the poor youth was playing pranks in the body, or whether he were haunting in the spirit those who had most to do with his untimely end.   This was the purport, or rather the no-purport, of the charge.

The jury were absent for a very short time, and as it leaked out afterwards, their intelligence did not rise above the idea that the young gentleman was thick with they Frenchies who wanted to bring in murder and popery, warming-pans and wooden shoes. He called stoning poultry a trifle, so of what was he not capable? Of course he spited the poor young chap, and how could the fact be denied when the poor ghost had come back to ask for his blood?

So the awful suspense ended with ' Guilty, my lord.'

' Of murder or manslaughter ? '

' Of murder.'

The prisoner stood as no doubt he had faced Turkish batteries.

The judge asked the customary question whether he had any reason to plead why he should not be condemned to death.

' No, my lord.   I am guilty of shedding Peregrine Oakshott's blood, and though I declare before God and man that I had no such purpose, and it was done in the heat of an undesigned struggle, I hated him enough to render the sentence no unjust one. I trust that God will pardon me, if man does not.'

The gentlemen around drew the poor old father out of the court so as not to hear the final sentence, and Anne, half stunned, was taken away by her uncle, and put into the same carriage with him. The old man held her hands closely and could not speak, but she found voice. 'Sir, sir, do not give up hope. God will save him. I know what I can do. I will go to Princess Anne. She is friendly with the King now. She will bring me to tell him all.'

Hurriedly she spoke, her object, as it seemed to be that of every one, to keep up such hope and encouragement as to drown the terrible sense of the actual upshot of the trial. The room at the George was full in a moment of friends declaring that all would go well in the end, and consulting what to do. Neither Sir Philip nor Dr. Woodford could be available, as their refusal to take the oaths to King William made them marked men. The former could only write to the Imperial

Ambassador, beseeching him to claim the prisoner as an officer of the Empire, though it was doubtful whether this would be allowed in the case of an Englishman born. Mr. Fellowes undertook to be the bearer of the letter, and to do his best through Archbishop Tenison to let the King know the true bearings of the case. Almost in pity, to spare Anne the misery of helpless waiting, Dr. Woodford consented to let her go under his escort, starting very early the next morning, since the King might immediately set off for the army in Holland, and the space was brief between condemnation and execution.

Sir Edmund proposed to hurry to Carisbrooke Castle, being happily on good terms with that fiery personage, Lord Cutts, the governor of the Isle of Wight as well as a favoured general of the King, whose intercession might do more than Princess Anne's. Moreover, a message came from old Mr. Cromwell, begging to see Sir Edmund. It was on behalf of Major Oakshott, who entreated that Sir Philip might be assured of his own great regret at the prosecution and the result, and his entire belief that the provocation came from his unhappy son. Both he and Richard Cromwell were having a petition for pardon drawn up, which Sir Henry Mildmay and almost all the leading gentlemen of Hampshire of both parties were sure to sign, while the sheriff would defer the execution as long as possible. Pardons, especially in cases of duelling, had been marketable articles in the last reigns, and there could not but be a sigh for such conveniences. Sir Philip wanted to go at once to the jail, which was very near the inn, but consented on strong persuasion to let his son-in-law precede him.

Anne longed for a few moments to herself, but durst not leave the poor old man, who sat holding her hand, and at each interval of silence saying how this would kill the boy's mother, or something equally desponding, so that she had to talk almost at random of the various gleams of hope, and even to describe how the little Duke of Gloucester might be told of Philip and sent to the King, who was known to be very fond of him. It was a great comfort when Dr. Woodford came and offered to pray with them.

By and by Sir Edmund returned, having been making arrangements for Charles's comfort. Ordinary prisoners were heaped together and miserably treated, but money could do something, and by application to the High Sheriff, permission had been secured for Charles to occupy a private room, on a heavy fee to the jailor, and for his friends to have access to him, besides other necessaries, purchased at more than their weight in gold. Sir Edmund brought word that Charles was in good heart; sent love and duty to his father, whom he would welcome with all his soul, but that as Miss Woodford was—in her love and bravery—going so soon to London, he prayed that she might be his first visitor that evening.

There was little more to do than to cross the street, and Sir Edmund hurried her through the flagged and dirty yard, and the dim, foul hall, filled with fumes of smoke and beer, where melancholy debtors held out their hands, idle scapegraces laughed, heavy degraded faces scowled, and evil sounds were heard, up the stairs to a nail-studded door, where Anne shuddered to hear the heavy key turned by the coarse, rude-looking warder, only withheld from insolence by the presence of a magistrate.   Her escort tarried outside, and she saw Charles, his rush-light candle gleaming on his gold lace as he wrote a letter to the ambassador to be forwarded by his father.

He sprang up with outstretched arms and an eager smile.   'My brave sweetheart! how nobly you have done.   Truth and trust. It did my heart good to hear you.'

Her head was on his shoulder.   She wanted to speak, but could not without loosing the flood of tears.

'Faith entire,' he went on ; 'and you are still striving for me.'

'Princess Anne is——' she began, then the choking came.

'True!' he said.   'Come, do not expect the worst.   I have not made up my mind to that!   If the ambassador will stir, the King will not be disobliging, though it will probably not be a free pardon, but Hungary for some years to come—and you are coming with me.'

'If you will have one who might be—may

have been—your death. Oh, every word I said seemed to me stabbing you;' and the tears would come now.

'No such thing! They only showed how true my love is to God and me, and made my heart swell with pride to hear her so cheering me through all.'

His strength seemed to allow her to break down. She had all along had to bear up the spirits of Sir Philip and Lady Archfield, and though she had struggled for composure, the finding that she had in him a comforter and support set the pent-up tears flowing fast, as he held her close.

'Oh, I did not mean to vex you thus!' she said.

'Vex! no indeed! 'Tis something to be wept for. But cheer up, Anne mine. I have often been in far worse plights than this, when I have ridden up in the face of eight big Turkish guns. The balls went over my head then, by God's good mercy. Why not the same now? Ay! and I was ready to give all I had to any one who would have put a pistol to my head and got me out of my misery, jolting along on the way to the

Iron Gates. Yet here I am! Maybe the Almighty brought me back to save poor Sedley, and clear my own conscience, knowing well that though it does not look so, it is better for me to die thus than the other way. No, no; 'tis ten to one that you and the rest of you will get me off. I only meant to show you that supposing it fails, I shall only feel it my due, and much better for me than if I had died out there with it unconfessed. I shall try to get them all to feel it so, and, after all, now the whole is out, my heart feels lighter than it has done these seven years. And if I could only believe that poor fellow alive, I could almost die content, though that sounds strange. It will quiet his poor restless spirit any way.'

'You are too brave. Oh! I hoped to come here to comfort you, and I have only made you comfort me.'

'The best way, sweetest. Now, I will seal and address this letter, and you shall take it to Mr. Fellowes to carry to the ambassador.'

This gave Anne a little time to compose herself, and when he had finished, he took the candle, and saying, 'Look here,' he held it to the wall, and they read, scratched on the rough bricks, 'Alice Lisle, 1685.   This is thankworthy.'

'Lady Lisle's cell!   Oh, this is no good omen!'

'I call it a goodly legacy even to one who cannot claim to suffer wrongfully,' said Charles.   'There, they knock—one kiss more—we shall meet again soon.   Don't linger in town, but give me all the days you can.   Yes, take her back, Sir Edmund, for she must rest before her journey.   Cheer up, love, and do not lie weeping all night, but believe that your prayers to God and man must prevail one way or another.'

CHAPTER XXXI

' Three ruffians seized me yestermorn,
Alas ! a maiden most forlorn ;
They choked my cries with wicked might,
And bound me on a palfrey white.'
S. T. COLERIDGE

YET after the night it was with more hope than despondency, Anne, in the February morning, mounted *en croupe* behind Mr. Fellowes's servant, that being decided on as the quickest mode of travelling. She saw the sun rise behind St. Catherine's Hill, and the gray mists filling the valley of the Itchen, and the towers of the Cathedral and College barely peeping beyond them. Would her life rise out of the mist?

Through hoar - frosted hedges, deeply crested with white, they rode, emerging by and by on downs, becoming dully green above, as the sun touched them, but white below. Suddenly, in passing a hollow, overhung by two or three yew-trees, they found themselves surrounded by masked horsemen. The servant on her horse was felled, she herself snatched off and a kerchief covered her face, while she was crying, 'Oh sir, let me go! I am on business of life and death.'

The covering was stuffed into her mouth, and she was borne along some little way; then there was a pause, and she freed herself enough to say, 'You shall have everything; only let me go;' and she felt for the money with which Sir Philip had supplied her, and for the watch given her by King James.

'We want you; nothing of yours,' said a voice. 'Don't be afraid. No one will hurt you; but we must have you along with us.'

Therewith she was pinioned by two large hands, and a bandage was made fast over her eyes, and when she shrieked out, 'Mr. Fellowes! Oh! where are you?' she was answered—

'No harm has been done to the parson. He will be free as soon as any one comes by. 'Tis you we want. Now, I give you fair notice, for we don't want to choke you; there's no one to hear a squall. If there were, we should gag you, so you had best be quiet, and you shall suffer no hurt. Now then, by your leave, madam.'

She was lifted on horseback again, and a belt passed round her and the rider in front of her. Again she strove, in her natural voice, to plead that to stop her would imperil a man's life, and to implore for release. 'We know all that,' she was told. It was not rudely said. The voice was not that of a clown; it was a gentleman's pronunciation, and this was in some ways more inexplicable and alarming. The horses were put in rapid motion; she heard the trampling of many hoofs, and felt that they were on soft turf, and she knew that for many miles round Winchester it was possible to keep on the downs so as to avoid any inhabited place. She tried to guess, from the sense of sunshine that came through her bandage, in what direction she was being carried, and fancied it must be southerly. On—on—on—still the turf. It seemed absolutely endless. Time was not measurable under such circumstances, but she fancied noon must have more than passed, when the voice that had before spoken said, 'We halt in a moment, and shift you to another horse, madam ; but again I forewarn you that our comrades here have no ears for you, and that cries and struggles will only make it the worse for you.'   Then came the sound as of harder ground and a stop— undertones, gruff and manly, could be heard, the peculiar noise of horses' drinking ; and her captor came up this time on foot, saying, ' Plaguy little to be had in this accursed hole ; 'tis but the choice between stale beer and milk.   Which will you prefer ?'

She could not help accepting the milk, and she was taken down to drink it, and a hunch of coarse barley bread was given to her, with it the words, ' I would offer you bacon, but it tastes as if Old Nick had smoked it in his private furnace.'

Such expressions were no proof that gentle blood was lacking, but whose object could her abduction be—her, a penniless dependent ? Could she have been seized by mistake for some heiress ?   In that moment's hope she asked, ' Sir, do you know who I am—

Anne Woodford, a poor, portionless maid, not——'

'I know perfectly well, madam,' was the reply. 'May I trouble you to permit me to mount you again?'

She was again placed behind one of the riders, and again fastened to him, and off they went, on a rougher horse, on harder ground, and, as she thought, occasionally through brushwood. Again a space, to her illimitable, went by, and then came turf once more, and by and by what seemed to her the sound of the sea.

Another halt, another lifting down, but at once to be gathered up again, and then a splashing through water. 'Be careful,' said the voice. A hand, a gentleman's hand, took hers; her feet were on boards—on a boat; she was drawn down to sit on a low thwart. Putting her hand over, she felt the lapping of the water and tasted that it was salt.

'Oh, sir, where are you taking me?' she asked, as the boat was pushed off.

'That you will know in due time,' he answered.

Some more refreshment was offered her

in a decided but not discourteous manner, and she partook of it, remembering that exhaustion might add to her perils. She perceived that after pushing off from shore sounds of eating and low gruff voices mingled with the plash of oars. Commands seemed to be given in French, and there were mutterings of some strange language. Darkness was coming on. What were they doing with her? And did Charles's fate hang upon hers?

Yet in spite of terrors and anxieties, she was so much worn out as to doze long enough to lose count of time, till she was awakened by the rocking and tossing of the boat and loud peremptory commands. She became for the first time in her life miserable with sea-sickness, for how long it was impossible to tell, and the pitching of the boat became so violent that when she found herself bound to one of the seats she was conscious of little but a longing to be allowed to go to the bottom in peace, except that some great cause—she could hardly in her bewildered wretchedness recollect what—forbade her to die till her mission was over.

There were loud peremptory orders, oaths, sea phrases, in French and English, sometimes in that unknown tongue. Something expressed that a light was directing to a landing-place, but reaching it was doubtful.

'Unbind her eyes,' said a voice; 'let her shift for herself.'

'Better not.'

There followed a fresh upheaval, as if the boat were perpendicular; a sudden sinking, some one fell over and bruised her; another frightful rising and falling, then smoothness; the rope that held her fast undone; the keel grating; hands apparently dragging up the boat. She was lifted out like a doll, carried apparently through water over shingle. Light again made itself visible; she was in a house, set down on a chair, in the warmth of fire, amid a buzz of voices, which lulled as the bandage was untied and removed. Her eyes were so dazzled, her head so giddy, her senses so faint, that everything swam round her, and there that strange vision recurred. Peregrine Oakshott was before her. She closed her eyes again, as she lay back in the chair.

'Take this; you will be better.' A glass was at her lips, and she swallowed some hot drink, which revived her so that she opened her eyes again, and by the lights in an apparently richly curtained room, she again beheld that figure standing by her, the glass in his hand.

'Oh!' she gasped. 'Are you alive?'

The answer was to raise her still gloved hand with substantial fingers to a pair of lips.

'Then—then—he is safe! Thank God!' she murmured, and shut her eyes again, dizzy and overcome, unable even to analyse her conviction that all would be well, and that in some manner he had come to her rescue.

'Where am I?' she murmured dreamily. 'In Elf-land?'

'Yes; come to be Queen of it.'

The words blended with her confused fancies. Indeed she was hardly fully conscious of anything, except that a woman's hands were about her, and that she was taken into another room, where her drenched clothes were removed, and she was placed in a warm, narrow bed, where some more warm nourishment was put into her mouth with a spoon, after which she sank into a sleep of utter exhaustion. That sleep lasted long. There was a sensation of the rocking of the boat, and of aching limbs, through great part of the time; also there seemed to be a continual roaring and thundering around her, and such strange misty visions, that when she finally awoke, after a long interval of deeper and sounder slumber, she was incapable of separating the fact from the dream, more especially as head and limbs were still heavy, weary, and battered. The strange roaring still sounded, and sometimes seemed to shake the bed. Twilight was coming in at a curtained window, and showed a tiny chamber, with rafters overhead and thatch, a chest, a chair, and table. There was a pallet on the floor, and Anne suspected that she had been wakened by the rising of its occupant. Her watch was on the chair by her side, but it had not been wound, and the dim light did not increase, so that there was no guessing the time; and as the remembrance of her dreadful adventures made themselves clear, she realised with exceeding terror that she must be a prisoner, while the evening's apparition relegated itself to the world of dreams.

Being kidnapped to be sent to the plantations was the dread of those days. But if such were the case, what would become of Charles? In the alarm of that thought she sat up in bed and prepared to rise, but could nowhere see her clothes, only the little cloth bag of toilet necessaries that she had taken with her.

At that moment, however, the woman came in with a steaming cup of chocolate in her hand and some of the garments over her arm. She was a stout, weatherbeaten, kindly-looking woman with a high white cap, gold earrings, black short petticoat, and many-coloured apron. '*Monsieur veut savoir si mademoiselle va bien?*' said she in slow, careful French, and when questions in that language were eagerly poured out, she shook her head, and said, '*Ne comprends pas.*' She, however, brought in the rest of the clothes, warm water, and a light, so that Anne rose and dressed, exceedingly perplexed, and wondering whether she could be in a ship, for the sounds seemed to say so, and there was no corresponding motion. Could she be in France? Certainly the voyage had seemed interminable, but she did not think it *could* have been long enough for that, nor that any person in his senses would try to cross in an open boat in such weather. She looked at the window, a tiny slip of glass, too thick to show anything but what seemed to be a dark wall rising near at hand. Alas! she was certainly a prisoner! In whose hands? With what intent? How would it affect that other prisoner at Winchester? Was that vision of last night substantial or the work of her exhausted brain? What could she do? It was well for her that she could believe in the might of prayer.

She durst not go beyond her door, for she heard men's tones, suppressed and gruff, but presently there was a knock, and wonder of wonders, she beheld Hans, black Hans, showing all his white teeth in a broad grin, and telling her that Missee Anne's breakfast was ready. The curtain that overhung the door was drawn back, and she passed into another small room, with a fire on the open hearth, and a lamp hung from a beam, the walls all round covered with carpets or stuffs of thick glowing colours, so that it was like the inside of a tent.   And in the midst, without doubt, stood Peregrine Oakshott, in such a dress as was usually worn by gentlemen in the morning—a loose wrapping coat, though with fine lace cuffs and cravat, all, like the shoes and silk stockings, worn with his peculiar daintiness, and, as was usual when full-bottomed wigs were the rule in *grande tenue*, its place supplied by a silken cap.   This was olive-green with a crimson tassel, which had assumed exactly the characteristic one-sided Riquet-with-a-tuft aspect.   For the rest, these years seemed to have made the slight form slighter and more wiry, and the face keener, more sallow, and more marked.

He bowed low with the foreign courtesy which used to be so offensive to his contemporaries, and offered a delicate, beringed hand to lead the young lady to the little table, where grilled fowl and rolls, both showing the cookery of Hans, were prepared for her.

'I hope you rested well, and have an appetite this morning.'

'Sir, what does it all mean? Where am I?' asked Anne, drawing herself up with the native dignity that she felt to be her defence.

'In Elf-land,' he said, with a smile, as he heaped her plate.

'Speak in earnest,' she entreated. 'I cannot eat till I understand. It is no time for trifling! Life and death hang on my reaching London! If you saved me from those men, let me go free.'

'No one can move at present,' he said. 'See here.'

He drew back a curtain, opened first one door and then another, and she saw sheets of driving rain, and rising, roaring waves, with surf which came beating in on the force of such a fearful gust of wind that Peregrine hastily shut the door, not without difficulty. 'Nobody can stir at present,' he said, as they came into the warm bright room again. 'It is a frightful tempest, the worst known here for years, they say. The dead-lights, as they call them, have been put in, or the windows would be driven in. Come and taste Hans's work; you know it of old. Will you drink tea? Do you remember how your mother came to teach mine to brew it, and how she forgave me for being graceless enough to squirt at her ?'

There was something so gentle and reassuring in the demeanour of this strange being that Anne, convinced of the utter hopelessness of confronting the storm, as well as of the need of gathering strength, allowed herself to be placed in a chair, and to partake of the food set before her, and the tea, which was served without milk, in an exquisite dragon china cup, but with a saucer that did not match it.

'We don't get our sets perfect,' said Peregrine, with a smile, who was waiting on her as if she were a princess.

'I entreat you to tell me where we are!' said Anne.   'Not in France ?'

'No, not in France!   I wish we were.'

'Then—can this be the Island ?'

'Yes, the Island it is,' said Peregrine, both speaking as South Hants folk; 'this is the strange cave or chasm called Black Gang Chine.'

'Black Gang!   Oh! the highwaymen, the pirates!   You have saved me from them.

Were they going to send me to the plantations?'

'You need have no fears. No one shall
touch you, or hurt you. You shall see no
one save by your own consent, my queen.'

'And when this storm is passed—Oh!' as
a more fearful roar and dash sounded as if the
waves were about to sweep away their frail
shelter—'you will come with me and save
Mr. Archfield's life? You cannot know——'

'I know,' he interrupted; 'but why should
I be solicitous for his life? That I am here
now is no thanks to him, and why should I
give up mine for the sake of him who meant
to make an end of me?'

'You little know how he repented. And
your own life? What do you mean?'

'People don't haunt the Black Gang
Chine when their lives are secure from Dutch
Bill,' he answered. 'Don't be terrified, my
queen; though I cannot lay claim, like
Prospero, to having raised this storm by my
art magic, yet it perforce gives me time to
make you understand who and what I am,
and how I have recovered my better angel
to give her no mean nor desperate career.

It will be better thus than with the sudden-
ness with which I might have had to act.'

A new alarm seized upon Anne as to his
possible intentions, but she would not forestall
what she so much apprehended, and, sensible
that self-control alone could guard her, since
escape at present was clearly impossible, she
resigned herself to sit opposite to him by the
ample hearth of what she perceived to be a
fisherman's hut, thus fitted up luxuriously
with, it might be feared, the spoils of the sea.

The story was a long one, and not by any
means told consecutively or without interruption, and all the time those eyes were upon
her, one yellow the other green, with the
effect she knew so well of old in childish days,
of repulsion yet compulsion, of terror yet
attraction, as if irresistibly binding a reluctant
will.   Several times Peregrine was called off
to speak to some one outside the door, and
at noon he begged permission for his friends
to dine with them, saying that there was no
other place where the dinner could be taken
to them comfortably in this storm.

CHAPTER XXXII

SEVEN YEARS

It was between the night and day,
  When the Fairy King has power,
That I sunk down in a sinful fray,
And 'twixt life and death was snatched away
  To the joyless Elfin bower.'
                                    SCOTT.

THIS motto was almost the account that the twisted figure, with queer contortions of face, yet delicate feet and hands, and dainty utterance, might have been expected to give, when Anne asked him, 'Was it you, really?'

'I—or my double?' he asked. 'When?'

She told him, and he seemed amazed.

'So you were there? Well, you shall hear. You know how things stood with me —your mother, my good spirit, dead, my uncle away, my father bent on driving me to utter desperation, and Martha Browning laying her great red hands on me——'

'Oh, sir, she really loved you, and is far wiser and more tolerant than you thought her.'

'I know,' he smiled grimly. 'She buried the huge Scot that was killed in the great smuggling fray under the Protector, with all honours, in our family vault, and had a long-winded sermon preached on my untimely end. Ha! ha!' with his mocking laugh.

'Don't, sir! If you had seen your father then! Why did no one come forward and explain?'

'Mayhap there were none at hand who knew, or wished to meddle with the law,' he said. 'Well, things were beyond all bearing at home, and you were going away, and would not so much as look at me. Now, one of the few sports my father did not look askance at was fishing, and he would endure my being out at night with, as he thought, poor man, old Pete Perring, who was as stern a Puritan as himself; but I had livelier friends, and more adventurous. They had connections with French free-traders for brandy and silks, and when they found I was one with them, my French tongue was a boon to them, till I came to have a good many friends among the Norman fishermen, and to know the snug hiding-places about the coast. So at last I made up my mind to be off with them, and make my way to my uncle in Muscovy. I had raised money enough at play and on the jewels one picks up in an envoy's service, and there was one good angel whom I meant to take with me if I could secure her and bind her wings. Now you know with what hopes I saw you gathering flowers alone that morning.'

Anne clasped her hands; Charles had truly interfered with good cause.

'I had all arranged,' he continued; 'my uncle would have given you a hearty welcome, and made our peace with my father, or if not, he would have left us all his goods, and secured my career. What call had that great lout, with a wife of his own too, to come thrusting between us? I thought I should make short work of him, and give him a lesson against meddling—great unlicked cub as he was, while I had had the best training at Berlin and Paris in fencing ; but somehow those big strong fellows, from their very clumsiness, throw one out.   And he meant mischief—yes, that he did.   I saw it in his eyes.   I suppose his sulky rustic jealousy was a-fire at a few little civilities to that poor little wife of his.   Any way, when he bore me down like the swing of a windmill, he drove his sword home.   Talk of his being innocent! Why should he never look whether I were dead or alive, but fling me headlong into that pit ?'

Anne could not but utter her eager defence, but it was met with a sinister smile, half of scorn, half of pity, and as she would have gone on, ' Hush ! your pleading only fills up the measure of my loathing.'

Her heart sank, but she let him go on, listening perhaps less attentively as she considered how to take him.

' In fact,' he continued, ' little as the lubber knew it, 'twas the best he could have done for me.   For though I never looked for such luck as your being out in the court at that hour, I did think the chance not to be lost of visiting the garden or the churchyard, and there were waiting in the vault a couple of stout Normans, who were to come at my whistle. It seems that when I came tumbling down in their midst, senseless and bleeding like a calf, they did not take it quite so easily as your champion above, but began doing what they could for me, and were trying to staunch the wound, when they heard a trampling and a rumbling overhead, and being aware that our undertaking might look ugly in the sight of the law, and thinking this might be pursuers, they carried me off with all speed, not so much as stopping to pick up the things that have made such a commotion. Was there any pursuit ?'

'Oh no; it must have been the hay-makers.'

'No doubt. The place was in no great favour with our own people; they were in awe of the big Scot, who is in comfortable quarters in my grave, and the Frenchmen could not have found their way thither, so it was let alone till Mistress Martha's researches. So I came to myself in the boat in which they took me on board the lugger that was waiting for us ; and instead of making for Alderney, as I had intended, so as to get the knot safely tied to your satisfaction, they sailed straight for Havre. They had on board a Jesuit father, whom I had met once or twice among the Duke of Berwick's people, but who had found Portsmouth too hot to hold him in the frenzy of Protestant zeal on the Bishops' account. He had been beset, and owed his life, he says, to the fists of the Breton and Norman sailors, who had taken him on board. It was well for me, for I doubt if ever I was tough enough to have withstood my good friends' treatment. He had me carried to a convent in Havre, where the fathers nursed me well; and before I was on my legs again, I had made up my mind to cast in my lot with them, or rather with their Church.'

'Oh!'

'I had been baulked of winning the one being near whom my devil never durst come. And blood-letting had pretty well disposed of him. I was as meek and mild as milk under the good fathers. Moreover, as my good friend at Turin had told me, and they repeated it, such a doubly heretical baptism as mine was probably invalid, and accounted for my being as much a vessel of wrath as even my father was pleased to call me.   There was the Queen's rosary drawing me too.   Everything else was over with me, and it seemed to open a new life.   So, bless me, what a soft and pious frame I was in when they christened me, water, oil, salt and all, on what my father raged at folks calling Lammas Day, but which it seems really belongs to St. Peter in the Fetters.   So I was named Pierre or Piers after him, thus keeping my own initial.'

'Piers! oh! not Piers Pigwiggin?'

'Pierre de Pilpignon, if you please.   I have a right to that too; but we shall come to it by and by.   I can laugh now, or perhaps weep, over the fervid state I was in then, as if I had trodden down my snake, and by giving up everything—you, estate, career, I could keep him down.   So it was settled that I would devote myself to the priesthood—don't laugh!—and I was ordered off to their seminary in London, partly, I believe, for the sake of piloting a couple of fathers, who could not speak a word of English.   It was, as they rightly judged, the last place where my father would think of looking for me, but they did not as rightly judge that we should long keep possession there. Matters grew serious, and it was not over safe in the streets. There was a letter of importance from a friend in Holland, carrying the Prince of Orange's hypocritical Declaration, which was to be got to Father Petre or the King on the night— Hallowmas Eve it was—and I was told off to put on a secular dress, which I could wear more naturally than most of them, and convey it.'

'Ah, that explains!'

'Apparition number one! I guessed you were somewhere in those parts, and looked up at the windows, and though I did not see you, I believe it was your eyes that first sent a thrill through me that boded ill for Roman orders. After that we lived in a continual state of rumours and alarms, secret messages and expeditions, until I, being strong in the arm and the wind and a feather-weight, was one of those honoured by rowing the Queen and Prince across the river. M. de St. Victor accepted me. He told me there would be two nurses, but never knew or cared who they were, nor did I guess, as we sat in the dark, how near I was to you. And only for one second did I see your face, as you were entering the carriage, and I blessed you the more for what you were doing for Her Majesty.'

He proceeded to tell how he had accompanied the Jesuit fathers, on their leaving London, to the great English seminary at Douai, and being for the time convinced by them that his feelings towards Anne were a delusion of the enemy, he had studied with all his might, and as health and monotony of life began to have their accustomed effect in rousing the restlessness and mischievousness of his nature, with all the passions of manhood growing upon him, he strove to force them down by fasting and scourging. He told, in a bitter, almost savage way, of his endeavours to flog his demon out of himself, and of his anger and disappointment at finding Piers Pilgrim in the seminary of Douai, quite as subject to his attacks as ever was Perry Oakshott under a sermon of Mr. Horncastle's.

Then came the information among the students that the governor of the city, the

Marquis de Nidemerle, had brought some English gentlemen and ladies to visit the gardens. As most of the students were of British families there was curiosity as to who they were, and thus Peregrine heard that one was young Archfield of the Hampshire family, with his tutor, and the lady was Mistress Darpent, daughter to a French lawyer, who had settled in England after the Fronde. Anne's name had not transpired, for she was viewed merely as an attendant. Peregrine had been out on some errand in the town, and had a distant view of his enemy as he held him, flaunting about with a fine lady on his arm, forgetting the poor little pretty wife whom no doubt he had frightened to death.'

'Oh! you little know how tenderly he speaks of her.'

'Tenderly!—that's the way they speak of me at Oakwood, eh? Human, not to say elf, nature, could not withstand giving the fellow a start. I sped off, whipped into the Church, popped into a surplice I found ready to hand, caught up a candle, and!— Little did I think who it was that was hanging on his arm. So little did I know it that my heart began to be drawn to St. Germain, where I still imagined you. Altogether, after that prank, all broke out again. I entertained the lads with a few more freaks, for which I did ample penance, but it grew on me that in my case all was a weariness and a sham, and that my demon might get a worse hold of me if I got into a course of hypocrisy. They were very good to me, those fathers, but Jesuits as they were, I doubt whether they ever fathomed me. Any way, perhaps they thought I should be a scandal, but they agreed with me that their order was not my vocation, and that we had better part before my fiend drove me to do so with dishonour. They even gave me recommendations to the French officers that were besieging Tournay. I knew the Duke of Berwick a little at Portsmouth, and it ended in my becoming under-secretary to the Duke of Chartres. A man who knows languages has his value among Frenchmen, who despise all but their own.'

Peregrine did not enter into full details of this stage of his career, and Anne was not fully informed of the habits that the young Duke of Chartres, the future Regent Duke of Orleans, was already developing, but she gathered that, what the young man called his demon, had nearly undisputed sway over him, and she had not spent eight months at St. Germain without knowing by report of the dissolute manners of the substratum of fashionable society at Paris, even though outward decorum had been restored by Madame de Maintenon. Yet he seemed to have been crossed by fits of vehement penitence, and almost the saddest part of the story was the mocking tone in which he alluded to these.

He had sought service at the Court in the hope of meeting Miss Woodford there, and had been grievously disappointed when he found that she had long since returned to England. The sight of the gracious and lovely countenance of the exiled Queen seemed always to have moved and touched him, as in some inexplicable manner her eyes and expression recalled to him those of Mrs. Woodford and Anne ; but the thought had apparently only stung him into the sense of being forsaken and abandoned to his own devices or those of his evil spirit.

One incident, occurring some three years previously, he told more fully, as it had a considerable effect on his life. 'I was attending the Duke in the gardens at Versailles,' he said, 'when we were aware of a great commotion. All the gentlemen were standing gazing up into the top of a great chestnut-tree, the King and all, and in the midst stood the Abbé de Fénelon with his little pupils, the youngest, the Duke of Anjou, sobbing piteously, and the Duke of Burgundy in a furious passion, stamping and raging, and only withheld from rolling on the ground by the Abbé's hand grasping his shoulder. "I will not have him killed! He is mine," he cried. And up in the tree, the object of all their gaze, was a monkey with a paper fluttering in his hand. Some one had made a present of the creature to the King's grandsons; he was the reigning favourite, and having broken his chain, had effected an entrance by the window into the King's cabinet, where after giving himself the airs of a minister of state, on being interrupted, he had made off through the window with an important document, which he was affecting to peruse at his leisure, only interrupting himself to hurl down leaves or unripe chestnuts at those who attempted to pelt him with stones, and this only made him mount higher and higher, entirely out of their reach, for no one durst climb after him. I believe it was a letter from the King of Spain ; at any rate the whole Cabinet was in agony lest the brute should proceed to tear it into fragments, and a musqueteer had been sent for to shoot him down. I remembered my success with the monkey on poor little Madam Archfield's back — nay, perhaps 'twas the same, my familiar taking shape. I threw myself at the King's feet, and desired permission to deal with the beast. By good luck it had not been so easy as they supposed to find a musquet fit for immediate use, so I had full time. To ascend the tree was no more than I had done many times before, and I went high in the branches, but cautiously, not to give Monsieur le Singe the idea of being pursued, lest he should leap to a bough incapable of supporting me. When I had reached a fork tolerably high, and where he could see me, I settled myself, took out a letter, which fortunately was in my pocket, read it with the greatest deliberation, the monkey watching me all the time, and finally I proceeded to fold it neatly in all its creases. The creature imitated me with its black fingers, little aware, poor thing, that the musqueteer had covered him with his weapon, and was waiting for the first sign of tearing the letter to pull the trigger, but withheld by a sign from the King, who did not wish to sacrifice his grandson's pet before his eyes. Finally, after finishing the folding, I doubled it a second time, and threw it at the animal. To my great joy he returned the compliment by throwing the other at my head. I was able to catch it, and moreover, as he was disposed to go in pursuit of his plaything, he swung his chain so near me that I got hold of it, twisted it round my arm, and made the best of my way down the tree, amid the " Bravos!" started by the royal lips themselves, and repeated with ecstasy by all the crowd, who waved their hats, and made such a hallooing that I had much ado to get the

monkey down safely ; but finally, all dis-
hevelled, with my best cuffs and cravat torn
to ribbons, and my wig happily detached,
unlike Absalom's, for it remained in the tree,
I had the honour of presenting on my knee
the letter to the King, and the monkey to the
Princes.   I kissed His Majesty's hand, the
little Duke of Anjou kissed the monkey, and
the Duke of Burgundy kissed me with arms
round my neck, then threw himself on his
knees before his grandfather to ask pardon
for his passion.   Every one said my fortune
was made, and that my agility deserved at
least the *cordon bleu*.   My own Duke of
Chartres, who in many points is like his
cousin, our late King Charles, gravely assured
me that a new office was to be invented for
me, and that I was to be *Grand Singier du
Roi*.   I believe he pushed my cause, and so
did the little Duke of Burgundy, and finally
I got the pension without the office, and a
good deal of occasional employment besides,
in the way of translation of documents.
There were moments of success at play.
Oh yes, quite fairly, any one with wits about
him can make his profit in the long-run among

the Court set. And thus I had enough to purchase a pretty little estate and château on the coast of Normandy, the confiscated property of a poor Huguenot refugee, so that it went cheap. It gives the title of Pilpignon, which I assumed in kindness to the tounges of my French friends. So you see, I have a station and property to which to carry you, my fair one, won by myself, though only by catching an ape.'

He went on to say that the spot had been chosen advisedly, with a view to communication with the opposite coast, where his old connection with the smugglers was likely to be useful in the Jacobite plots. 'As you well know,' he said, 'my father had done his utmost to make Whiggery stink in my nostrils, to say nothing of the kindness I have enjoyed from our good Queen; and I was ready to do my utmost in the cause, especially after I had stolen a glimpse of you, and when Charnock, poor fellow, returning from reconnoitring among the loyal, told me that you were still unmarried, and living as a dependent in the Archfields' house. Our headquarters were in Romney Marsh, but it was as well to have, as it were, a back door here, and as it has turned out it has been the saving of some of us.'

'Oh, sir! you were not in that wicked plot?'

'Nay; surely *you* are not turned Whig.'

'But this was assassination.'

'Not at all, if they would have listened to me. The Dutchman is no bigger than I am. I could have dropped on him from one of his trees at Hampton Court, or through a window, *via presto*, and we would have had him off by the river, given him an interview to beg his uncle's pardon, and despatched him for the benefit of his asthma to the company of the Iron Mask at St. Marguerite; then back again, the King to enjoy his own again, Dr. Woodford, archbishop or bishop of whatever you please, and a lady here present to be Marquise de Pilpignon, or Countess of Havant, whichever she might prefer. Yes, truly those were the hopes with which I renewed my communications with the contraband trade on this coast, a good deal more numerous since the Dutchman and his wars have raised the duties and driven many good men to holes and corners.

'Ever since last spring, when the Princess Royal died, and thus extinguished the last spark of forbearance in the King's breast, I have been here, there, and everywhere—Romney Marsh, Drury Lane, Paris, besides this place and Pilpignon, where I have a snug harbour for the yacht, *Ma Belle Annik*, as the Breton sailors call her. The crew are chiefly Breton; it saves gossip; but I have a boat's crew of our own English folk here, stout fellows, ready for anything by land or sea.'

'The Black Gang,' said Anne faintly.

'Don't suppose I have meddled in their exploits on the road,' he said, 'except where a King's messenger or a Royal mail was concerned, and that is war, you know, for the cause. Unluckily my personal charms are not easily disguised, so that I have had to lurk in the background, and only make my private investigations in the guise of my own ghost.'

'Then so it was you saved the dear little Philip?' said Anne.

'The Archfield boy? I could not see a

child sent to his destruction by that villain
Sedley, whoever were his father, for he
meant mischief if ever man did. 'Twas
superhuman scruple not to hold your peace
and let him swing.'

'What was it, then, on his cousin's part?'

Peregrine only answered with a shrug.
It appeared further, that as long as the con-
spirators had entertained any expectation of
success, he had merely kept a watch over
Anne, intending to claim her in the hour of
the triumph of his party, when he looked to
enjoy such a position as would leave his
brother free to enjoy his paternal inheritance.
In the failure of all their schemes, through
Mr. Pendergrast's denunciation, Sir George
Barclay, and one or two inferior plotters, had
succeeded in availing themselves of the assistance of the Black Gang, and had been conducted by Peregrine to the hut that he had
fitted up for himself. Still trusting to the
security there, although his name of Piers
Pilgrim or de Pilpignon had been among
those given up to the Privy Council, he had
insisted on lingering, being resolved that an
attempt should be made to carry away the

woman he had loved for so many years. Captain Burford had so disguised himself as to be able to attend the trial, loiter about the inn, and collect intelligence, while the others waited on the downs. Peregrine had watched over the capture, but being unwilling to disclose himself, had ridden on faster and crossed direct, traversing the Island on horseback, while the captive was rounding it in the boat. 'As should never have been done,' he said, 'could I have foretold to what stress of weather you would be exposed while I was preparing for your reception. But for this storm—it rages louder than ever—we would have been married by a little parson whom Burford would have fetched from Portsmouth, and we should have been over the Channel, and my people hailing my bride with ecstasy.'

'Never!' exclaimed Anne. 'Can you suppose I could accept one who would leave an innocent man to suffer?'

'People sometimes are obliged to accept,' said Peregrine. Then at her horrified start, 'No, no, fear no violence; but is not something due to one who has loved you through exile all these years, and would lay down his life for you? you, the only being who overcomes his evil angel!'

'This is what you call overcoming it,' she said.

'Nay; indeed, Mistress Anne, I would let the authorities know that they are hanging a man for murdering one who is still alive if I could; but no one would believe without seeing, and I and all who could bear witness to my existence would be rushing to an end even worse than a simple noose. You were ready enough to denounce him to save that worthless fellow.'

'Not ready. It tore my heart. But truth is truth. I could not do that wickedness. Oh! how can you? This *is* the prompting of the evil spirit indeed, to expect me to join in leaving that innocent, generous spirit to die in cruel injustice. Let me go. I will not betray where you are. You will be safe in France; but there will yet be time for me to bear witness to your life. Write a letter. Your father would thankfully swear to your handwriting, and I think they would believe me. Only let me go.'

' And what then becomes of the hopes of a lifetime ?' demanded Peregrine. ' I, who have waited as long as Jacob, to be defrauded now I have you ; and for the sake of the fellow who killed me in will if not in deed, and then ran away like a poltroon leaving you to bear the brunt !'

' He did not act like a poltroon when he saved the life of his general, or when he rescued the colours of his regiment, still less when he stood up to save me from the pain of bearing witness against him, and to save a guiltless man,' cried Anne, with flashing eyes.

Before she had finished her indignant words, Hans was coming in from some unknown region to lay the cloth for supper, and Peregrine, with an imprecation under his breath, had gone to the door to admit his two comrades, who came into the narrow entry on a gust of wind as it were, struggling out of their cloaks, stamping and swearing.

In the middle of the day they had been much more restrained in their behaviour. There had at that time been a slight clearance in the sky, though the wind was as furious as ever, and they were in haste to despatch the meal and go out again to endeavour to stand on the heights and to watch some vessels that were being tossed by the storm. Almost all the conversation had then been on the chances of their weathering the tempest, and the probability of its lasting on, and they had hurried away as soon as possible. Anne had not then known who they were, and only saw that they were fairly civil to her, and kept under a certain constraint by Pilpignon, as they called their host. Now she fully knew the one who was addressed as Sir George to be Barclay, the prime mover in the wicked scheme of assassination of which all honest Tories had been so much ashamed, and she could see Captain Burford to be one of those bravoes who were only too plentiful in those days, attending on dissolute and violent nobles.

She was the less inclined to admit their attentions, and shielded herself with a grave coldness of stately manners; but their talk was far more free than at noon, suggesting the thought that they had anticipated the meal with some of the Nantz or other liquors that seemed to be in plenty.

They began by low bows of affected reverence, coarser and worse in the ruffian of inferior grade, and the knight complimented Pilpignon on being a lucky dog, and hoped he had made the best use of his time in spite of the airs of his duchess. It was his own fault if he were not enjoying such fair society, while they, poor devils, were buffeting with the winds, which had come on more violently than ever. Peregrine broke in with a question about the vessels in sight.

There was an East Indiaman, Dutch it was supposed, laying-to, that was the cause of much excitement. 'If she drives ashore our fellows will neither be to have nor to hold,' said Sir George.

'They will obey me,' said Peregrine quietly.

'More than the sea will just yet,' laughed the captain. 'However, as soon as this villainous weather is a bit abated, I'll be off across the Island to do your little errand, and only ask a kiss of the bride for my pains; but if the parson be at Portsmouth there will be no getting him to budge till the water is smooth. Never mind, madam, we'll have a merry wedding feast, whichever side of the water it is.   I should recommend the voyage first for my part.'

All Anne could do was to sit as upright and still as she could, apparently ignoring the man's meaning.   She did not know how dignified she looked, and how she was daunting his insolence.   When presently Sir George Barclay proposed as a toast a health to the bride of to-morrow, she took her part by raising the glass to her lips as well as the gentlemen, and adding, ' May the brides be happy, wherever they may be.'

' Coy, upon my soul,' laughed Sir George. ' You have not made the best of your opportunities, Pil.'   But with an oath, ' It becomes her well.'

' A truce with fooling, Barclay,' muttered Peregrine.

' Come, come, remember faint heart—no lowering your crest, more than enough to bring that devilish sparkle in the eyes, and turn of the neck ! '

' Sir,' said Anne rising, ' Monsieur de Pilpignon is an old neighbour, and understands how to respect his most unwilling guest.   I wish you a good-night, gentlemen. Guennik, *venez ici, je vous prie.'*

Guennik, the Breton boatswain's wife, understood French thus far, and comprehended the situation enough to follow willingly, leaving the remainder of the attendance to Hans, who was fully equal to it. The door was secured by a long knife in the post, but Anne could hear plainly the rude laugh at her entrenchment within her fortress and much of the banter of Peregrine for having proceeded no further. It was impossible to shut out all the voices, and very alarming they were, as well as sometimes so coarse that they made her cheeks glow, while she felt thankful that the Bretonne could not understand.

These three men were all proscribed traitors in haste to be off, but Peregrine, to whom the yacht and her crew belonged, had lingered to obtain possession of the lady, and they were declaring that now they had caught his game and given him his toy, they would brook no longer delay than was absolutely necessitated by the storm, and married or not married, he and she should both be carried off together, let the damsel-errant give herself

what haughty airs she would.   It was a weak
concession on their part to the old Puritan
scruples that he might have got rid of by this
time, to attempt to bring about the marriage.
They jested at him for being afraid of her,
and then there were jokes about gray mares.

The one voice she could not hear was
Peregrine's, perhaps because he realised more
than they did that she was within ear-shot,
and besides, he was absolutely sober ; but she
thought he silenced them ; and then she heard
sounds of card-playing, which made an accompaniment to her agonised prayers.

CHAPTER XXXIII

'Come, Lady ; while Heaven lends us grace,
   Let us fly this cursed place,
   Lest the sorcerer us entice
   With some other new device.
   Not a word or needless sound
   Till we come to holier ground.
   I shall be your faithful guide
   Through this gloomy covert wide.'

MILTON.

NEVER was maiden in a worse position than that in which Anne Woodford felt herself when she revolved the matter. The back of the Isle of Wight, all along the Undercliff, had always had a wild reputation, and she was in the midst of the most lawless of men. Peregrine alone seemed to have any remains of honour or conscience, and apparently he was in some degree in the hands of his associates. Even if the clergyman came, there was little hope in an appeal to him. Naval chaplains bore no good reputation, and Portsmouth and Cowes were haunted by the scum of the profession. All that seemed possible was to commit herself and Charles to Divine protection, and in that strength to resist to the uttermost. The tempest had returned again, and seemed to be raging as much as ever, and the delay was in her favour, for in such weather there could be no putting to sea.

She was unwilling to leave the stronghold of her chamber, but Hans came to announce breakfast to her, telling her that the Mynheeren were gone, all but Massa Perry; and that gentleman came forward to meet her just as before, hoping 'those fellows had not disturbed her last night.'

'I could not help hearing much,' she said gravely.

'Brutes!' he said. 'I am sick of them, and of this life. Save for the King's sake, I would never have meddled with it.'

The roar of winds and waves and the beat of spray was still to be heard, and in the manifest impossibility of quitting the place

and the desire of softening him, Anne listened
while he talked in a different mood from the
previous day. The cynical tone was gone, as
he spoke of those better influences. He
talked of Mrs. Woodford and his deep
affection for her, of the kindness of the good
priests at Havre and Douai, and especially
of one Father Seyton, who had tried to
reason with him in his bitter disappointment
and savage penitence on finding that 'behind
the Cross lurks the Devil,' as much at Douai
as at Havant. He told how a sermon of the
Abbé Fénelon's had moved him, and how he
had spent half a Lent in the severest penance,
but only to have all swept away again in the
wild and wicked revelry with which Easter
came in. Again he described how his heart
was ready to burst as he stood by Mrs.
Woodford's grave at night and vowed to
disentangle himself and lead a new life.

'And with you I shall,' he said.

'No,' she answered; 'what you win by a
crime will never do you good.'

'A crime! 'Tis no crime. You *know* I
mean honourable marriage. You owe no
duty to any one.'

'It is a crime to leave the innocent to undeserved death,' she said.

'Do you love the fellow?' he cried, with a voice rising to a shout of rage.

'Yes,' she said firmly.

'Why did not you say so before?'

'Because I hoped to see you act for right and justice sake,' was Anne's answer, fixing her eyes on him.   'For God's sake, not mine.'

'Yours indeed!   Think, what can be his love to mine?   He who let them marry him to that child, while I struggled and gave up everything.   Then he runs away—*runs away* —leaving you all the distress; never came near you all these years.   Oh yes! he looks down on you as his child's governess! What's the use of loving him?   There's another heiress bespoken for him no doubt.'

'No.   His parents consent, and we have known one another's love for six years.'

'Oh, that's the way he bound you to keep his secret!   He would sing another song as soon as he was out of this scrape.'

'You little know!' was all she said.

'Ay!' continued Peregrine, pacing up and

down the room, 'you know that all that was wanting to fill up the measure of my hatred was that he should have stolen your heart.'

'You cannot say that, sir. He was my kind protector and helper from our very childhood. I have loved him with all my heart ever since I durst.'

'Ay, the great straight comely lubbers have it all their own way with the women,' said he bitterly. 'I remember how he rushed headlong at me with the horse-whip when I tripped you up at the Slype, and you have never forgiven that.'

'Oh! indeed I forgot that childish nonsense long ago. You never served me so again.'

'No indeed, never since you and your mother were the first to treat me like a human being. You will be able to do anything with me, sweetest lady; the very sense that you are under the same roof makes another man of me. I loathe what I used to enjoy. Why, the very sight of you, sitting at supper like the lady in *Comus*, in your sweet grave dignity, made me feel what I am.

and what those men are.   I heard their jests with your innocent ears.   With you by my side the Devil's power is quelled.   You shall have a peaceful, beneficent life among the poor folk, who will bless you; our good and gracious Queen will welcome you with joy and gratitude; and when the good time comes, as it must in a few years, you will have honours and dignities lavished on you. Can you not see what you will do for me?'

'Do you think a broken-hearted victim would be able to do you any good?' said she, looking up with tears in her eyes.   'I *do* believe, sir, that you mean well by me, in your own way, and I could, yes, I can, be sorry for you, for my mother did feel for you, and yours has been a sad life; but how could I be of any use or comfort to you if you dragged me away as these cruel men propose, knowing that he who has all my heart is dying guiltless, and thinking I have failed him!' and here she broke down in an agony of weeping, as she felt the old power in his eyes that enforced submission.

He marched up and down in a sort of passion.   'Don't let me see you weep for him! It makes me ready to strangle him with my own hands!'

A shout of 'Pilpignon!' at the door here carried him off, leaving Anne to give free course to the tears that she had hitherto been able to restrain, feeling the need of self-possession. She had very little hope, since her affection for Charles Archfield seemed only to give the additional sting of jealousy, 'cruel as the grave,' to the vindictive temper Peregrine already nourished, and which certainly came from his evil spirit. She shed many tears, and sobbed unrestrainingly till the Bretonne came and patted her shoulder, and said, '*Pauvre, pauvre!*' And even Hans looked in, saying, 'Missee Nana no cry, Massa Perry great herr—very goot.'

She tried to compose herself, and think over alternatives to lay before Peregrine. He might let her go, and carry to Sir Edmund Nutley letters to which his father would willingly swear, while he was out of danger in Normandy. Or if this was far beyond what could be hoped for, surely he could despatch a letter to his father, and for such a price she *must* sacrifice herself, though it cost her

anguish unspeakable to call up the thought
of Charles, of little Philip, of her uncle, and
the old people, who loved her so well, all
forsaken, and with what a life in store for her!
For she had not the slightest confidence in
the power of her influence, whatever Peregrine might say and sincerely believe at
present.   If there were, more palpably than
with all other human beings, angels of good
and evil contending for him, swaying him
now this way and now that; it was plain from
his whole history that nothing had yet availed
to keep him under the better influence for
long together; and she believed that if he
gained herself by these unjust and cruel
means the worst spirit would thereby gain
the most absolute advantage.   If her heart
had been free, and she could have loved him,
she might have hoped, though it would have
been a wild and forlorn hope; but as it was,
she had never entirely surmounted a repulsion from him, as something strange and
unnatural, a feeling involving fear, though
here he was her only hope and protector, and
an utter uncertainty as to what he might do.
She could only hope that she might pine

away and die quickly, and *perhaps* Charles Archfield might know at last that it had been for his sake. And would it be in her power to make even such terms as these?

How long she wept and prayed and tried to 'commit her way unto the Lord' she did not know, but light seemed to be making its way far more than previously through the shutters closed against the storm when Peregrine returned.

'You will not be greatly troubled with those fellows to-day,' he said; 'there's a vessel come on the rocks at Chale, and every man and mother's son is gone after it.' So saying he unfastened the shutters and let in a flood of sunshine. 'You would like a little air,' he said; ''tis all quiet now, and the tide is going down.'

After two days' dark captivity, Anne could not but be relieved by coming out, and she was anxious to understand where she was. It was, though only in March, glowing with warmth, as the sun beat against the cliffs behind, of a dark red-brown, in many places absolutely black, in especial where a cascade, swelled by the rains into imposing size, came roaring, leaping, and sparkling down a sheer precipice. On either side the cove or chine was closely shut in by treeless, iron-coloured masses of rock, behind one of which the few inhabited hovels were clustered, and the boat which had brought her was drawn up. In front was the sea, still lashed by a fierce wind, which was driving the fantastically shaped remains of the great storm cloud rapidly across an intensely blue sky. The waves, although it was the ebb, were still tremendous, and their roar re-echoed as they reared to fearful heights and broke with the reverberations that she had heard all along. Peregrine kept quite high up, not venturing below the washed line of shingle, saying that the back draught of the waves was most perilous, and in a high wind could not be reckoned upon.

'No escape!' he said, as he perceived Anne's gaze on the inaccessible cliff and the whole scene, the wild beauty of which was lost to her in its terrors.

'Where's your ship?' she asked.

'Safe in Whale Chine. No putting to sea yet, though it may be fair to-morrow.'

Then she put before him the first scheme she had thought out, of letting her escape to Sir Edmund Nutley's house, whence she could make her way back, taking with her a letter that would prove his existence without involving him or his friends in danger. And eagerly she argued, 'You do not know me really! It is only an imagination that you can be the better for my presence.' Then, unheeding his fervid exclamation, 'It was my dear mother who did you good. What would she think of the way in which you are trying to gain me?'

'That I cannot do without you.'

'And what would you have in me? I could be only wretched, and feel all my life—such a life as it would be—that you had wrecked my happiness. Oh yes! I do believe that you would try to make me happy, but don't you see that it would be quite impossible with such a grief as that in my heart, and knowing that you had caused it? I know you hate him, and he did you the wrong; but he has grieved for it, and banished himself. But above all, of this I am quite sure, that to persist in this horrible evil of leaving him to die, because of your revenge, and stealing me away, is truly giving Satan such a frightful advantage over you that it is mere folly to think that winning me in such a way could do you any good. It is just a mere delusion of his, to ruin us both, body and soul. Peregrine, will you not recollect my mother, and what she would think? Have pity on me, and help me away, and I would pledge myself never to utter a word of this place nor that could bring you and yours into danger. We would bless and pray for you always.'

'No use,' he gloomily said. 'I believe you, but the others will never believe a woman. No doubt we are watched even now by desperate men, who would rather shoot you than let you escape from our hands.'

It seemed almost in connection with these words that at that moment, from some unknown quarter, where probably there was an entrance to the Chine, Sir George Barclay appeared with a leathern case under his arm. It had been captured on the wreck, and contained papers which he wanted assistance in deciphering, since they were in Dutch, and he believed them to be either despatches or bonds, either of which might be turned to profit. These were carried indoors, and spread on the table, and as Anne sat by the window, dejected and almost hopeless as she was, she could not help perceiving that, though Peregrine was so much smaller and less robust than his companions, he exercised over them the dominion of intellect, energy, and will, as if they too felt the force of his strange eyes ; and it seemed to her as if, supposing he truly desired it, whatever he might say, he must be able to deliver her and Charles ; but that a being such as she had always known him should sacrifice both his love and his hate seemed beyond all hope, and ' Change his heart ! Turn our captivity, O Lord,' could only be her cry.

Only very late did Burford come back, full of the account of the wreck and of the spoils, and the struggles between the wreckers for the flotsam and jetsam. There was much of savage brutality mated with a cool indifference truly horrible to Anne, and making her realise into what a den of robbers she had fallen, especially as these narratives were diversified by consultations over the Dutch letters and bills of exchange in the wrecked East Indiaman, and how to turn them to the best advantage. Barclay and Burford were so full of these subjects that they took comparatively little notice of the young lady, only when she rose to retire, Burford made a sort of apology that this little business had hindered his going after the parson. He heard that the Salamander was at the castle, and redcoats all about, he said, and if the *Annik* could be got out to-morrow they must sail any way; and if Pil was still so squeamish, a Popish priest could couple them in a leash as tight as a Fleet parson could. And then Peregrine demanded whether Burford thought a Fleet parson the English for a naval chaplain, and there was some boisterous laughter, during which Anne shut herself up in her room in something very like despair, with that one ray of hope that He who had brought her back from exile before would again save her from that terrible fate.

She heard card-playing and the jingle of

glasses far into the night, as she believed, but it seemed to her as if she had scarcely fallen asleep before, to her extreme terror, she heard a knock and a low call at her door of 'Guennik.' Then as the Bretonne went to the door, through which a light was seen, a lantern was handed in, and a scrap of paper on which the words were written: 'On second thoughts, my kindred elves at Portchester shall not be scared by a worricow. Dress quickly, and I will bring you out of this.'

For a moment Anne did not perceive the meaning of the missive, the ghastly idea never having occurred to her that if Charles had suffered, the gibbet would have been at Portchester. Then, with an electric flash of joy, she saw that it meant relenting on Peregrine's part, deliverance for them both. She put on her clothes with hasty, trembling hands, thankful to Guennik for helping her, pressed a coin into the strong toil-worn hand, and with an earnest thrill of thankful prayer opened the door. The driftwood fire was bright, and she saw Peregrine, looking deadly white, and equipped with slouched hat, short wrapping cloak, pistols and sword at his belt, dark lantern lighted on the table, and Hans also cloaked by his side. He bent his head in salutation, and put his finger to his lips, giving one hand to Anne, and showing by example instead of words that she must tread as softly as possible, as she perceived that he was in his slippers, Hans carrying his boots as well as the lantern she had used. Yet to her ears the roar of the advancing tide seemed to stifle all other sounds. Past the other huts they went in silence, then came a precipitous path up the cliff, steps cut in the hard sandy grit, but very crumbling, and in places supplemented by a rude ladder of sticks and rope. Peregrine went before Anne, Hans behind. Each had hung the lantern from his neck, so as to have hands free to draw her, support her, or lift her, as might be needful. How it was done she never could tell in after years. She might jestingly say that her lightened heart bore her up, but in her soul and in her deeper moments she thought that truly angels must have had charge over her. Up, up, up! At last they had reached standing ground, a tolerably level space, with another high cliff seeming to rise behind it. Here it was lighter—a pale streak of dawn was spreading over the horizon, both on sky and sea, and the waves still leaping glanced in the light of a golden waning moon, while Venus shone in the brightening sky, a daystar of hope.

Peregrine drew a long breath, and gave an order in a very low voice in Dutch to Hans, who placed his boots before him, and went off towards a shed. 'He will bring you a pony,' said his master. 'Excuse me;' and he was withdrawing his hand, when Anne clasped it with both hers, and said in a voice of intense feeling—

'Oh, how can I thank you and bless you! This *is* putting the Evil Angel to flight.'

''Tis you that have done it! You see, I cannot do the wicked act where you are,' he answered gloomily, as he turned aside to draw on his boots.

'Ah! but you have won the victory over him!'

'Do not be too sure. We are not out of reach of those rascals yet.'

He was evidently anxious for silence, and

Anne said no more. Hans presently brought from some unknown quarter a little stout pony bridled and saddled ; of course not with a side saddle, but cloaks were arranged so as to make a fairly comfortable seat for Anne, and Peregrine led the animal on the ascent to St. Catherine's Down. It was light enough to dispense with the lanterns, and as they mounted higher the glorious sight of daybreak over the sea showed itself—almost due east, the sharp points of the Needles showing up in a flood of pale golden light above and below, with gulls flashing white as they floated into sunlight, all seeming to Anne's thankful heart to be a new radiance of joy and hope after the dark roaring terrors of the Chine.

As they came out into the open freedom of the down, with crisp silvery grass under their feet, the breadth of sea on one side, before them fertile fields and hills, and farther away, dimly seen in gray mist, the familiar Portsdown outlines, not a sound to be heard but the exulting ecstasies of larks, far, far above in the depths of blue, Peregrine dared to speak above his breath, with a question

whether Anne were at ease in her extemporary
side saddle, producing at the same time a slice
of bread and meat, and a flask of wine.

'Oh, how kind! What care you take of
me!' she said. 'But where are we going?'

'Wherever you command,' he said. 'I
had thought of Carisbrooke. Cutts is there,
and it would be the speediest way.'

'Would it not be the most dangerous for
you?'

'I care very little for my life after this.'

'Oh no, no, you must not say so. After
what you are doing for me you will be able
to make it better than ever it has been.
This is what I thought. If you would bring
me to some place whence I could reach Sir
Edmund Nutley's house at Parkhurst, his
servants would help me to do the rest, even
if he be not there himself. I would never
betray you! You know I would not! And
you would have full time to get away to your
place in Normandy with your friends.'

'You care?' asked he.

'Of course I do!' exclaimed she. 'Do I
not feel grateful to you, and like and honour
you better than ever I could have thought?'

'You do?' in a strange choked tone.

'Of course I do. You are doing a noble, thankworthy thing. It is not only that I thank you for *his* sake, but it is a grand and beautiful deed in itself; and if my dear mother know, she is blessing you for it.'

'I shall remember those words,' he said, 'if—' and he passed his hand over his eyes. 'See here,' he presently said; 'I have written out a confession of my identity, and explanation that it was I who drew first on Archfield. It is enough to save him, and in case my handwriting has altered, as I think it has, and there should be further doubt, I shall be found at Pilpignon, if I get away. You had better keep it in case of accidents, or if you carry out your generous plan. Say whatever you please about me, but there is no need to mention Barclay or Burford; and it would not be fair to the honest free-traders here to explain where their Chine lies. I should have brought you up blindfold, if I could have done so with safety, not that *I* do not trust you, but I should be better able to satisfy those fellows if I ever see them again, by telling them I have sworn you to secrecy.'

Then he laughed. 'The gowks! I won all those Indian bonds of them last night, but left them in a parcel addressed to them as a legacy.'

Anne took the required pledge, and ventured to ask, 'Shall I say anything for you to your father?'

'My poor old father! Let him know that I neither would nor could disturb Robert in his inheritance, attainted traitor as the laws esteem me. For the rest, mayhap I shall write to him if the good angel you talk of will help me.'

'Oh do! I am sure he would rejoice to forgive. He is much softened.'

'Now, we must hush, and go warily. I see sheep, and if there is a shepherd, I want him not to see us, or point our way. It is well these Isle of Wight folk are not early risers.'

CHAPTER XXXIV

LIFE FOR LIFE

'Follow Light, and do the Right—for man can half-control
his doom—
Till you find the deathless Angel seated in the vacant
tomb.

Forward, let the stormy moment fly and mingle with the
Past.
I that loathed, have come to love him.   Love will conquer
at the last.'

TENNYSON.

ON they had gone in silence for the most part, avoiding villages, but as the morning advanced and they came into more inhabited places, they were not able entirely to avoid meeting labourers going out to work, who stared at Hans's black face with curiosity. The sun was already high when they reached a cross-road whence the massive towers of Carisbrooke were seen above the hedges, and another turn led to Parkhurst.   They paused

a moment, and Anne was beginning to entreat
her escort to leave her to proceed alone, when
the sound of horses' feet galloping was heard
behind them.   Peregrine looked back.

'Ah!' he said.   'Ride on as fast as you
can towards the castle.   You will be all right.
I will keep them back.   Go, I say.'

And as some figures were seen at the end
of the road, he pricked the pony with the
point of his sword so effectually that it bolted
forward, quite beyond Anne's power of check-
ing it, and in a second or two its speed was
quickened by shouts and shots behind.   Anne
felt, but scarcely understood at the moment,
a sharp pang and thrill in her left arm, as the
steed whirled her round the corner of the
lane and full into the midst of a party of
gentlemen on horseback coming down from
the castle.

'Help! help!' she cried.   'Down there.'

Attacks by highwaymen were not un-
common experiences, though scarcely at eight
o'clock in the morning, or so near a garrison,
but the horsemen, having already heard the
shots, galloped forward.   Perhaps Anne
could hardly have turned her pony, but it

chose to follow the lead of its fellows, and in a few seconds they were in the midst of a scene of utter confusion. Peregrine was grappling with Burford trying to drag him from his horse. Both fell together, and as the auxiliaries came in sight there was another shot and two more men rode off headlong.

'Follow them!' said a commanding voice. 'What have we here?'

The two struggling figures both lay still for a moment or two, but as some of the riders drew them apart Peregrine sat up, though blood was streaming down his breast and arm. 'Sir,' he said, 'I am Peregrine Oakshott, on whose account young Archfield lies under sentence of death. If a magistrate will take my affidavit while I can make it, he will be safe.'

Then Anne heard a voice exclaiming: 'Oakshott! Nay—why, this is Mistress Woodford! How came she here?' and she knew Sir Edmund Nutley. Still it was Peregrine who answered—

'I captured her, in the hope of marrying her, but that cannot be—I have brought her back in all safety and honour.'

'Sir! Sir, indeed he has been very good to me. Pray let him be looked to.'

'Let him be carried to the castle,' said the commander of the party, a tall man sunburnt to a fiery red. 'Is the other alive?'

'Only stunned, my lord, I think, and not much hurt,' was the answer of an attendant officer; 'but here is a poor blackamoor dead.'

'Poor Hans! Best so perhaps,' murmured Peregrine, as he was lifted. Then in a voice of alarm, 'Look to the lady, she is hurt.'

'It is nothing,' cried she. 'O Mr. Oakshott! that this should have happened!'

'My lord, this is the young gentlewoman I told you of, betrothed to poor young Archfield,' said Sir Edmund Nutley.

Lord Cutts, for it was indeed William's favoured 'Salamander,' took off his plumed hat in salutation, and both gentlemen perceiving that she too was bleeding, she was solicitously invited to the castle, to be placed under the charge of the lieutenant-governor's wife. She found by this time that she was in a good deal of pain, and thankfully accepted the support Sir Edmund offered her, when he dismounted and walked beside her pony, while explanations passed between them. The weather had prevented any communication with the mainland, so that he was totally ignorant of her capture, and did not know what had become of Mr. Fellowes. He himself had been just starting with Lord Cutts, who was going to join the King for his next campaign, and they were to represent the case to the King. Anne told him in return what she dared to say, but she was becoming so faint and dazed that she was in great fear of not saying what she ought; and indeed she could hardly speak, when after passing under the great gateway, she was lifted off her horse, at the door of the dwelling-house, and helped upstairs to a bedroom, where the wife of the lieutenant-governor, Mrs. Dudley, was very tender over her with essences and strong waters, and a surgeon of the suite almost immediately came to her.

'Oh!' she exclaimed, 'you should be with Mr. Oakshott.'

The surgeon explained that Mr. Oakshott would have nothing done for him till he had fully made and signed his deposition, in case the power should afterwards be wanting.

So Anne submitted to the dressing of her hurt, which was only a flesh wound, the bone being happily untouched. Both the surgeon and Mrs. Dudley urged her going to bed immediately, but she was unwilling to put herself out of reach ; and indeed the dressing was scarcely finished before Sir Edmund Nutley knocked at the door to ask whether she could admit him.

'Lord Cutts is very desirous of speaking with you, if you are able,' he said. 'Here has this other fellow come round, declaring that Oakshott is the Pilpignon who was in the Barclay Plot, and besides, the prime leader of the Black Gang, of whom we have heard so much.'

'The traitor!' cried Anne. 'Poor Mr. Oakshott was resolved not to betray him! How is he—Mr. Oakshott, I mean ?'

'The surgeon has him in his hands. We will send another from Portsmouth, but it looks like a bad case. He made his confession bravely, though evidently in terrible suffering, seeming to keep up by force of will till he had totally exonerated Archfield and signed the deposition, and then he fainted, so that I thought him dead, but I fear he has more to go through.   Can you come to the hall, or shall I bring Lord Cutts to you ?   We must hasten in starting that we may bring the news to Winchester to-night.'

Anne much preferred going to the hall, though she felt weak enough to be very glad to lean on Sir Edmund's arm.

Lord Cutts, William's high-spirited and daring officer, received her with the utmost courtesy and kindness, inquired after her hurt, and lamented having to trouble her, but said that though he would not detain her long, her testimony was important, and he begged to hear what had happened to her.

She gave the account of her capture and journey as shortly as she could.

'Whither was she taken ?'

She paused.   'I promised Mr. Oakshott for the sake of others——' she said.

'You need have no scruples on that score,' said Lord Cutts.   'Burford hopes to get off for the murder by turning King's evidence, and has told all.'

'Yes,' added Sir Edmund; 'and poor Oakshott managed to say, "Tell her she need keep nothing back.   It is all up."'

So Anne answered all the questions put to her, and they were the fewer both out of consideration for her condition, and because the governor wanted to take advantage of the tide to embark on the Medina.

In a very few hours the Archfields would have no more fears.   Anne longed to go with Sir Edmund, but she was in no state for a ride, and could not be a drag.   Sir Edmund said that either his wife would come to her at once and take her to Parkhurst, or else her uncle would be sure to come for her. She would be the guest of Major and Mrs. Dudley, who lived in the castle, the actual Lord Warden only visiting it from time to time; and though Major Dudley was a stern man, both were very kind to her.

As a Whig, Major Dudley knew the Oakshott family, and was willing to extend his hospitality even to the long-lost Peregrine. The Lord Warden, who was evidently very favourably impressed, saying that there was no need at present to treat him as a prisoner, but that every attention should be paid to him, as indeed he was evidently a dying man. Burford and another of his associates were to be carried off, handcuffed, with the escort to Winchester jail, but before the departure, the soldiers who had been sent to the Chine returned baffled; the place was entirely deserted, and Barclay had escaped.

Anne allowed herself to be put to bed, being indeed completely exhausted, and scarcely able to think of anything but the one blessed certainty that Charles was safe, and freed from all stigma. When, after the pain in her arm lulled enough to allow her to sleep, she had had a few hours' rest, she inquired for Peregrine, she heard that for many hours the surgeon had been trying to extract the balls, and that they considered that the second shot had made his case hopeless, as it was in the body. He was so much exhausted as to be almost unconscious; but the next morning, when Anne, against the persuasions of her hostess, had risen and been dressed, though still feeling weak and shaken, she received a message, begging her to do him the great kindness of visiting him.

Deadly pale, almost gray, as he looked, lying so propped with pillows as to relieve his shattered shoulder, his face had a strange look of peace, almost of relief, and he smiled at her as she entered. He held out the hand he could use, and his first word was of inquiry after her hurt.

'That is nothing—it will soon be well; I wish it were the same with you.'

'Nay, I had rather cheat the hangman. I told those doctors yesterday that they were giving themselves and me a great deal of useless trouble. The villains, as I told you, could not believe we should not betray them, and meant to make an end of us all. It's best as it is. My poor faithful Hans would never have had another happy moment.'

'But you must be better, Peregrine,' for his voice, though low, was steady.

'There's no living with what I have here,' he said, laying his hand on his side; 'and—I dreamt of your mother last night.' With the words there was a look of gladness exceeding.

'Ah! the Evil Angel is gone!'

'I want your prayers that he may not

come back at the last.'   Then, as she clasped her hands, and her lips moved, he added, 'There were some things I could only say to you.   If they don't treat my body as that of an attainted traitor, let me lie at your mother's feet.   Don't disturb the big Scot for me, but let me rest at last near her.   Then tell Robin 'tis not out of want of regard for him that I have not bequeathed Pilpignon to him, but he could do no good with a French estate full of Papists ; and there's a poor loyal fellow, living ruined at Paris—a Catholic too —with a wife and children half starved, to whom it will do more good.'

'I meant to ask—Shall a priest be sent for ?   Surely Major Dudley would consent.'

'I don't know.   I have not loved such priests lately.   I had rather die as near your mother as may be.'

' Miss Woodford,' said a voice at the door, and going to it, Anne found herself clasped in her uncle's arms.   With very few words she led him to the bedside, and the first thing he said was 'God bless you, Peregrine, for what you have done.'

Again Peregrine's face lighted up, but fell

again when he was told of the Portsmouth
surgeon's arrival at the same time, saying
with one of his strange looks that it was
odd sort of mercy to try to cure a man for
Jack Ketch, but that he should baffle them
yet.

'Do not set your mind on that,' said Dr.
Woodford, 'for Lord Cutts was so much
pleased with you that he would do his utmost
on your behalf.'

'Much good that would do me,' said poor
Peregrine, setting his teeth as his tormentor
came in.

Meantime, in Mrs. Dudley's parlour, while
that good lady was assisting the surgeon at
the dressing, Anne and her uncle exchanged
information. Mr. Fellowes had arrived on
foot at about noon, with his servant, having
only been released after two hours by a
traveller, and having been deprived both of
money and horses, so that he could not
proceed on his journey, besides that he had
given the alarm about the abduction, and
raised the hue and cry at the villages on his
way. There had been great distress, riding
and searching, and the knowledge had been

kept from poor Charles Archfield in his prison. Mr. Fellowes had gone on to London as soon as possible, and Dr. Woodford had just returned from a fruitless attempt to trace his niece, when Sir Edmund Nutley and Lord Cutts appeared, with the joyful tidings, which, however, could be hardly understood.

Nothing, Dr. Woodford said, could be more thorough than the vindication of Charles Archfield. Peregrine had fully stated that the young man had merely interposed to prevent the pursuit of Anne Woodford, that it was he himself who had made the first attack, and that his opponent had been forced to fight in self-defence. Lord Cutts had not only shown his affidavit to Sir Philip, but had paid a visit to the Colonel himself in his prison, had complimented him highly on his services in the Imperial army, only regretting that they had not been on behalf of his own country, and had assured him of equal, if not superior rank, in the British army if he would join it on the liberation that he might reckon upon in the course of a very few days.

'How did you work on the unhappy young

man to bring about this blessed change?' asked the Doctor.

'Oh, sir, I do not think it was myself. It was first the mercy of the Almighty, and then my blessed mother's holy memory working on him, revived by the sight of myself. I cannot describe to you how gentle, and courteous, and respectful he was to me all along, though I am sure those dreadful men mocked at him for it. Do you know whether his father has heard?'

'Robert Oakshott is gone in search of him. He had set off to beat up the country, good old man, to obtain signatures to the petition in favour of our prisoner, and Robert expected to find him with Mr. Chute at the Vine. It is much to that young man's credit, niece, he was so eager to see his brother that he longed to come with me himself; but he thought that the shock to his father would be so great that he ought to bear the tidings himself. And what do you think his good wife is about? Perhaps you did not know that Sedley Archfield brought away jail fever with him, and Mrs. Oakshott, feeling that she was the cause by her hasty action, has taken lodgings for him in Winchester, and is nursing him like a sister. No. You need not fear for your colonel, my dear maid. Sedley caught the infection because he neither was, nor wished to be, secluded from the rest of the prisoners, some of whom were, I fear, only too congenial society to him. But now tell me the story of your own deliverance, which seems to me nothing short of miraculous.'

The visit of the Portsmouth surgeon only confirmed Peregrine's own impression that it was impossible that he should live, and he was only surviving by the strong vitality in his little, spare, wiry frame. Dr. Woodford, after hearing Anne's story, thought it well to ask him whether he would prefer the ministrations of a Roman Catholic priest; but whether justly or unjustly, Peregrine seemed to impute to that Church the failure to exorcise the malignant spirit which had led him to far worse aberrations than he had confessed to Anne. Though by no means deficient in knowledge or controversian theology, as Dr. Woodford soon found in conversation with him, his real convictions were all as to what personally affected him, and his strong Protestant ingrain education, however he might have disavowed it, no doubt had affected his point of view. He had admired and been strongly influenced by the sight of real devotion and holiness, though as his temptations and hatred of monotony recurred, he had more than once swung back again. Then, however, he had been revolted by the perception of the concessions to popular superstition and the morality of a wicked state of society. His real sense of any religion had been infused by Mrs. Woodford, and to her belongings, and the faith they involved, he was clinging in these last days.

Dr. Woodford could not but be glad that thus it was, not only on the penitent's own account, but on that of the father, who might have lost the comfort of finding him truly repentant in the shock of finding a Popish priest at his bedside. And indeed the contrition seemed to have gathered force in many a past fit of remorse, and now was deep but not unhopeful.

In the evening the father and brother arrived. The Major was now an old man, hale indeed, and with the beauty that a pure, self-restrained life often sheds on an aged man. He was much shaken, and when he came in, with his own white hair on his shoulders, and actually tears in his eyes, the look that passed between them was like nothing but the spirit of the parable so often, but never too often, repeated.

Peregrine, who never perhaps had spent a happy or fearless hour with him, and had dreaded his coming, felt probably for the first time the mysterious sense of home and peace given by the presence of those between whom there is the tie of blood. Not many words passed; he was hardly in a state for them, but from that time, he was never so happy as when his father and brother were beside him; and they seldom left him, the Major sitting day and night by his pillow attending to his wants, or saying words of prayer.

The old man had become much softened, by nothing more perhaps than watching the way in which his daughter-in-law dealt with the manifestations of the Oakshott imp nature in her eldest child.

'If I had understood,' he said to Dr.

Woodford. 'If I had so treated that poor boy, never would he have been as he is now.'

'You acted according to your conscience.'

'Ah, sir! a man does not grow old without learning that the conscience may be blinded, above all by the spirit of opposition and party.'

'I will not say there were no mistakes,' said the Doctor; 'and yet, sir, the high standard, sound principle, and strong faith he learnt from you and your example have prevailed to bear him through.'

The Major answered with a groan, but added, 'And yet, even now, stained as he tells me he is, and cut off in the flower of his age, I thank my God and his Saviour, and after Him, you and yours, that I am happier about him than I have been these eight and twenty years.'

With no scruple, Major Oakshott threw his heart into the ministrations of Dr. Woodford, which Peregrine declared kept at bay the Evil Angel who more than once seemed to his consciousness to be striving to make him despair, while friend and father brought him back to the one hope.

From time to time Anne visited him for a short interval, always to his joy and gratitude. There was one visit at last which all knew would be the final one, when she shared in his first and last English Communion.   As she was about to leave him, he held her hand, and signed to her to bend down to hear him better.   'If you can, let good Father Seyton at Douai know that peace is come—the Evil One beaten, thanks to Him who giveth us the victory—and I thank them all there—and ask their prayers.'

'I will, I will.'

Some one at the door said, 'May I come in?'

There was a sunburnt face, a head with long brown hair, a white coat.

'Archfield?' asked Peregrine.   'Come, send me away with pardon.'

''Tis yours I need;' and as Charles knelt by the bed the two faces, one all health, the other gray and deathly, were close together. 'You have given your life for mine, and given *her*.   How shall I thank you?'

'Make her happy.   She deserves it.'

Charles clasped her hand with a look that

was enough. Then with a strange smile, half sweetness, half the contortion of a mortal pang, the dying man said, 'May she kiss me once?'

And when her lips had touched the cold damp brow—

'There— My fourth seven. At last! The change is come. Old—impish—evil— self left behind. At last! Thanks to Him who treads down Satan under our feet. Thanks! Take her away now.'

Charles took her away, scarce knowing where they went,—out into the spring sunshine, on the slopes above the turf bowling-green, where the captive King had beguiled his weary hours. Only then would awe and emotion let them speak, though his arm was round her, her hand in his, and his first words were, as he looked at the scarf that still bore up her arm, 'And this is what you have borne for me?'

'It is all but healed. Don't think of it.'

'I shall all my life! Poor fellow, he might well bid me deserve you. I never can. 'Tis to you I owe all. I believe, indeed, the ambassador might have claimed me, but he is so tardy that probably I should have been hanged long before the proper form was ready; and it would have been to exile, and with a tainted name. You have won for me the clearing of name and honour—home, parents and child and all, besides your sweet self.'

'And it was not me, but he whom we so despised and dreaded. Had I not been seized, I could only have implored for you.'

'I know this, that if you had not been what you are, my boy would have borne a dishonoured name, and we should never have been together as now.'

It was in truth their first meeting in freedom and security as lovers; but it could only be in a grave, quiet fashion, under the knowledge that he, to whom their re-union was chiefly owing, was breathing out the life he had sacrificed for them. Thus they only gently and in a low voice went over their past doings and feelings as they walked up and down together, till Dr. Woodford came in the sunset to tell them that the change so longed for had come in peace, and with a smile that told of release from the Evil Angel.

Peregrine's wish was fulfilled, and he was buried in Portchester Churchyard at Mrs. Woodford's feet. This time it was Mr. Horncastle, old as he was, who preached the funeral sermon, the *In Memoriam* of our forefathers ; and by special desire of Major Oakshott took for his text, ' At evening time there shall be light.' He spoke, sometimes in a voice broken, as much by feeling as by age, of the childhood blighted by a cruel superstition, and perverted, as he freely made confession, by discipline without comprehension, because no confidence had been sought. Then ensued a tribute of earnest, generous justice to her who had done her best to undo the warp in the boy's nature, and whose blessed influence the young man had owned to the last, through all the temptations, errors, and frenzies of his life. Nor did the good man fail to make this a means of testifying to the entire neighbourhood, who had flocked to hear him, all that might be desirable to be known respecting the conflict at Portchester, actually reading Peregrine's affidavit, as indeed was due to Colonel Archfield, so as to prove that this was no mere pardon, though technically it had so to stand, but actual acquittal. Nor was the struggle with evil at the end forgotten, nor the surrender alike of love and of hatred, as well as of his own life, which had been the final conquest, the decisive passing from darkness to light.

It was a strange sermon according to present ideas, but not to those who had grown up to the semi-political preaching of the century then in its last decade; and it filled many eyes with tears, many hearts with a deeper spirit of that charity which hopeth all things.

A month later Charles Archfield and Anne Jacobina Woodford were married at the little parish church of Fareham. Sir Philip insisted on making it a gay and brilliant wedding, in order to demonstrate to the neighbourhood that though the maiden had been his grandson's governess, she was a welcomed and honoured acquisition to the family. Perhaps too he perceived the error of his middle age, when he contrasted that former wedding, the work of worldly conventionality, with the present. In the first, an

unformed, undeveloped lad, unable to understand his own true feelings and affections had
been passively linked to a shallow, frivolous,
ill-trained creature, utterly incapable of growing into a helpmeet for him ; whereas the
love and trust of the stately-looking pair, in
the fresh bloom of manhood and womanhood,
had been proved in the furnace of trial, so
that the troth they plighted had deep foundation for the past, and bright hope for the
future.

Nor was anybody more joyous than little
Philip, winning his Nana for a better mother
to him than his own could ever have been.

It was in a blue velvet coat that Colonel
Archfield was married.   He had resigned his
Austrian commission ; and though the 'Salamander' was empowered to offer him an
excellent staff appointment in the English
army, he decided to refuse.   Sir Philip
showed signs of having been aged and shaken
by the troubles of the winter, and required his
son's assistance in the care of his property,
and little Philip was growing up to need a
father's hand, so that Charles came to the
conclusion that there was no need to cross

the old Cavalier's dislike to the new regime, nor to make his mother and wife again suffer the anxieties of knowing him on active service, while his duties lay at home.

Sedley Archfield, after a long illness, owed recovery both in body and mind to Mrs. Oakshott, and by her arrangement finally obtained a fresh commission in a regiment raised for the defence of the possessions of the East India Company.   And that the poor changeling was still tenderly remembered might be proved by the fact that when the bells rung for Queen Anne's coronation there was one baby Peregrine at Fareham and another at Oakwood.

THE END

Printed by R. & R. CLARK, *Edinburgh.*